ONCE TWO HEROES

ALSO BY CALVIN BAKER

Naming the New World

ONCE TWO HEROES

Calvin Baker

Viking

VIKING

Published by the Penguin Group

Penguin Putnam Inc., 375 Hudson Street, New York, New York 10014, U.S.A.

Penguin Books Ltd, 80 Strand, London WC2R 0RL, England

Penguin Books Australia Ltd, 250 Camberwell Road, Camberwell,
    Victoria 3124, Australia

Penguin Books Canada Ltd, 10 Alcorn Avenue,
    Toronto, Ontario, Canada M4V 3B2

Penguin Books India (P) Ltd, 11 Community Centre, Panchsheel Park,
    New Delhi - 110 017, India

Penguin Books (N.Z.) Ltd, Cnr Rosedale and Airborne Roads, Albany,
    Auckland, New Zealand

Penguin Books (South Africa) (Pty) Ltd, 24 Sturdee Avenue,
    Rosebank, Johannesburg 2196, South Africa

Penguin Books Ltd, Registered Offices:
Harmondsworth, Middlesex, England

First published in 2003 by Viking Penguin,
a member of Penguin Putnam Inc.

10   9   8   7   6   5   4   3   2   1

PUBLISHER'S NOTE
This is a work of fiction. Names, characters, places, and incidents either are the product
of the author's imagination or are used fictitiously, and any resemblance to actual persons,
living or dead, business establishments, events, or locales is entirely coincidental.

LIBRARY OF CONGRESS CATALOGING-IN-PUBLICATION DATA
Baker, Calvin.
    Once two heroes / Calvin Baker.
        p.   cm.
    ISBN 0–670–03164–X (alk. paper)
    I. Title.
    PS3552.A3997 O53 2003
    813'.54—dc21   2002025885

This book is printed on acid-free paper. ∞
Printed in the United States of America
Set in Minion with Bauer display
Designed by Carla Bolte

For Ariane and Ricardo

ONCE TWO HEROES

1946

PROLOGUE: THE DEAD MAN

He is a man like any other of his country, heroic, and even the stars in the sky might have hummed out and whispered his name. You're nobody's sap, and nothing at all like a homespun—what's that word they got?—eugenicist, but to see him in uniform brings a sentiment that wells and crinkles your eyes. He is why you live in near freedom.

Besides the war, he has been twice touched by history: when he was a boy, in a kiss from a great prophet; and, after he came home, by a starlet of the stage and silver screen. There is an aloofness in his carriage. Still, he has no qualm calling any honest man friend.

Tonight he drives his brand-new motorcar across the connected roadways of America. Well, not quite new, it was made in 1941, before production stopped, and had sat unsold on the dealer's lot ever since, but it has seen miles all the same. He is returning to the Golden State, whence his trip began. He touches the gas pedal and lets the ribbon of highway pull him home to California.

1

You can tell by the way the dusk shadows his face that his business on the East Coast did not go well. Here in the countryside, though, the soft silhouette of trees, and quiet contours of the otherwise flat ground, still his mind, and he is able to keep many desperate thoughts at bay. No matter how he was treated in Washington, his pride is stronger than anger and shame, and he smiles at thoughts of a wife and loving relatives. Warm, unconditional family. They wait for him, and in a week he will be back with them. Just one more week, he tells himself again, and I will be home.

He manages to forget for a moment the knot in his stomach that has sat there since he first realized, on top of his other worries, what chance he takes being a Negro driving through the Deep South alone. He hopes his uniform will protect him, the evening skies blanket his journey, and the countryside lie still to let him pass.

"Not quite destiny manifest," his father used to say, growing nostalgic when they lived in farthest-away lands, "but richer and wider than any one man will ever know." It is beautiful down south as well, and he concentrates on the peaceful expanse around him, the clear, opulent night reflecting off puddles from an earlier rain still gathered in the empty fields that dazzle his eyes and keep him awake.

When he first left the capital, he thought he would take his time getting back, because he wasn't sure he would know what to tell his family. Now he knows they will help him recover and remember himself. He will swim then with his wife in the warmth of the ocean at Long Beach, and he will care less, will count himself lucky, if he never sees the graypink evil of the Atlantic again.

He—by name, Mather Henry Rose—smiles across the beauty of the Old Confederacy, into the Mississippi stillness. He feels again the thrill he felt as a boy when seeing a new place for the first time, instead of the thoughts that punctured him before. The moon above the world holds them both, man and country, with untold tenderness.

He pulls off the road at a filling station in Lauderdale County, just west of Meridian, and honks his horn, then steps out to stretch his legs. He leaves the lights on and walks a piece along the shoulder of the road, in the weeds between fields and asphalt, looking deep into Southern November with tired eyes. The world has a finite imagination for landscapes, he tells himself, taking a few basic patterns and repeating them from locale to locale, even across continents. Even though he has never been to Mississippi, Mather feels himself in one of those places he has known before. He cannot remember where, but knows it held some special meaning, whose marker no amount of time or distance will ever remove from his blood. He feels in this moment, as the night comes along, as close as he ever will again to being at ease with his life. He breathes the crisp air, and holds it as deep in his lungs as a long-distance runner, before exhaling in light fogs that break apart on the eddies of a breeze.

There are reasons to have faith in the world, no matter what reasons it gives for doubt. He holds on to that as he comes back across the lot, and pushes all other thoughts away.

At the car, a boy, not quite thirteen, unscrews the bright, polished cap on the gas tank, and lets out a long whistle when he catches sight of Mather in the ax of light from the headlamps.

"You sure got a lot of medals on that uniform, mister," the boy says in his broad inland accent. "Why, I bet you got every one they give."

"A few," Mather answers. He does not condescend to the boy, but copies the warm liquidity of his speech, slipping into a light drawl all the same. He does not tell the boy he does, in fact, have every one they give except one.

"Where'd you win 'em all?" the boy asks as he finishes filling the car's tank with gas.

"Germany," Mather answers him. "It wasn't that hard. One day you'll win medals too."

"Not unless they give one for gasoline pumping," the kid says, conspiring with his malnourished eyes, "but if there was Nazis round here I'd sure as hell shoot 'em."

Mather laughs warmly. He is a likable child with an intelligent countenance, he thinks, if a little too willing to clown around. "Say, do you know how far it is until the next motel?" he asks, because he wants to make a little more distance before the end of the night but is worried about having to sleep in the car again, as he has had to whenever a vacancy turned into no vacancy when he tried to rent a room.

"No, sir, mister," the boy says. "It's Thanksgiving Eve, and most places are probably already closed. If you wait a minute, though, I can go ask Mr. Nathan." The boy screws the top back onto the gasoline tank and gives the smooth black paint a flick with his rag. "'Forty-one Zephyr, right?"

"Naw, just an old '39," Mather answers, flipping the kid a dollar he can barely afford to give, with an easy motion of his thumb.

"I know a Zephyr anywhere." The boy shakes his head and laughs as he turns to run back to the store, the coin jingling against odds and ends in the pockets of his three-quarter breeches.

"Hey," Mather calls after him, "ask if he knows where I might find something to eat as well."

"You got it, mister."

Mather leans against the side of the car and looks up at the sky choked to bursting with stars, waiting for the boy to return from this errand.

He pulls his hand down his unshaven face and stares at the spark of light from distant houses, then checks his watch and looks into the shopwindow to see what is keeping the kid so long.

Nathan Hampton sits behind the counter, half listening to something bluesy coming from the radio, counting the minutes until he can close up and go meet his buddies for a drink. "What you running so fast for, Frankie?" he asks when his young charge comes bolting through the door. "Slow down before you break something."

"Like what?" Frankie asks, looking around the bare store, which has not been improved upon since before the Depression.

"Like your ass," Nathan says. "Don't you sass me."

"There's a war hero outside say he need a room for the night," Frankie tells Nathan. "Tipped me a whole dollar too."

"Did he? Well, you better hand it on over."

"Come on, Mr. Nathan, he gave it to me."

"I said give it here," Nathan commands again with an impish smile. "It was a tip for the fine service this establishment provides, and I am in charge of the store, so just hand it over."

Frankie digs in his pocket, down past marbles, a bottle cap, and frayed bits of string, to pull up the coin. He hands his boss the tip, watching it glint for a moment under the bare lightbulb as it changes possession a second time, slipping out of his life into Nathan's pocket, where he might as well never even have heard of such a thing as a silver dollar.

Nathan pockets the coin with satisfaction. Tonight he, from time to time a king, will buy the first round. "Now," he says, standing up and pushing the tails of his faded green shirt back into his pants, "never let it be said that a Mississippian denied hospitality to a stranger." He looks at the clock. "Or that Mr. Hampton kept a child from his family. You better get on home."

"Okay," says Franklin, going to the back of the store to gather his hand-me-down jacket. "But you know that was my dollar."

"Why, you . . .," Nathan begins, but the boy is already in back, and when he looks out the window, that shiny car sits waiting for him. Maybe, he thinks, heading toward the door, there is more money to be had, or he can get the feller looking away long enough to do that tire scheme he learned a few months back.

He opens the door, pulls his uniform cap down around his ears, and walks into the cool night filled with the stray calling of late-season insects. He is ready to offer every inch of hospitality he knows, right down to his own bed, to whoever this stranger may be. If only there is another tip to be had.

When Nathan looks at Mather, though, there comes a blank hatred to his face you can all but touch.

"You the one who needs a room?"

"Just for the night."

"Frankie," he yells. "Frankie, get your evil black ass back out here."

The boy sulks out from the shop, not knowing what he has done wrong.

"This the man who told you he needs a room?" Nathan asks, glowering at the kid.

"Yessir," says Frankie.

"Well, why don't you tell him . . ." Nathan does not know what to tell him, or even why he feels so much malice toward the man, but he knows there is something in the stranger's presence taunting him, even beyond the fact that he walked all the way out here to wait on a colored.

"Why don't you leave the boy alone? You already took his dollar," Mather says, hating to see anyone done so wrong, least of all a child. There were nights when he would not have known what to say. Now the words fly from his mouth like second nature, regardless of what ground he is on.

"Well, where Negro soldiers sleep, I do not know," Nathan says, bothered by everything about the flashy soldier and his fancy car, and speaking to him in the Negro way of talking. "And I especially don't know of no place in the South where they take in uppity niggers in fancy automobiles." He stabs the gravel with a short kick of his foot, sending a pebble jumping across the otherwise silent lot. He follows it, as it comes to a halt, with a sadness to his eyes that touches on regret. He knows what challenge he brings.

The boy looks between the two men, Mr. Nathan—whom he has known ever since he can remember, but is sore with—and the stranger, who—simply with his presence, and a few warm words—made him feel something he knows he is not supposed to, not shame, but a secret and reckless pride. He doesn't know what else he might expect of him, but he does. He wants a gift like it was Christmas Eve instead of the night before Thanksgiving. Something that will maybe replace that dollar. To hear Nathan spoken to in a different voice. He feels this new, strange thing, and his chest presses down, as if an invisible hand has been placed there, as he realizes he expects and desires a treasure of violence.

He is disappointed, though, when Mather opens his mouth. "I'm sorry you feel that way," he says, backing down without response. "I'm just looking for a hotel, then to get up in the morning and keep driving to California."

The boy's heart drops to see the stranger abused and put back in his place like any life-loving sharecropper he has ever known. If Mr. Nathan can speak like that even to a hero coming home with a chest full of medals, then he knows he can speak that way to any Negro, and everything on earth is just as bad as his mother has always told him.

"Nigger like you always looking for trouble," Nathan says, unable to let go of the advantage he has been given. "If not for yourself, then for somebody else."

Mather looks at Nathan, sizing up the salmon-faced man, who is as ignorant and unwashed as the day he was born, and tries to measure the charge of force he might be capable of. He feels another surge inside himself, as his own eyes flare. He tells himself he should walk away. He cannot help or control, though, the words that come to his mouth, and take his tongue, because, even before Washington, he knew how little regard one man may have for another.

He looks at Nathan with the full measure of the anger that has been sitting in his mouth since he first stepped onto this land before the war. He touches the meaningless medals. "You mean these, boy?" he says to Nathan, like he was still speaking to the half-clothed child. "Let's see. I got this one for getting shot at, and these four for getting shot. This is for marksmanship, and this for being an all-around defender of freedom, who just happened to come back alive." He touches the last one and stops, unwilling to belittle it even though he no longer has faith in its sign. If it meant anything, there would be another next to it, but it holds for him the memory of those he fought with.

"Well, what about it, nigger?" Nathan points at the one he has seen on his brother. "Which white man's grave you rob it from?"

"Oh, this?" Mather asks, slitting his eyes at the white man. If he had a friend to stay with, or did not mind sleeping in the car, or if the boy knew anything other than the fields he had grown up with and had been able to direct him to a motel, or if he were less stubborn, or more afraid, or more willing to accept certain things. If many things, none of this would be happening. If he was not the man he was, he might not be here at all, with all hell breaking loose tonight. "This come flying out of Hitler's ass when I put my hand down his throat. General Patton cleaned it up personally, and gave it to me for winning him the Western Front."

Frankie's heart seizes up under that hidden hand, as cold drops of sweat fall down the small of his back under his coat, pulling his shirt tight against his skin. There is an uncommon strangeness in the air between the two men now. To see them, you would think they were old friends sharing a drink or laugh. He had wished before for violence; now he thinks he should not be hearing or seeing any of this. Colored and white ain't supposed to be talking to each other so, especially not that proper-speaking soldier making fun of Mr. Nathan, who is not so even in the way he acts. Franklin watches, trying to understand the quiet terror rocking through his blood, and wonders if the soldier, who he had thought before was big as the world, is making fun of him in some way too.

Mr. Nathan goes all quiet and soft, and now so has that war hero. Both of them sucking all the sound out of the world, like they're about to turn that noise at the end of speaking into something else. He wanted to see what would happen before; now he will settle for everything to go back the way it was five minutes ago. He knows it will not, though, when he sees his boss's hand reach into the oil-stained pocket of his breeches where he keeps his buck knife.

Frankie's sense of protection vanishes, and he wants to, knows he should, run away, but he cannot move, and watches Mr. Nathan's mouth for his next words, just as he had once watched the beautiful, frightening twists of a tornado ripping up distant homes from his bedroom window.

"Give it to me," Nathan says.

"Give?" Mather asks, with a glint of pleasure around his mouth. "You seem to me like a man used to taking what he wants. Now, why don't you reach over here and do like you did with this boy's coin."

Nathan looks at the black man and sees something that's halfway wild. He did not count on this, and is no longer sure of the situation, but he knows a crazy nigger ain't nothing to treat any less seriously than you would a mad dog.

His fingers wrap around the handle of the knife in his pocket. He looks at young Frankie, then out at the highway, and doesn't see anything around himself but blackness. Blackness of night, and blackness of Negro faces.

"Ah, hell, boy," he says to the stranger. "I was just playin' around. What's it to me if you wanna dress up in an army uniform and go round stealing cars."

Mather opens his mouth wide, throws his head back, and lets out a laugh, then laughs and laughs. "You got some funny people around here, Frankie," he says to the boy as he watches Nathan's tensing arm, waiting to see if that hand will jump out of its pocket.

Frankie feels a petrifaction moving from his legs to his mouth. The only movement he makes as the stranger laughs and Mr. Nathan reaches out his hunting knife is to open his eyes up wide.

This stillness holds him as the knife hollers through the air toward the soldier's windpipe, as if something more powerful than his own control of his legs wants him to see.

Mather eases to the side, out of the way of the blade, and Nathan turns around to charge at him again. The knife comes nearer this time, and Mather sees the white man is faster than he suspected.

When the blade hisses past his ear, he throws a hard punch that lands on Nathan's jawbone. He stands there, waiting for his assailant to recover and come at him again. This time, he does not bother to get out of the knife's way, but catches Nathan's arm, with the full rage of knowing this man wants to kill him.

Nathan struggles to free himself from Mather's grip, the two of them thrashing and turning around the point of the knife like catfish caught on the same string.

The knife falls free from Nathan's hand, and both of them dive to pick it up. As they reach for it, their eyes lock on to each other's. They are still held there when Mather jams the metal into his enemy's gut. He yanks it upward, and twists the handle. The white man's eyes make the same up-then-sideways motion as blood flies from his torso in dense, migratory bursts.

Frankie lets loose a scream, regaining control of his limbs at the same time, and takes off across the hoarfrosted fields into the stand of pine trees. His heart beats in skip-dash rhythms, as the image of what he has just seen chases him home. He swallows and pumps his legs faster, possessed for all the world with the golden, light-speed efficiency of a young Jesse Owens.

Mather gets up from the pavement of the Texaco station, feeling a great wave of release come over him. It is tranquillity come not from pleasure in killing, but in being still alive. He knows there is no other honor in this.

Not until the boy's copper-colored limbs disappear into the darkness, suffused with something realer than God, does he realize fully what he has done. He feels in a flash he has thrown something away.

He knows he must pay for this in guilt and inner turmoil. You cannot just kill a man for being a fool.

He looks at the pallid face of the man beneath him, then feels his own color, with the weight of knowing what has passed here, under the Line of Mason and Dixon, belongs to more than himself and the dying man. He realizes as well he does not have friends for many miles around. He listens to the soft twinkling of the Southern night, and knows he must get out of there.

"It is what any man would have done," he says to himself. "I was defending myself." He suspects, though, everyone else knew some secret code of conduct that would have never let the situation bloom.

It has blossomed nonetheless, and Mather Rose struggles to gather his senses. He has killed before, but never in rage, and never done anything that might be looked on as murder. He kicks the knife from its wound, and away from the body, then bends to retrieve it off the ground, trying not to look at the newborn agony frozen on the man's face. He wipes the steel blade and folds it into his waistband, where it gives him a protection he thinks he should have had with him all along. Too late for this hindsight, he gets back into his car with bloody hands and punches west on 80 as fast as he can.

On the radio, Sarah Vaughan sings "East of the Sun."

Mather's peacetime eyes shine out with a lonelier kind of fear than they have held before.

Under the Texaco sign, Nathan Hampton's last breaths chortle in his throat. He looks in agony at a view of death only dead men may see.

He rolls onto his belly and claws himself over the ground like a stricken animal creeping to a ditch to die. Two crickets call from somewhere out in the surrounding fields. They are all he hears, except the sound of his own gurgling effort for breath, until he makes it into the pattern of light falling across the lot from the store's window. He struggles inside, where he hears the same slow blues he had been listening to before wrenching its way through the room.

He props himself up and topples the phone down from the desk, then clicks at the cold metal cradle until he gets the operator. He begs her to send over help.

Meridian is a small place, with no more than its share of killing, but the woman is steady in the face of disaster and asks in a tender voice, "What has happened to you out there?"

"I've been stabbed. By a nigger," Nathan says, trying to answer her questions. "He's driving a brand-new Lincoln, heading west."

"What's he look like, honey?" the operator soothes and coaxes. "You just hang on, somebody'll be right there."

Nathan drops the phone and huddles against his desk, trying to stop the bleeding that rushes from his gut, and not watch as his own life weeps through his fingers. He shivers and shuts his eyes. "I didn't mean nothing by it," he thinks to himself, until he loses strength to sit upright, and his head lolls to the side. A thick foam, pink with blood, slides down the side of his face. It is the last blood he can spare. He curses everything. Exhales his last half-a-breath.

The sheriff and a deputy arrive to find him there, sprawled on the block tile. He is still warm, but "just as dead as he will ever be," the deputy says, dropping the flat-veined wrist back to the dirty floor.

"You know, I hate to say it, Sheriff," Richman continues, wiping his hands on a rag, "but old Nate might have had it coming." He, Richman, is a thickset man whose face shows its first signs of wrinkles, but he still turns his watery blue eyes to his boss for approval.

"Then don't say it," the sheriff scolds, no longer feeling the excitement of murder his young protégé does. "Nobody deserves dying like this."

"I'm not saying 'deserved.' I'm just saying you could see it coming from miles and miles away. . . . Too cozy with the Negroes," Richman goes on laconically. "After a while, it was just bound to happen."

"Be such as it might," Cox says, cutting the deputy off, "we have a murderer to catch, and we better get to him."

"How much of a head start do you think he has?"

"Fifteen, twenty minutes," the sheriff answers, looking around the store and down at the body again. "He will never make it out of Mississippi."

Mather slows down on the road to keep from attracting attention. He balances his foot carefully on the gas pedal and watches the empty space in front of him show itself in the headlights, before fading again to darkest, unconsoling calm.

When he sees a bright corona of light in his rearview mirror, he calculates the distance in his head and tells himself he still has half a hope. Maybe less than that. A fool's chance. But, like you, he will take it. Anything not to know too soon what else they will try to take from him.

He mashes the accelerator down as far to the floor as he can with his booted foot, knowing once the V-12 opens and gets up to speed nothing natural on four wheels can catch him.

The sheriff follows at a distance, going a little faster than before, but not fast enough to do any more than keep the distance between the two cars constant. "Don't you think . . . ," the deputy starts to say. The sheriff puts his finger to his lip and shushes his lieutenant. Richman understands and falls silent, matching the intent look on his boss's face. They are hunting.

The glossy black Zephyr caroms over the Red Hills of Mississippi as fast as it can now, but that corona in the mirror stays focused in Mather's eyes. His olive dress uniform is soaked through with sweat, holding him fast to the seat, and the hair at the back of his neck is standing on end. His stomach clenches and climbs to his throat, making him dizzy with nausea as he tries to will it to stay down.

He passes a sign for Pelahatchie, and on the other side of it, stares straight into a squadron of troopers and baying dogs. He does not know whether or not he should stop, but knows he cannot. He cannot stop any more than he could stop that man's swinging arm once it was set in motion, or any more than he could stop his own hand once it touched the blade that had tried to withdraw his life from its circle of being.

The dogs rise up restless, yelping, and one of the cops fires his gun in the air. Mather feels his hope dwindling as his stomach speaks to his brain in bona-fide gibberish. But he also feels the acute thrill of action take hold of him, and the headiness of odds stacked so precariously high that he is pushed close to the bone of his being, fully awake, in a state that begs to be called aroused. It is not that, though, but a nexus of loss and well-being. Come doom or safe passage, he cannot stop.

He has killed a man who came after him for nothing more than asking where he might find a motel. He will not be caught or give himself to them again. He has escaped from tighter corners than this. He is Mather Henry Rose. Hero of war. He only wants to get home.

Mather looks at the men and animals standing in the road, and the light coming closer in his mirror. He swerves from the roadway and sends the car flying over the fields, throwing up clumps of mud as it jolts wildly, trying to get away.

The rump of the Zephyr shimmies, daring the coppers to follow. They watch from the highway. They do not know his name, but Mather Rose doesn't even have a nigger's chance in the unforgiving swamp of red Mississippi mud.

Sheriff Cox shakes his head and lines his face, watching the car turn circles in the dirt. He knows there is no escape from that field, and waits until man and machine finally realize the futility of their effort. When they come to rest, in a tractionless patch of impromptu pond from this morning's rain, Cox unholsters his gun, then picks his way out to the murderer, motioning for deputy, roadblockers, and dogs to follow.

Mather is 165 pounds of frozen sweat slumped over the steering wheel with an instinct to live and, for whatever it might be worth, or chance it might hold, to wake up tomorrow. He does not move, but tells himself he has faced worse before, remembering rooms made of bullets. He forces his mind to carve some sanctuary within itself of blankness, or way of escape, and his face falls unnaturally calm.

In a small room of his mother's house, Franklin breathes the smell of recently baked cornbread and pulls the blanket snug around his chin. It is the odor of all good things, and enough to make him forget for a moment he was ever anywhere else except here in his bed, without worry.

He daydreams for long seconds about everything that will be spread around the table for the next day's meal, and counts to himself the things he will be thankful for when it is his turn to rise and testify. I will be more thankful this year than any before, he says to himself, trying to barter away what he has just witnessed with promises to God. If You make that disappear, I will join church this Sunday and get baptized.

He swears he will rise early to collect the morning eggs, and perform the chores he would otherwise have to be told a dozen times to do. He projects images of himself scattering feed to the chickens in their coop behind the house, then dressing and accompanying his mother to the church house, as proof of how good he can be. He pulls his blanket closer, asking the divine to reverse recent history.

It is from deep within this cocoon of anxiety that he hears his mother yell his name.

"I'll be right there," he calls back to her, turning on his side under the blankets but remaining otherwise still.

"Franklin," she shouts again from the front of the house, "get in here."

He has heard it in her trembling voice and is not surprised when the lights come on in his room and he sees the police officer. He feels the heaviness of his secret and a terror close to guilt push down on him as he looks at the large man in his beige uniform, with the gun, and nightstick, and handcuffs ringing his waist on their thick leather belt like one of those trains around Christmas trees he has seen in the newspaper.

"Were you working out at the filling station earlier tonight?" Richman asks, staring down at the boy.

"Yessir," Frankie says sheepishly, sitting up in his bed, "but Mr. Nathan let me come home early."

"Now, why would he do that?" the policeman demands, as the boy gets out of bed and pulls on a sweater in the chilly room.

"I don't know," Frankie answers. "I suppose on account of Thanksgiving." He is surprised by how evenly the words come out. It is his voice, but the words sound alien to his ears, bolder than he knew was in him.

The deputy reddens at the collar and scowls. "Don't you smart-ass me, boy. If you don't tell me what you saw, I'll unleash something so bad around here, every nigger in Meridian will feel it."

"Franklin," his mother says, "a man was killed. You better tell the officer if you saw something."

"I didn't have nothing to do with it," Frankie says, looking at his mother, and speaking too fast. "The man just wanted to know where he could find a room, but Mr. Nathan started calling him out of his name for no good reason, then turn around and go after him with a knife."

"Don't lie to me, boy," Richman shouts, his nostrils pulsing out, then retracting back into place. "You know what happens to liars."

"That's the God's truth," Frankie tells him, hating to tell a cop anything, but nervous with the thought of what he knows can happen if he doesn't.

He cannot tell about his own emotions, but he can still remember that silver dollar and shouts out, in a recess from fear, just what he thinks. "Mr. Nathan started it, but he couldn't finish."

The deputy's hand is sharp on the boy's face before the words are even in the air good. Frankie stands there with tears at the corner of his eyes, but does not utter another word. "That's all for right now," the deputy says, still feeling the tingling in his fingers from the blow to the boy's face.

Frankie's mother sighs a measure of relief, following Richman to the front door, until he stops and turns back to the boy. "I suspect we will be seeing each other again, by and by," he says with a malevolent twist of his mouth. "Maybe by then you'll be ready to tell the truth." He nods, and Frankie knows, one way or another, he is coming back.

Frankie stares at the ceiling, listening to the policeman make his way out of the house and into his car.

Across town Mather still measures his odds. A ring of brightest fire shines in the sky above Mississippi. It is the moon above the world. It holds each and guides their thoughts with clarity to make any un-dead thing contemplate the meaning of life.

I

A LIFE AND TIMES OF M. H. ROSE

1940

ONE

When the *Taio Mary* approaches Los Angeles Harbor, Mather does not have anything left to his name other than his traveling trunk, a faded address printed on an old blue envelope, and a copy of the *South China Daily News* he has found aboard. He had set sail from Paris two months earlier on a passenger ship headed to New York via London. Instead, he arrives on a cargo vessel from Japan, having gone the long way round the world and managing to spend all of his money on such things as are available to a young traveler in the ports of the East.

He mourns his foolishness less, though, when he wakes from his Asian misadventures, and the grinding monotony of life aboard ship, to a view of the Pacific more wondrous than any map could suggest. He stares out at the even sea and a skyline above the city's hills that is just as becalmed, just as mystically blue. After a life spent in the crowded capitals of Europe, he can scarcely believe such a clear view of the sky exists anywhere in the world. He has trouble equating it with the country his father always swore never to return to, and swore with enough intent that he was still sitting in their Montmartre flat as war renewed her claim on Europe and sent refugees fleeing through the streets, even beneath their own window, in search of safety.

In the untainted morning light of Los Angeles, it is hard for Mather to remember there is war anywhere in the world, let alone that in all likelihood it will soon engulf him as well.

He goes belowdecks and collects his remaining trunk, then re-surfaces to watch the crew dock the ship. As he waits at the top of the gangplank, he feels impressive after his long voyage and prepared for anything the morning or this country may extend to him.

In the terminal he looks around at the other passengers who have just arrived from sea and separates himself out as he heads to the customs line for citizens. He hands his passport over to the immi-grations officer, and accepts it back with the jubilation of beginning a new adventure. He walks out into the main terminal with this ela-tion and no thought other than the heady sensation of arrival. He trusts some natal instinct will steer him safely to the address on the envelope, his family's house in West Adams.

When he sees a tall, correct, but loose-limbed man in a cream suit holding a sign, he remembers suddenly the letter he mailed from Bombay. Both men break into a smile when their eyes meet. The sign says "Rose," and Mather leaves his trunk where it is to make his way through the crowd. "Uncle Wallace?" he asks, holding out his hand.

The older man walks beyond Mather's hand and pulls him into an intense embrace. "Welcome home, Nephew." And the way Wallace says "nephew" bears no trace of the tentativeness with which Mather had called him "uncle." He says "nephew" and it restores the word, making Mather hear it as if for the first time, with the sudden understanding that family is not just his mother and father, but a whole synaptic system whose loves, claims, and right to miss one were real. Mather, who had not known this before, is on the sharp edge of tears. There are reunions such as this going on all over the terminal as the day heats up and the sound of ship horns breaks throughout the harbor.

"Thank you," Mather says, filled with this new sense of belonging.

When they leave the station, onto Port Street, Uncle Wallace makes small talk, asking about his trip as he loads the trunk into the back of the biggest car Mather has ever seen.

"Well, this is Los Angeles," Wallace says, waving toward the windshield as they drive north on Figueroa, away from the shipyard and warehouses. "Is it what you imagined so far?"

"No," Mather answers, his body and brain trying to assimilate their new surroundings and the excitement he feels, "better. It is nothing like Europe at all."

"How about Asia?" Wallace asks slyly.

Mather does not know how to explain his irresponsibility. He had not truly understood that there were people awaiting him on the other end of his voyage, because when he left Paris he had told himself he was now on his own. "That," he says, hesitating. "Well . . ."

"Showing up five weeks late, going thousands of miles the wrong way round the world," Wallace says, making Mather feel that he is claiming that other part of uncle as well, that right to reprimand. "And, on top of it all, with no idea of what would be waiting for you."

He sulks in his seat, feeling just as he would if he were getting a lecture from his father. He knows his actions must appear reckless and self-indulgent, but he is also certain they have been in the service of something greater, something monumental that will eventually forgive him for what he has done.

"Well," Wallace says, shaking his head and showing an amusement that lets Mather relax, "you're not the first Rose to do that. Your grandfather Henry . . ."

"Once walked from Shreveport to Oakland," Mather says, finishing the sentence, as he realizes his uncle has a sense of humor, despite his stern bearing.

"Oh, you know it already." Wallace smiles at his youthful nephew. "Good, because if you didn't it would be a shameful thing."

"Uncle Wallace," Mather tells him, "I probably couldn't find Shreveport or Oakland on a map, but I know Henry Rose once walked from one to the other."

The two of them laugh together, and Wallace is overjoyed that his only nephew is finally home. That when his brother's son did not know quite what to do or how to do it, he has come to him. That he has arrived already knowing some of the things he should. "Just like a Rose, goddamnit. I tell you, just like a Rose."

Mather has been in many places, and more in the last weeks, but when he walks into the large, cool living room of the sumptuous pink house in West Adams, he feels that nothing he has ever known matches its ease and tranquillity. It is at once formal and relaxed, as if the people who live in it understand the size of their home as an invitation, not a barrier.

"Mother," Wallace calls, closing the door and leading Mather through the rooms, "guess what the tide brought in?"

If Mather had just learned that morning he is linked to people other than his parents, he quickly finds the extent of that linkage. From all over the house, cousins, and aunts, and uncles, and friends, and once-removeds materialize with shouts and jokes and joyful calls of reunion, because even if he does not remember them, from the time his parents brought him here for a visit when he was a child, he feels immediately how much he belongs among them.

"Come here, let me look at you," his grandmother Vidia says, bringing the entire hive from the full pandemonium his arrival has excited to a hushed frenzy.

Mather walks over to the white-haired woman seated against the wall in a high-backed chair, who presides over the gathering like an indulgent queen mother.

"Why, if you don't look just like Walter when he was nineteen," she says approvingly. "Now, what took you so long getting here?"

He is in real trouble, and everyone watches to see how he will respond.

"Oh, wait, before I forget," Mather stalls, escaping the question as he runs back out to the car to get the gift he has brought for her. He wishes he had thought before spending all of his money to buy gifts enough to spread among the entire clan. He had no idea, though, there were so many of them, because his father always mentioned their names as if they were scattered as far away as he was and the family in America was only his uncle and grandmother.

He struggles back inside with the packages he has brought for the two of them. "This is for you, Grandmother; I bought it in China," he says, handing to her a large, carefully wrapped box he has removed from his trunk.

"What do I want with gifts at my age?" she asks, but you can tell she's positively delighted, both at the present itself and in knowing, even though the boy was raised in France, he is still well mannered, still remembers his grandmother.

"Uncle Wallace, this is for you," Mather says, giving Wallace the smaller of the two boxes he has brought in from the car.

Wallace opens a case of Japanese whiskey as Mather's grandmother finally gets open her gift, with the aid of an eager grandchild, and takes the lid off of a shimmering rainbow of Chinese silks that unfurl and flutter around the room in the hands of his female cousins and the aunts. Great bolts of silk, yellow and blue embroidered with saffron thread, green sashes printed with flowers, pure red, and red entwined with orange, unwind from hand to hand, stretching across the room, or form impromptu sarongs in the palm-shaded living room.

One of the male relatives helps Wallace open a bottle of the Japanese whiskey, as someone warns, "It's too early to be drinking. It's not even one of the clock yet," and someone else, "Cousin Mather, where's your beret?," and, "I'm telling you, Mather Henry looks just like little Jason," but, "He's got Vidia's smile," and one of the cousins puts on Count Basie swinging like no tomorrow, and "Mather, y'all got this in France?," but, "Do they lindy-hop over there?," as the party spills out of the house onto the patio, where the scent of hickory smoke mingles with the eucalyptus and lemon trees, and with the swing, and the laughter, as plates materialize, and, "Mather, how do you say 'celebration' in French?"

"One home and just two more to go," Uncle Wallace says, hugging him again and knuckling the top of his nephew's head.

"Well, they better get here soon, before Eleuthua drinks up every-thing in the state of California."

"Mather, when are your parents going to leave that damn coun-try?" There is a silence, as if someone has pronounced aloud a taboo word.

"Is there really going to be another war?"

TWO

Mather keeps a close eye trained on the events in Europe, but he is amazed by how readily the low-slung sprawl of Los Angeles absorbs him into its imagination. In the short weeks he has been here, he has become the toast of their social circle, and his cousins' friends see him as one of the most eligible young men among them. Because they have sensed their friends' eagerness, the cousins form a protective barrier around him, taking pleasure in the boost to their own status that having a cousin from France affords them.

By the end of these three weeks, however, Mather's initial excitement has waned completely, and he finds he cannot bear another round of partygoing, or the constricted rigidness of his family's circle. If anything, he would rather be out exploring the fabled riches of the city, and enjoying the freedom of movement he is used to. When his cousin Eunice comes into the kitchen that morning, he is

already making himself coffee, having planned to go out before anyone else could rise and stop him.

"You're up early," Eunice says, taking cups from the cabinet, and
pushing him away from the range. "Sit down, I'll finish making it."

"Just restless," Mather says, moving over to the kitchen table as
Eunice takes the handle of the coffeepot from his hands.

"Do you take whole milk or Pet milk?" she asks, pouring the
steaming liquid into a silver-rimmed coffee cup.

"What's Pet milk?"

"It's condensed."

"Whole," he says, "lots of it."

"Cold or warm?"

"Warm."

"What's wrong with you this morning?" she wants to know, looking at Mather's distracted face as he stares out the window. "Are you
bored of us already?"

"Not you," Mather says, "but that party last night, I don't think
I've ever met a duller bunch of people in my life." Don't they know
what's happening?

"You haven't," Eunice says under her breath as she gives him his
coffee, and checks over her shoulder. Eunice is his uncle Wallace's
oldest daughter, and of the cousins, she is the one he has grown closest to, but he has been too polite to tell her what he thinks of their
friends. "They're one of the richest families in California, and some
of the most useless people you will ever meet in your life," she gos-
sips, happy to find he feels as she does about the people life has im-
posed on her. "Don't tell her I told you, but Lydia has a crush on
Arnold Stokes. But I know you didn't hate them so much last night

you couldn't wait to get up this morning to start complaining about them again."

"No. I was thinking about my parents," Mather replies, giving the true reason for his sleepless night.

"Whether they'll be okay?"

"Not that," he says, though he has worried about it as well. "The war is still a long way from Paris. I was wondering why they would leave here and never come back." Despite feeling hemmed in at times by his family here, he has also found a vitality in Los Angeles he had not expected.

"People have reasons," Eunice says. "Nobody here talks about it much, except to say Uncle Walter walks on water and he lives in France. My father told me he had sworn since they were young he would leave this country, but whenever they talk about you all, they act like he just went to the store to buy milk." Mather knows what Eunice says is true. It is how his father spoke at home of their relatives overseas, so that family for him has always had an aspect of the mythic, and people's reasons for doing things were always "because he could," or "because he had to." He looks around the sunny kitchen and tries to imagine his father in these rooms, but finds he cannot, because his father is so much less careful than this house.

"How does Uncle Walter talk about us?" Eunice asks.

"In French," Mather says, "but with love; never anything bad. He saves all his swearing for the once or twice a year when he might have something to say about Americans.

"I still don't understand how someone can just pick up and cut themselves off like that." He knows the reasons in the abstract, but, in the kitchen of the home where his father grew up, which is grander than their own in Paris, he cannot imagine there was anything diffi-cult about his life.

"Is it really better over there?" Eunice asks. "I mean for us?"

"Not as far as I can tell," Mather jokes, looking out to the patio and courtyard behind the house. His own life has been comfort-able—his mother, in fact, pushed him in a carriage well past the time he could walk, and all his life his father has told him, like scold-ing, he didn't know how lucky he was—but he has been taught money is not a thing to be taken for granted. He suspects his uncle, though, of being loaded.

"You know I don't mean for making money. I mean for being . . ." Eunice hesitates, looking down at her slender fingers. "I don't know—for being a person."

"I wish I knew, Cousin," he says, looking at Eunice and realizing there are things she knows that he never will. She, he thinks, looking at her delicate form, knows properly what it means to be Negro American. He only knows that it is what he is. He has no other point of reference outside his family and their small colony in a foreign city.

"Well, you'll find out soon enough," Eunice says, going to the stove for another cup of coffee. "But I bet I know one thing that isn't better in Europe, and I'm going to show you tonight."

"What's that?" Mather asks.

"Central Avenue on Saturday night. Nobody anywhere knows how to have a good time like they do on Central Avenue. They even danced away the Depression over there."

"I'm not so sure about that," Mather says, taking up the rivalry.

"What don't you know?" his uncle Wallace asks, entering the kitchen in his broad-striped pajamas and dressing gown.

"Daddy," says Eunice, looking up at her father, "those are positively the ugliest pajamas anyone has ever seen."

"I know," Wallace says proudly, kissing Eunice on the cheek. "They were a birthday present from my daughter."

"Which daughter? Not this one."

"Are you calling your father a liar?"

"Mather . . . ," says Eunice.

"I'm staying out of this one."

"Smart man." Wallace nods.

"Oh, Daddy, before I forget, can Mather take Lydia and me to the Somerville tonight?"

"He may," Wallace says, enjoying the morning's levity. "Especially since Sunday is his last day to sleep in."

"Whaddya mean, Uncle Wallace?"

"I just thought you might like to learn a little about the butter-and-egg business," Wallace answers, taking up his paper.

"Daddy," Eunice argues on his behalf, "I think Cousin Mather would rather lead a life of leisure."

"This true, son?" Wallace arches his brow with mock concern.

"Absolutely, Daddy-o," Mather says, using one of the new words he learned that week.

"Well, why didn't you say so? We've never had an international playboy in the family."

"Who's an international playboy?" his aunt Sorra asks as she walks into the room and goes to the refrigerator to begin preparing breakfast.

"Reverend Daniels," Eunice says. "Didn't you hear?"

"Dear, don't spread rumors."

"Aunt Sorra, are you married yet?" Mather asks.

"Wallace, do you hear how this boy talks to me? Right off the boat and already with a mouth as fresh as . . ."

"Butter and eggs?!" Mather and Eunice burst into simultaneous laughter.

"Keep it up and the two of you are going to laugh your way right into the Colored Waifs' Home," Uncle Wallace says, taking Sorra's side. But a grin creeps across his face as he watches Sorra with her premature old-maid's demeanor.

Sorra ignores them to start breakfast; they sit all around the table teasing each other and trading gossip as the morning grows late. So that, when Vidia wakes up, and comes downstairs into the kitchen, it is to this gaiety of sound, and the smell of breakfast already made.

She opens the door on the room with a sense of well-being, thinking all is as right with the world as it was when her husband was alive. She knows soon everyone will be where they are supposed to. They will be here, safe.

That evening, Mather glows with the same sense of expectation as he puts on the suit he bought earlier in the day, and counts the money Uncle Wallace has given him, with the admonishment to live it up before he learns how it is made. He will, and prepares for Saturday night with the feeling he always had before going to hear a great band play, or the first time he walked over the bridges and quays of the Seine as a child, or before a kiss, when his newly beloved's face was pressed close enough so that he could taste her breath but not yet her lips. He forgets for an evening about the war, simply to bask in the energy of Los Angeles. He is not vain, but passes his hands over his head again, smoothing a little more Dixie Peach into his already po-maded hair. He winks at himself in the mirror, less narcissistic than in an admission that he looks and feels as good as he ever has. When he heads downstairs and catches sight of Lydia and Eunice in the hall, he feels even better. He feels charmed.

As they drive through the evening streets with the top down on Wallace's convertible, they all do. Eunice produces a pack of Chesterfields and passes them around. Lydia leans forward and turns the radio up a little louder. They are happy. They are free in the city tonight.

More than simply the spoiled children of a Negro butter-and-egg king, they are as intelligent, beautiful, and young as any carload of souls on the road tonight. Because of this, they feel like aristocrats in their own right—part of a natural aristocracy who have been given much, but who will also offer everything in return. They are golden.

Each knows it is a precarious wonderland. Mather because a war is coming. Eunice and Lydia know other reasons, but are adept enough at pushing them away. Tonight they are as hopeful as the world is old.

Eunice takes another Chesterfield from the pack, telling Mather to make a turn at the next red light, as Lydia preens in her compact and touches her freshly marcelled hair. The convertible speeds through the streets, a little faster than they need to be driving, but not so fast that a passerby can't get a good long look at the figure they cut, which is just a little more sophisticated than they really are. They are going dancing at the Somerville on Central Avenue.

"Don't you mean the next light?" Mather asks. "Why do people always tell you to turn at the next red light?"

"Because they mean the next red light," Eunice says, flicking ash out the window. "Tonight I don't want to stop. I don't care if we have to go to Boston and back, just no red lights."

They will make their way to the club driving, against Lydia's protestations, with no better directions than the whim of the street-lights.

"I like it," Mather says as they head over the Hills and down again past the Hollywood Bowl. "A woman after my own heart."

"If you weren't my cousin . . . ," Eunice says, making coy moon-eyes at him. She halfway means it too. He is the brother she never had, and their characters could not be any more similar if they had grown up in the same house. Mather feels this as well, and thinks, as he looks at her, there are not enough words for love in any of the languages he knows. His and Eunice's for each other has been in-stant and real, as siblings long lost to each other. Because of this sep-aration, and because it is love, he knows the charge it bears is not without Eros. It is platonic, and well containable, one of the many unnamed subspecies of love; still, it is Eros.

"If I weren't your cousin, I'd be the chauffeur," he says.

"A man in uniform." Eunice flirts with her dark lashes.

"You two are sick," Lydia jests, sticking her finger down her throat in the back seat.

"Sorry, Sis," says Mather. "Haven't ya heard? I'm in the commod-ity business as of Monday."

"Mather, are you really going to do it?" Lydia asks. "Work at the office?"

"Why not?" he answers her. "What else should I do?"

"Nothing else," she says. "Daddy is going to be so happy." They will be happy as well. With Mather there to take over the business, it will mean a sense of continuity. They will all be well cared for and well loved as they are tonight.

When they arrive at the Somerville, Mather feels the things he loves about the city being added to. He has never seen so many, or so many kinds, of colored people together at the same time in all his life. Montmartre was populated by artists, musicians, and the professional class his father belonged to. They gathered often enough, and even formed a community. But for the most part they lived their lives as members of French society at large. When they did come together, on holidays, or grand social occasions, the assemblage was, more often than not, one of many different cultures, as their friends and lovers came with them. So they were less Negro gatherings than meetings of a colorful international body.

He loved them, but the Somerville Hotel was more varied by far in the examples and kinds of Negro life it contained. All of Colored Los Angeles, in fact, seemed to be in that room, ranging in age from young to old, as opposed to the Montmartre scene, where one seldom saw anyone who was not in his or her prime.

Mather thinks he has found the wellspring of the energy and buzz produced at Zellis or Chez Florence, which he had always thought possible only in communities of the exiled. To feel it here tonight is to him like being in Paris, but running deeper, as if it were infinitely replenishable, and without the sense of being special or apart. It is also better than Paris, to his mind, because it feels permanent. This room, he thinks, will never be any different from what it is at this moment, while the artists and personalities who made Paris itself always gave the impression they might at any moment pack and move away, leaving nothing behind except their names, and memory of their style.

And style there is in this room. Even in his new suit, Mather feels underdressed when he takes in the other patrons, who seem to him balanced in a beautiful lattice of public and private, care and happenstance, but all with a faith in and care for grace. It is nowhere else in the whole of Los Angeles, but in the Somerville, and he feels the room expand with it until it is without edges. As he makes his way through the crowd, he senses himself growing into it, until he feels larger than he ever has before.

When they have finished their first round of highballs and the band strikes up again, there is something else Mather feels as well. He sees a woman with thick black hair parted down the center, and soft, liquid brown eyes, dancing three-quarters of the way out onto the polished wooden floor. She is with another man, but Mather is mesmerized, because when he catches her eye he has the sensation she is dancing not for him, but to him. She is not a great dancer. It does not matter to Mather, because she dances toward him and toward something in him. She catches sight of him watching her and smiles, and Mather feels himself lift from his chair. When she looks away, he begins to fall but does not touch the ground.

He waits for an opportunity to approach her, as Eunice and Lydia tease him, Lydia telling him she is not from their crowd. He does not answer them, but himself, when he says, "She is from mine." He is nineteen, and you cannot tell him anything to slow him down. When the band finishes a cover of "I've Got the World on a String," he takes his chance. He approaches her and asks for the next dance, then moves with her in a good feast of wanting.

He looks at her and appreciates her effort to keep time, as he tries to do the same. He looks at her with lust as her hips slip in time against the fabric of her skirt, and the two of them move in awkward sincerity, both with the knowledge that the dance matters less than that they dance.

They speak with their bodies. Cut me, I will not guard myself from you, but because my blood may be loosened so simply, and because I know this, or because I am less than twenty and do not yet know this quite, I know you will not harm me. Only the inhuman could wish to cause their suffering, because to dare this openness, Mather knows, is to be a real human being, and who cannot love that? He is fond of books but not overly so. When he looks at her, though, he loves what he sees with an intensity of feeling so festive, wide, and unending, it approaches the intellectual. He smiles as her face glows in the heat of the club, and makes his way ever nearer to her.

She smiles at him in turn, and it prompts them both to an ease of love and a willingness to love that nothing else except heart's thinking and thought's heart can decode. Beautiful, this. When he touches her bare skin above the strapless gown for the first time, he feels he has triumphed for a moment, over the darkness. Over the goddamned. Over the goddamned darkness that oppresses and drives off the instinct to be human. And it refreshes his own sense of the possible, prompting him toward even greater openness. Toward renewal. She rests her head on his chest, and Mather Henry Rose holds Mercedes Trumbull in his arms. He is in love—without an obstacle on earth.

"How will I see you again?" he asks at the end of their dance, when she tells him she doesn't have a phone.

"You're going to have to call on me," she says, taking a precious bone-white card from her purse and tucking it into his lapel pocket before slipping away into the crowd, back to the table of friends she is out with for the night. Mather follows her with his eyes, hoping she will turn around to smile at him again.

Mercedes does not, but as she makes her way across the room to her table, there is a smile on her face to light the Pacific Rim.

Mather goes back to his own table, where he finds Lydia declining an invitation from a man who has asked her to dance.

"What was wrong with him?" he asks, when her admirer has slunk off.

"What was so right about her?"

"Touché. Where did Eunice go?"

"She's out there." Lydia motions toward the floor with a look of devastating boredom.

"What about you?" he asks. "Why aren't you dancing?"

"I don't know anyone here," she says. "I couldn't imagine dancing with a complete stranger." He does not know if she intends it, but Mather hears reproach in her voice. Reproach for him, for Eunice, for the whole room that is not where she wants to be.

"Lydia Rose," he says, trying to lighten her mood, and extending his hand, "allow me to present Mather Rose."

"Don't be silly." Lydia shoos him, refusing his outstretched hand.

Mather sits down next to his younger cousin and raises a finger for the waiter, who makes his way over to take their order for another round. Mather turns back to Lydia, still not understanding the sudden temper that has overtaken her. "What's wrong?" he asks carefully, because he has seen her bad moods ruin other nights. "I thought you wanted to come out."

"I did," she says. "I was hoping someone would be here."

"Who is that?" he asks. "It wouldn't be Arnold Stokes, would it?"

"Don't make fun of me," Lydia pouts, trying to throw off her bad mood even as she slips deeper into it. "It doesn't matter. On second thought, maybe I would like that dance."

Mather agrees, and leads Lydia to the dance floor, where they find a space next to Eunice and the man she is dancing with. They move without enthusiasm, until Eunice abandons her partner to join them.

"Hey, no cutting in," Lydia protests.

"You don't even notice we're here," Eunice says, with a hand in Mather's and another in Lydia's, as they turn lindy-hopping into a dance of three, not caring what spectacles they make.

"So—who is she?" Eunice asks Mather when he takes both her hands and swings her as she and Lydia have taught them.

"She who?" Eunice doesn't have the chance to answer before he has turned to Lydia and spins her.

"You're going to make your new girlfriend jealous," Lydia says.

"Who?" Mather asks Lydia, returning to Eunice.

"She you were dancing with."

"I don't know what you're talking about."

"That girl sitting over there cutting her eyes at us."

"What girl?" They go on getting sillier and sillier as the dance winds down, then make their way back to their table, where those highballs are waiting for them. Mather sips his drink and scans the room again for Mercedes, but she is gone.

He gets up to search for her in the crowded hall. He cannot find her. When he comes back from his mission, he finds both his cousins still at the table, Eunice with a look of exhaustion in her face, and Lydia lovelorn as all get-out. He looks back at the thinning crowd and knows it is time to go home. If he were alone, he might go looking for the next place, but he knows he has found, and is full on, everything one night can hold.

They make their way to the car, and the three of them wait for the long double line of automobiles ahead of them to move on through the packed streets.

"He didn't show up," Lydia says again, twirling a gardenia from the table bouquet between her fingers.

"It's okay." Eunice turns around over the seat to hug her little sister, as the last strains of music wafting from the other clubs on the avenue begin to fade away. The honking of horns increases through the early-morning streets, covering the sound of Jelly Roll Morton's "Deep Creek," but a few notes surface from the din, making lucid the world, as the music splits open and covers Central for that moment no one will ever remember, before vanishing.

"Do you think," Lydia asks, pulling her hair back into place as they wait to go home, "that he thinks I'm ugly?" Mather's heart breaks for her in this moment, because she is too beautiful to tell.

"He's a natural fool if he does," Eunice says. "Who could not love you, Lydia?"

Who indeed, he wonders, could not love them all?

THREE

Mather wakes up late the next day and goes downstairs, where he passes Uncle Wallace, his gray head bent down in front of the radio.

"Mather," Wallace says, nodding toward the box. His nephew pauses, then stops to listen. That is all.

He listens in turmoil and the hazy residue of last night's drinks as the announcer reports Germany's invasion of France from the north. Uncle Wallace shakes his head heavily when the news report ends. "They have to come home," he says, walking off to get his car keys.

He returns and tells Mather to come with him, and the two of them drive to the Western Union office, where Wallace sends off a simple telegram: IT IS TIME TO COME HOME FULL STOP YOU CAN'T JUST SIT THERE STOP WAITING FOR THEM FULL STOP YOU MUST GET OUT OF THERE STOP NOW FULL STOP

When the doorbell rings later that evening, Mather waits anxiously in his room until his uncle calls him. "I can't read it," Wallace says, handing Mather his father's reply to their telegram.

"*Nous sommes bien,*" Mather begins. But from the moment he sees the first word of French on the pale-yellow sheaf, he knows they are not returning. He bites his lip, willing a calm. Because Uncle Wallace cannot. Wallace lets his feeling of devastation flow freely. Mather is not ashamed of this, but he does not think it will do anything for them now.

"He's stubborn, Uncle Wallace," he says, sitting down next to his father's brother on one of the high stools at the island between the dining room and kitchen. "But he's not stupid. He's stubborn and tough."

"They're going to die over there," says Wallace, who has been following the news as doggedly as Mather.

He hears the word "there" and understands it, as his uncle does, to be the other side of the world, instead of the place where he grew up. He realizes that it is, in fact, exactly the other side of the world. He feels this helplessness, but refuses to believe the worst of what he knows.

What he tells himself is, they will get out in time; beneath that he feels a sadness of guilt and selfishness for having left them "there."

"What does he have against us?" asks Wallace, who, instead of swearing and cursing his brother, stills holds him in the brave romantic light he always has. But he knows he has measured the situation correctly, and takes Walter's refusal to return as anger directed at the family, instead of the world.

"You didn't do anything, Uncle Wallace," Mather reasons. "He is still there for his own reasons. Maybe it isn't as bad as we think. If it is, they will leave."

"And come home?" Wallace asks with an edge of anger now that keeps his voice from losing control. "If he leaves, will he come back here?"

"Yes," Mather says.

"Well, when he gets here, he's going to have to eat a whole heap of crow," says Uncle Wallace, trying to make light of his worries. He wipes his hand across his face. "When your father gets back to Los Angeles, it's going to be one helluva sad day for crows."

Mather goes to sleep that night worried about his parents and the friends he has left behind. But when he dreams of them, they are all together again. He knows they will be here in time.

This thought is the only thing that makes it possible for him to get out of bed when his uncle knocks at his door at an insane hour the following morning to take him to work.

When he enters Rose and Sons for the first time, something in him lights up as Wallace shows him around the warehouse.

"This is where your father and I really grew up," Wallace says, leading Mather through the dark industrial building. "Nothing but hard work made all of this." He walks him around the rest of the cavernous room, then hands Mather a pair of thick work gloves when they reach a loading dock out back. "Do you have it in you to keep building?" he asks, nodding at the burly men moving crates from trucks parked in the alley.

"I do," Mather replies, rolling up the sleeves of his white dress shirt and sliding his hands into the rubber-tipped gloves. He had expected his uncle to put him to work in the office, but he lines up with the rest of the men on the platform and strains to move his first box. He watches from the corner of his eyes as the other men transport their loads easily across the gray floor, while he struggles under the weight of a lesser load. By the time he gets across the room, two half-moons of sweat darken the underarms of his dress shirt, and he feels an awful strain in his muscles. But he does his best to disguise the effort it has cost him and hurries back to grab another crate, as his uncle goes into the office.

By noon, his thoughts have turned back to his parents, and he feels his emotions pushing to the surface, pincering his heart as the boxes have the muscles of his arms. He falls behind in his work, and gazes at the pile of unmoved crates climbing higher and higher in front of him.

"Are you going to cry, or are you going to move those fucking boxes?" Wallace yells when he returns to the dock at lunchtime to check on Mather.

"I'm going to lift them," Mather says, not knowing what has turned his uncle so hard all of a sudden, and shocked to hear him, who was so gentle at home, swear.

"Good," Wallace says, leaving him again under the intense sun baking the red bricks in the alley, "'cause that's all a man can do in this world."

He thinks less about France that spring, as he goes to work learning the business of commodities, beginning with how to unload them from the truck every morning before the sun comes up. He moves them as they come down from the San Fernando Valley, up from San Diego, or in from the refrigerated railcars, in which they had been shipped from as far away as Ohio. It is back-breaking work. Performed, he learns, by men who do not fear, or who cannot afford to fear, looking four o'clock square in the face and getting up to demand everything of their backs. As the days wear on, he throws himself into it as well as any of them. Because as he works he knows, and his uncle is not shy about reminding him, that he is not only unloading boxes, he is also handling a thread that goes back to his grandfather, who walked out past where the road ended to make his way to California, extended through his uncle and father, and binds him to his cousins. He is a Rose.

Mather's parents had always encouraged his sense of sensitivity and intelligence, but as he works out on the dock, he begins to see that a man in the world who is only sensitive or smart would know no end of tears.

His uncle pushes him, and he pushes himself even harder, to the point of exhaustion each night, so that when he goes to bed all he feels are the calluses growing on his hands, as they crab up under the ghost weight of their labor, and the ache of raw muscles telling him this is really what it is to be a man.

He scarcely remembers anymore his idle first days, or thinks anymore how big everything is. "Lifting boxes til your balls hurt," is what he writes back to his friend Henri, who sends him a letter telling him things are getting worse in France, then asking, for the sake of comparison, what it is like in America.

When Uncle Wallace moves him, months later, from the loading dock to the office, Mather misses the camaraderie he has won with the men who took the electric streetcar to work every morning and toiled alongside him in the chill air before the sun came up.

Not all of his time on the dock, of course, was so determined. When he dropped his first crate of eggs, because he was daydreaming instead of paying attention to his work, it was one of the worst moments he had known.

As he stared at the slick scramble of yolks, whites, and shells on the dirty warehouse floor, a sharp sense of chagrin walled in him, and climbed all the higher because he had dropped a prized box of extra-large browns from Corcoran. Work on the dock came to a standstill as all around him the men went silent. "Why doesn't anyone say anything?" he asked himself, heading to get a broom to clean up the mess.

When he had walked a few paces, he heard a voice behind him say, "Don't hang your head, boy." It was his supervisor, Joe. "If you never break an egg, it just means you never carried one."

Mather realized they had treated him until then like the boss's nephew. Even if he had been careful never to behave like anything other than one of the guys, their warmth and camaraderie toward him had been reserved. With Joe's words, he gained a sense of how they were when he was not around. He had been determined to outperform everyone, but was now thankful to be accepted like any other worker who has been on the job only a short time and had a mishap. Not only did he feel an easing of the tension he hadn't realized until then had been present, but also found the older man's wisdom applicable to other parts of his life.

It is at the end of the week after this mishap that he decides to call on Mercedes for the first time. He has held her address since the night at the Somerville, because he lacked the courage to proceed. He is not shy around women, but he feared ruining his chance if he acted too hastily. His night of dancing with her was still perfect in his mind, and he suspected only disappointment could follow.

He decides, as he leaves work for the week, that there is no perfect next move. He will simply stop by, as he was invited to, and proceed from there.

After he gets his pay from his uncle, he folds the bills into his pocket and weighs the coins in his hands, then asks one of the guys for directions. When he has washed the stink and sweat of produce from his skin, and changed into street clothes, he walks out of the building onto the midday sidewalk and, since he has driving privileges only on the weekend, boards the electric streetcar. He feels a kind of confidence he has not known before, looking at the thick skin of his hands and work-broken nails.

Only weeks before, he would have been likely to think of his current mission in the language of Romantic and classical poets he had read at the *lycée*. But after endless days of going to bed with no thought other than having to get up and work in the morning, he finds himself thinking like any other man who has spent the week killing himself to gain the few dollars in his pocket. He wants a woman, and he cannot think of anything besides the way Mercedes felt pressed against his arms. When he exits the streetcar, he knows he does not just want a woman, he wants her.

Mather Rose calls on Mercedes Trumbull for the first time as young men have always called on young women, with his hair carefully combed, his tie impeccably knotted, and a trickle of sweat escaping from behind his ear. He had been cocksure of himself on the streetcar, but he approaches the one-story bungalow in Watts nervous as any suitor in the history of courtship.

The wooden house is neat but unpainted, with a weathered trellis framing the garden that runs along the side of the house facing the street. Mather walks up the pathway and across the little lawn, musters his resolve, straightens his tie again, then knocks at the door as casually as he can will himself to do.

The door opens, and Mercedes stands before him, dressed, in overcoat and red cloche hat, to go out on her daily errands. Mather looks at her and knows he has come at the wrong time. He feels himself crash to the ground.

"Hi," he says, pressing ahead and reintroducing himself anyway. "We met, at the Somerville."

"Uh-huh," Mercedes answers, extending her hand with the smallest hint of coyness, "I remember."

In his mind he says things that are practiced and debonair, but all he can manage is, "Well, you look busy." As the words escape his mouth, he feels all of his courage wasted, like a bashful boy shrinking from a pretty girl on the first day of school. He wants to pull them back and start again with that night at the Somerville. He has circled the globe alone, and he has held his own against the burly men and boxes on the loading dock, but this one woman makes all his breath slip away.

She is only eighteen and he a year older, but he knows exactly what he's doing. When she speaks, he hears something in her voice like nothing he has ever known, like a woman who believes there's something deeper, like a woman determined to think for herself. He wants to win her love. Why must that be so difficult? he thinks, holding his nerves in abeyance. "When can I come by again?"

From the time she was fourteen, Mercedes has had young men, and a few less than young, stand at the garden path outside the door of the little wooden bungalow, and she has dismissed just as many as have stood there. Both because she had drilled into her the trouble a young girl who was not careful could find herself in, and because she was beautiful and had the bad habit the beautiful share of always wanting to know what that beauty was worth and might gain; whether it might not always be valued at just a bit more than the offer in hand. She wanted to know if it was worth the price in princes and kingdoms paid in fairy tales. She looks at him sweating and knows that he is not a wolf, but also that he will not be moved. She wonders if this is what all princes are made of.

She is haughtier than on the night of their dance, but he also has that condition of a handsome man who has been pampered all his life, and is used to the reserve of regality and its aspirants. The barriers of beauty that intimidated and prevented others from approaching either of them too easily is recognized by the other, as they stand in front of the little house, not as a character flaw but as a commonality of shared sensibilities. He carries within him not only this power, she thinks, looking at him, but also a grace.

Mather's heart beats wilder, as he tries his best to hold it in check, because he sees in her something other than beauty. He smiles and hopes, without knowing it, to speak to it.

She thinks, as she looks at his handsome face and the vulnerability that cuts through his confidence, that he is the most intriguing man she has ever met. Whether or not all of this was only narcissism on both their parts matters less than what it has produced.

"If you like, you can walk me," she says, looking at him shyly in the face of her uncharacteristic boldness.

"Mercedes, who's at the door?" a woman's voice calls from inside the house.

"No one," she replies, trying to exit, as a small Indian-looking woman comes up behind her to scowl at Mather.

"Hello"—Mather extends his hand to her—"pleased to meet you."

"Hi," the little Indian lady answers him coolly.

"This is Mather," Mercedes introduces them. "He's just walking me to the store."

"Well, hurry back," Mercedes's grandmother tells her protectively as the two young people start down the little step that was the entirety of the front porch, then adds something in what Mather recognizes as Spanish.

"It was a pleasure meeting you," Mather says again, and it is hard to tell which of them looks the more in control and who has more butterflies in the stomach as Mather and Mercedes walk out through the yard, and the old woman stands on the front doorstep watching them head down the street.

Despite what feels to him like his clumsiness with Mercedes, Mather is too sophisticated to ask anything that doesn't need justifying, or simply might be none of his business. His cousins are both experts at deciphering the morphology of human faces, but the only differences he can tell are between the French. He can tell, for example, a French person with Polish roots from one with Italian origins, and between the French and other Europeans.

In Los Angeles he only knows the difference between Negroes, Orientals, Mexicans, and whites, and, as his cousins have pointed out, he is not even always successful there. He cannot, for instance, tell a white Mexican from a white Angelino. And although he is Negro, he has been spoken to in Spanish on several occasions, or greeted with too much enthusiasm by white people his cousins later identified to him as "noncommittal." When he asks what that is, they tell him it is a Negro who passes as white most of the time, but feels guilty about it and reveals himself to colored people he thinks will not judge him. Mather has had many such people unveil themselves to him in Los Angeles. So many, in fact, it has made him wonder whether this is what would have become of his own grandchildren had he stayed in France.

"She thought you were cute," Mercedes says, translating her grandmother's words for Mather.

"Oh," is all Mather can manage, because his mind is still dwelling on the ambiguities of Los Angeles, as he thinks of the little Mexican woman and tries to read Mercedes's sculpted face for signs of not-Negroness, whatever that might be.

"She's black," Mercedes answers his unspoken question. He realizes his silence has made her uncomfortable and self-conscious, but also that he has heard her words with relief. Where before he would not have cared about anything except the curve of her body under its dress and the perfume that wafts from her and moves through the air to seduce him, he now belongs to Negro Los Angeles and his family's society. To date someone who is not of it would cause tension, as he knows from when Lydia pointed out people who were from the wrong crowd. To date someone not from within it, who was darker-skinned than he was, would cause fear. To date someone not from within his circle who was black as the queen of spades and not even Negro would be a little complicated in a society hesitant of outsiders and sensitive to the gradients of skin color even within itself. But to date a beautiful Negro girl with big brown eyes who was as dark as midnight water was to be the envy of any man. Because, he knew, men would kill for women as light as his grandmother or dark as his mother, but everything in the middle had to fend for itself.

Mather finds this all, by turns, amusing, fascinating, touching, and deeply disturbing, especially as it works on him. He has grown up in a space where it was taught as being beside the point, and has not yet found a way to negotiate these things—his love for Negroes and Negro company with the quiet hysteria for color that seeps through them, as well it does through anything else. He has found himself not immune to this, and prizes Mercedes not only for her hauteur and sable-brown eyes, but also for her flawless skin.

Mercedes is bejeweled with darkness, and Mather walks through the streets next to her with a charge of wanting that is more than desire. He has never thought about anything in terms of needing before, but, just as working for his money has made him realize its value, being next to her makes him think beyond the present, squeezing him against something larger than himself to what life requires and reaches for. He walks with her through the South Central streets struck by how simple it is.

As they stroll, Mercedes shares with him little tidbits from the history of Los Angeles, and her own life. "Everyone knows California used to be in Mexico," she says, because she has never had a visitor from out of town before and doesn't know how much he does or does not know. "But no one knows over half of its founders were Negro Mexicans."

Mather certainly did not know. He did not even know there were Negro Mexicans, but as he adds it to a list of things to ask Eunice about, Mercedes goes on telling him how her parents met, when the Captain, her grandfather, still owned the ranch and her mother fell in love with a gringo Negro cowboy from Tejas. "Texas," she teases.

As he hears this story, and others about the early city, he senses in her voice how proud she is of her place in it. It makes him feel more and more a part of it and closer to her, especially since he understands that a story about how one's parents met is an invitation to candor. He also feels her story easing his transition from expatriate to native, as he learns those things only Angelinos know. He knows how lucky he is.

"It was first called El Pueblo de Nuestra Señora la Reina de los Angeles," Mercedes tells him as her grandmother had once told her, "the City of Our Queen of Angels." And because she shares that with him, as they walk past the liquor stores and barber shops on the South Central corners filled with migrant men unable to find jobs, in the future he will also now and again call the city by its ancient name. It makes him feel it is a place watched over, and so everyone in it has the right to hope. It means as well, Mather supposes, looking for the courage to take Mercedes's hand, that all who knew her name might petition directly to the city's Queen. He does so now, as he will on other days, just as, eventually, Spanish will become for him the language of great love.

As they walk down 107th and Mercedes points out the Watts Towers, Mather looks up at the fantasy of mussel shells, mirrors, and glass that decorate the loops and squiggles of the spires. He reaches out to touch her hand, quoting a line from the Romantics that has always served him well in the past.

"Not so fast," she says, seeing through his smoothness and taking a half-step away. Perhaps he isn't so intriguing after all, she thinks, just some guy who wants what all men wanted.

What she tells her mother that night, though, not willing to admit her disappointment or involve her family any more in the affairs of her heart than they already were, is, "I think he's really smart."

Mercedes's dating and prospects for marriage are issues of communal interest in the Trumbull household. All of the old families who descended from the settlers have fallen on ruin as they have, leaving no eligible young men from their old circle who might, or might be willing to, make a good match to Mercedes. Her mother has been disappointed so many times in her own life, and lived in such a state of agitation, that her desires by now come down to three things only: to see her daughter remain a virgin until she is married, to see her daughter not get pregnant before she weds, and to see her daughter wed before losing her virginity and getting impregnated by the city. If she could open one eye and have that wish come true, then her second-most-fervent desire was for her daughter to make a good marriage, to see that her daughter married a man with money, and to see to it that her daughter was neither a failure nor a fool at love and did not marry a bum, so that while in the beginning her wish had only been to see her daughter not devoured by Watts, but married to a nice man, it had grown, as little mustachioed thirteen-year-old manboys first started showing up on the front porch, to six trinity points of devotion.

"Does he have any land?" asks the little Indian, who still equates all wealth with land, and remembers the day the Captain's ranch was foreclosed on. "What good is a man without acres? What does he do?"

"He works in a factory. . . ."

"Dios mío."

"His father's a doctor," Mercedes says, "and his uncle owns the factory."

"Well, how much land do they have?"

"Mercedes, what does he look like?" her mother asks.

"Nice-looking, medium complexion . . ."

"He's blacker than my boot," the grandmother says.

"He grew up in Paris."

"He's an African."

"Well, if you like him, Mercedes . . . ," her mother says, doing her best to release her daughter from her own and her mother's anxieties as she removes the dishes from the table. She takes the information about his family as cause to think, perhaps, her daughter will not be a fool or a failure at love after all.

"Like mother, like daughter," the grandmother says, adjusting her little vest, which was a throwback to the previous century, and accepting her role in the house as the fallen martyr of another age. "At least he's not a cowboy."

Even Mercedes's grandmother, though, is won over by Mather's charm and good breeding the first time he is invited to the house for dinner.

It is Saturday, and he has use of the car for the weekend. He was not at his best during their last encounter, but knows, from the way he has been unable to get her out of his mind, he must try again and move slower, because the very way he thinks about the world changes when he is near her. When he left her, he kept hearing her voice in his head, and it reminded him of goodness, like a woman who has grown up close to God. He wants to be near it, but also to keep it sheltered. He does not know where this instinct in him comes from, but he does not want her to know what struggle the world is.

He drives to Watts and calls on Mercedes again, inviting her out to lunch. She accepts, and the two of them drive up through the elegiac air of the San Gabriel Mountains for a picnic. He finds himself more at ease today, and she finds him more sincere.

When he brings her home, they are still unready to part, finding they get along much better on their second date than on the first, and go to sit in the little garden.

As it grows late, Mercedes's mother, who has spied them once or twice from the kitchen window, comes outside with a pitcher of lemonade. She thinks she knows by looking at Mather that her prayers for her daughter have been answered. Aside from his being handsome and engaging, even with the hint of rebelliousness, he has something in his face that strikes her as kindness.

"Mercedes," she says, as a seeming afterthought, on her way back into the house, "why don't you invite Mather to stay for dinner."

Mather is still wearing the tropical aloha shirt he had picked up when his ship stopped in Hawaii, and at first demurs, claiming he is not dressed for dinner. Mercedes persists, though, then finally looks at him as if she has lost all interest. It is the look she will use in the future whenever she thinks he is being too fussy about a thing, or simply wants her way.

She is self-conscious, though, about the menu, because there has been no time to shop, and even more worried about how her grandmother might behave, but she is also used to improvising and determined to have a nice evening. Mather is impressed by her spirit as he watches her help with the preparations, and finds himself picturing what it would be like if she were making dinner for him alone.

Mercedes is amused by how helpless he is as he tries to offer help, but also finds she likes the way he looks at her, so that by the time dinner is served Mather, Mercedes, and her mother each think they had been the first to see the early signs of a shared future in the house that day.

If Mercedes worried about how her grandmother would receive Mather, she need not have. When Flora, her mother, announced to the old lady they were having a guest for dinner, the older woman immediately began pushing them from their tasks, to take over preparation of the meal herself, roasting the tomatillos, rehydrating the chipotles, broiling the meats, and, finally, placing fresh flowers out on the table. When she finishes, she goes off to dress for dinner, and returns having changed into one of her long crepe gowns and a pair of satin shoes. Her arms are covered, nearly to the elbow, with gold bracelets the Captain gave her, and when she sits, they fill the air with a delightful ringing. She feels tonight as she did when her daughter, instead of granddaughter, was young, and they opened the *rancho* to visitors, as for a cotillion.

Mather, being a good guest, is careful at dinner to pay attention to each of his hosts in equal measure, but perhaps a bit more to Doña Silvia, who overflows tonight with a livelier temper than anyone had seen her in for years.

Mercedes and her mother are pleased with her mood, but trade looks of surprise and amusement across the table throughout the meal. When Mercedes returns from seeing her guest to the door, her *abuelita* is a little tipsy when she confesses to them, "He reminds me of the Captain."

When he arrives home later that night, Mather is as large as on the evening he first danced with Mercedes, as if nothing could be wrong in the world.

When he goes up to his room, he finds an envelope waiting for him on his bed, with a postmark from a small mountain town. He recognizes the handwriting on the envelope as that of his best friend, Henri.

Inside, he finds a short note informing him they did not have time to send it, and is confused until he looks at the interior of the envelope and sees his mother's handwriting. He carefully slits the sides of the mailer and begins reading his mother's beautiful script.

The Germans took the city on June 14, she writes, and we were forced to flee south on the road to Morocco. It is the same stream of people, he would remember, who had been flowing through the streets since the war first began pushing down from the north and east that spring, in cars and carts laden with such things as one saves at the last minute. His father, the doctor, saved nothing but the bag containing the elementary tools of his trade that he kept beside his desk. If not for her, she wrote on, they would have had nothing useful at all, but been adrift in that human tide without any of the necessities of life.

As they went south, their progress was hindered by the triage he performed and the children he delivered. "Imagine," she writes, "almost a dozen children born between Paris and Marseille." Even when they left the city, it had not truly dawned on them that France was defeated, but by the time they reached the port, it was equally hard to imagine there had ever been an armistice after the last war.

She then went on at length to give him practical advice—did he remember to change his socks? Was he keeping his nails clean?— intended to add an air of normalcy to the letter, but that only makes Mather look at his hands and wonder whether they were his mother's or father's that trembled under the yellow light of his bedside lamp.

They had enemies in that city, she reminded him, but they also had friends. By the time he received her letter, what with the mail being so unpredictable at the moment, they would probably be in the middle of the Atlantic. He looks at the postmark on the envelope again, then the date on the wall calendar, before finishing the letter.

The last line is in another hand, and its words are both warm with filial love and cold in their practicality. "If we do not make it," his father writes, "remember, you have a dream to keep."

Mather puts the letter down and feels an irregular skip of time. He looks at the ceiling of his room again, thinking of his parents on the leaky boat in the middle of the sea, and remembers them again as they were when he left, and tries to figure out his father's words, until the moment stretches out indefinitely and that night seems to last a lifetime. So, where only a month earlier he had been a young man, without a single real worry, as it grows early in the June morning and he gets up to go back to work, every space inside him vibrates with the energy of accepting his new responsibility. Mather feels his brain punctured with the awareness of how frivolous he has been before. He feels the psalm of his youth ended.

If he had worked hard in his first months on the job, he finds now he can invest even more in his tasks, as if work might keep the turbulence of good and evil fortune in their proper balance. He works like a man without much time left, putting in longer and longer hours, trying to stretch them; trying to learn everything possible from his uncle. He needs to unlock the secrets of both butter and adulthood. He works to kill time and transport his worries.

Uncle Wallace is pleased by Mather's enthusiasm and new ideas when he suggests taking fuller advantage of the refrigerated railcars, after discovering a wholesaler in Tennessee who undersold their main California farms by pennies an egg. He negotiates with the railroad for better prices as their volume of traffic increases. He begins looking into the possibility of air-conditioned trucks so that they might distribute their wares to farther-flung places, then becomes determined to overcome their inability to win accounts beyond the South Central area of the city.

He returns to the house late at night, and walks through the construction his grandmother ordered when she learned his parents were on their way back to California. Just as he looks forward to showing them the transformation he has undergone, under his grandmother's careful supervision new rooms are being opened in the house, curtains are changed, the yard is relandscaped, and living arrangements reshuffled.

Her Walter is coming home after twenty years and two wars. Now all of her family, she says, going through the house giving instructions to workmen and relatives alike, will finally be there.

"Yes, Grandmother," Mather answers carefully, looking at the thinness of skin around her old eyes, "they will."

FOUR

When the Southwest Chief pulls into Union Station, the entire family waits in the great hall to meet them.

The passengers disembark under the noise of hope and reunion that spreads throughout the massive room, echoing the sound of lovers and families finding each other in the crowd below high up into the beams of the rafters. According to their letter, his parents' boat was supposed to dock in New York earlier that week, and this is the train they planned to take back to California. But as the last passenger enters the emptying hall, the family searches the rooms of the terminal but cannot find them.

Mather walks through the deserted station to the ticket window, his shoe leather reverberating in the hollow air, to ask the attendant whether his parents made the train in New York. The man keeps at his work under the brass light, then finally tells Mather they did not, before pulling down the shade over the glass.

When he reports this to the rest of the family, they all try to take the news in stride. "Well, they will be on the next one," Wallace says, keeping a careful eye on his mother. But as they make their way home on the freeway, a heaviness sits over them all.

They return to a house full of the same partygoers who greeted Mather when he arrived. When these visitors have dispersed, leaving them alone in the rooms, no one in the family says anything as they turn in for the night. They will be here on the next train, Mather tells himself lying in his bed. It has taken nearly two years from their first letter until they finally left Europe for good, so another small delay should be nothing to worry over. He tries to, but cannot sleep.

At five the next morning, he rises and returns to work. He toils the entire day under a fog nothing he does seems able to lift.

He leaves work early for the first time, which for him means promptly when his shift ends, still exhausted from the night before. He gets into the car to go home and rest. On the way, he stops at the station again, and waits outside as another train comes in from New York. When his parents do not appear, he tells himself it was a long shot anyway, and leaves the depot to make his way to West Adams, hoping there will be news of them there. He slumps in his seat and is driving along the evening highway, lost in thought, when his vision is split by lights in his rearview mirror. He looks over his shoulder to see a black-and-white Highway Patrol car approaching from behind.

He steers to the side of the road, then rolls his window down and asks the policeman what is the matter.

The cop leans through the window and scrutinizes him before asking where he is headed.

Mather answers politely, but his ears drum with humiliation. He can feel his blood pressure rising in the space between the two of them as the cop asks for the car's registration.

"Do you have identification?" the cop asks Mather after examining the vehicle's registration and finding it in order.

Mather reaches into his pocket and pulls out his driver's license, then hands it to the cop, who examines it for inordinately long.

While he examines it, Mather goes rigid, searching his mind for anything he might have done or anything that might be out of order with his papers. He then begins to search out his small failures, growing paranoid as the cop holds his identification under the flashlight, until he realizes there is nothing out of order. He begins to grow heated again, but cannot find the words to express what he feels; or, rather, what he feels is exactly to be without words.

"Take it easy, boy," the policeman says, giving the young man a slant-eyed look. "You know you were going over the speed limit."

Mather says nothing as the man gives him back his identification.

"I'm going to let you off with a warning this time, but you should watch it in the future."

In his mind, Mather begins to find words and curses the man, then curses the bitch who bore him, but he is silent as the policeman returns to his own car. He drives again under the mercury lights, dreaming the darkest revenge fantasies he has ever known, against anything that ever wore a uniform.

He is still in a foul, shaken mood when he arrives home and finds his family sitting in the living room, which was seldom occupied. He thinks for a moment his parents have come on some other train, but the silence that grips them tells him something terrible has happened. He looks from face to ashen face before asking his uncle Wallace what has happened. But he knows already.

"The boat sank," Wallace says, handing Mather the telegram that arrived at the house from the shipping company. Mather takes it and scans its lines, before crumpling the paper in his hand and hurling it across the room.

He had received a letter from an old friend earlier that week that painted the darkest picture, and told him just how his parents escaped. He knows now that, if the world they believed in, he believes in, is to exist, then he will have to go through this war to get it. It is the first time in his life he has felt anything like noble sentiment. "I'm going to join the war," he says, his hands clenching into determined fists with nothing in their path to punch. His chest heaves rapidly as he looks around the room, a film coming over his eyes.

"We're not in the war," Wallace replies with stern reason.

"Then I'll go back and join the Resistance," Mather answers, undeterred. "I don't have to fight for the U.S., I can go back and fight for France."

His uncle looks at him. "That's the most feckless thing I've ever heard," Wallace snaps. "What do you have to offer any army besides a target?"

Mather falls silent. He is a grown man. He does not have to argue for another man's approval.

"I need you at the office," Wallace says, backpedaling, both because it is true, and to balm his nephew's wounded pride. "If this war needs you, it has your address."

Mather looks at Wallace in anger, and asks him what he has ever had to fight for. Wallace laughs. Mather grows angrier and steps close to Wallace, within inches of his face, to challenge him, prompting Eunice to get up and come between them.

As she stands there holding out her arms between them, Wallace and Mather look at each other with inflated chests. Mather feels his arms still tight, lending power to his curled fists, as he sizes Wallace up. He knows he can defeat his uncle. The thought though feels barbed in his consciousness, and sends a sting of guilt to his balled hands, sapping some of the strength massing within them. Wallace sees the look in his nephew's face, and realizes the boy would lash out at anything before him right now. He watches Mather carefully, and knows what he measures now is his own power in the world. He is a strong boy, Wallace thinks, but he does not feel danger or threat, only sympathy. That his nephew has stepped so close and walked across a Rubicon without knowing it, and must now learn the source and limit of any man's strength. Wallace reaches past Eunice's arms as Mather tenses, and lays a warm hand on his nephew's face. He cannot protect him any longer.

Later that evening, when the women have retired and Wallace and Mather are alone in the dim living room, Wallace looks at his nephew and tries to estimate what he does and does not know. He has always thought the boy's life was charmed, but sees now he does know exactly what it has been, sheltered or not, as a Negro child in Paris. If he knows nothing about what it means to be a colored man, Wallace says to himself as he looks at Mather, then he has been failed. But if he knows too much: about the depths and abysses of human thought, then the world has mocked his brother and all their lives.

He knows neither he nor Walter has been able to keep their children from looking over the edge and into the canyon of what the world is capable of imagining, of what unsayable transactions are daily conducted, but hopes it has not reached out to clasp and hold his nephew in its undefinable maw.

He has walked his whole life over the hard floor of the factory, and worn a hole in his stomach the size of the bare patch he has paced in the bedroom rug. His brother walked that spring from Paris to Marseille, only to die in a floating hell. His own father had come down over the Rockies a full fifty-five years earlier, walking from Shreveport to Cajon Pass, and from there to the ocean, without a road to steer by.

Wallace wonders where his nephew will walk. He looks at Mather, then turns to stare at the eucalyptus and lemon trees shading the side windows in the courtyard.

"Ours is a fragile place in the world, Mather," Wallace says, still looking into the dark night. "Mine, yours, even those Germans'. Every man is here by some grace of balance, and all you see around you is an acknowledgment of the fineness of that balance, and the fear that it might tip.

"If a man happens to be a thinking man, or a deep-feeling fellow, then he lives just that much closer to tipping that balance, and causes just that much more fear in some people—who don't know what would happen if something shifted on the scales. But that balance is stronger than we think it is too, and not quite so fragile, but most people don't know that. If a man thinks and feels enough to not want to be held back by what somebody else thinks or doesn't think, feels or can't feel, well, you add it up and see how things start to totter.

"Now, if the man trying to think and see his own way just happens to be a Negro, then he must feel like he's living on an icicle, or one of those paper snowflakes children make from tissue paper. Your daddy looked around, then left here for good after the riots of 1919, because he saw it get colder instead of thawing, and he did not want to live his whole life in winter. Maybe can't no man escape it, but I'll be damned if I just sit back and watch you walk right into it."

Mather's father had never given him such clarity around why they did not live where they were supposed to, and his mother was always ambivalent about not being home. But as he thinks of the red-faced policeman attacking his pride down to the bone of being, and his parents in the middle of an ocean, forced to flee an authority with the same intent magnified a thousand times, and thousands of times again, he remembers a photo he once saw of his father in uniform, full-breasted with medals, and his refusal to engage the hand-to-hand humiliation that ultimately took his life, and he feels his father come to him in spirit. He knows he too will go to war.

When the doorbell rings, his face is still set with this resolve as he answers it. He is surprised when he opens it to see Mercedes there, but knew somehow it must be her. Just as, when she enters and looks at his face, she knows with a lover's instinct he is leaving her.

"I'm going to enlist," he tells her finally, as they sit in the court-yard behind the house, snuggling late into the night after he has told her the story of his parents' deaths. She straightens herself and moves a little away from him, to look at his face with her motionless eyes.

"When?" she asks at last, hating him for going away, and hating even more what takes him from her.

"Tomorrow morning."

"Does your family know?"

"I just told them," he says.

"Okay," she answers tentatively, because she has listened to him as the war in Europe was becoming more real in his mind than anything else, larger even, she fears, than his love for her.

"Will you wait for me?" he asks.

"I do not know," she says, bitterly. She does not care about what happens in the world, but about what becomes of him. "Maybe you won't have to fight," she says to herself. The words, however, find voice in the air in the form of her tears. They are not married, but she thinks she has an inkling of how widows feel. "You better come back."

She settles back into his arms and ceases to cry, but silently begins to pray for him.

He is twenty. He challenges history.

FIVE

It is gray and raining at the proving grounds. It rains from the time he arrives in late August, through the rest of the year. He grows comfortable with chill and dampness. He drills on the parade ground, under his heavy gear, waiting for the U.S. to enter the war.

Weeks after he first comes to the army, he is given a battery of tests, more tests than he knew existed, and they determine he is intelligent enough to be assigned to one of the Negro artillery units. Although he thinks he is ready for any unit, he first has to go through desensitivity training on top of his regular duties.

When he emerges from the guts of the fat red brick building, where the new training is held, there is a gloss in his eyes, and a full-body hunger for action as he waits for his assignment. He waits to take down Panzers. He waits for blood and revenge.

The fight has grown hot now on the supercontinent. It engulfs Czechoslovakia, Poland, France, Britain, Finland, Denmark, Norway, Belgium, Luxembourg, and the Netherlands. It is not for nothing this is being called the Second World War: It also inflames Latvia, Lithuania, Estonia, Italy, Ethiopia, Somaliland, Egypt, Romania, and Greece. Mather is a man of the world and has followed events closely, but some of the places the war goes to he never even knew existed; he marks them off on his map all the same, along with Yugoslavia, Lebanon, New Guinea, Syria, Russia, China, and Japan. So far. The United States has not entered. He is dying to get there, but satisfies himself with the knowledge that, as fire can jump water, so too will this thing come.

He eyes his map again and traces the route of his parents' escape into the pale-paper ocean, then sticks the last pin in its fat center and presses it with his thumb, until he has dented the corkboard beneath.

"Nothing but pimps and prostitutes now," his bunkmate, Private Bilkens, says, looking at Mather's map.

"So which are we?" Mather asks, looking at the impish gleam in Bilkens's light-brown face.

"We'll find out soon enough," Blix says, as Mather gets up to go to the latrine. "If you see a U-boat up in that somamabitch, though, we'll know something."

Bilkens is the son of a nightclub owner in Missouri, and has become Mather's closest friend during basic training. His sense of humor and laissez-faire help burn the days, and take Mather's mind from his impatience to get to the front. He knows at the front there is glory. He will wring it from a Nazi's neck.

Even though he has been desensitized, he still feels this deep coil that loosens and tightens as the tension builds in the world around them, and spends his extra time on the shooting range to help release it. The other men in the unit tease him when he comes back, having risen before reveille, singing to himself. Or when he runs extra laps after they have broken some infraction. It is teasing, but not making fun of, and he takes it well. Still, he keeps up his habits. He practices. He runs.

When they are at last given their assignment, at a base overseas, he knows the war has moved closer to them, and takes the train back down the coast to bid farewell to his family before leaving.

They have not seen him in three months, and when he arrives in uniform, they stifle the dissent they felt before he left and try to put on brave faces all around. They too know the war is close at hand.

After lunch in the West Adams house, he goes to visit Mercedes, wearing his new uniform, and the faint mustache he has been cultivating, to show off.

She makes a fuss as big as he had hoped for as they drive to the theater, then head back to his house for dinner. He sits straight in his seat, feeling invincible.

As they arrange themselves around the table for dinner, he touches the new mustache nonchalantly, and tries to catch up on what has gone on while he was away. Mercedes goes into the kitchen to help Eunice with the salad; his uncle Wallace talks to him about business; his grandmother and Aunt Sorra look at him as if he were the center of the globe. He feels in this room a perfect sense of security in the round world.

In back, in the kitchen, the radio plays while Eunice and Mercedes wash the greens and wait for the croutons to finish baking. When they hear the announcer's voice, Mercedes is the first to scream. Eunice does not, but drops an oversized bowl on the kitchen's yellow-and-white tile floor.

In the living room, Mather and Wallace ignore the noise from the back, but Sorra calls into the kitchen to ask if they need help in there. No. It's all right. When they come back to the table, Mercedes stands looking at Mather as everything else recedes around her.

She takes the deepest, slowest breath she can.

"What is it, dear?" Mather's grandmother asks. They speak. Japan just bombed a U.S. Navy base in the Pacific. We are in the war.

Mather's pulse races. He is ready to run back to his own base. The rest of the room fills with uneasy worry for him. Wallace, though, is angry. "Well, boy," he says, looking at Mather, "it looks like you just got your war." But it is not all anger. Maybe—he thinks, looking at his nephew in his new uniform, and the cut his eyes have taken on— they will fight this thing once and for all.

Wallace stands up and composes himself, then clinks his glass with the side of a fork. "I'd like us to rise," he says, looking across to Mather, as the few people around the table still seated rise to their feet. They take hold of each other's hands, and Wallace leads them in surprisingly eloquent prayer for a nonbeliever. "Lord, we ask You to bless this house and this nation," he says. "We ask that when our nephew leaves this house You leave it with him. We ask that the world You made may also be kept safe and free from the malice man from time to time bears his fellow. We ask that our better values and better hearts as men and mankind may prevail. And we ask that You judge them not, Lord, for they know not what they do. Finally, we ask You to help us to believe as we pray."

"Well," Mather says, as they sit and eat in agitation, "the sooner it's started, the sooner it's over."

No one asks him when that might be. What they do not need to ask, as a soothing patriotic fever comes to the table, telling them their sacrifices are not in vain, is who will win.

When he drives Mercedes home that night, Mather's thoughts are distant and unknown. She takes up his arm and puts it around her shoulder, then squeezes his hand.

He leans over to kiss her. With her here, he tells himself, my chances are better of returning.

When they stop in front of her house, she looks at him again and thinks he is the best-looking doughboy on earth.

Where she was distraught before, tonight she is as proud of him as she is sad. He is as important as kings and presidents, and braver, because he rises up to risk his safety for the words they only stake reputations on. He is as tall as the redwoods tonight. She will miss him, and hates the army for taking him away. He leaves for real this time. For war. She does not know how to say good-bye.

It is a year in the world that has unleashed another man from the boy he was when he left France. He feels the excitement of the war pulling him, and the drive to avenge what has been taken from him, knowing he will not rest until he has done this. This angry need courses through him with greater power than he knew existed inside him, but with her he is tender this evening as they make love in the car.

"Come to me," he says, but he moves closer to her instead to press his lips again against the full eight of her mouth. He hugs her buttocks with his hand and lifts her up from the seat. She holds his neck and keeps him close as she explores his slim waistline with her fingers. He moves his hand under her skirt and rolls her panties to the floor. She looks at the foggy windows, worried they will get caught, but he tells her there is no one to get caught by anymore. They are in the large front seat of a car, like teenagers, but he makes love to her as if she is already his wife.

When they climax, he breathes in again the sweet scent from the top of her head that overwhelms even the smell of sex lingering in the air, and the oil she uses to press her hair. The top of her head is the smell of love to him, and it penetrates everything else he knows. He will carry it with him over the ocean and over four years. He will protect that and come home to her. He will avenge his parents and keep them from taking anything else that is his. He kisses her again.

Two days later, it is time for him to report back to base. He leaves the house and puts his duffel bag in the back of the car, then gets in the passenger seat, as Wallace drives him to the train station. The two of them have been careful around each other the last few days, as the time for him to leave grew nearer and nearer, and Wallace grew more and more gruff.

When they stop in front of the station, though, Mather is surprised to see his uncle all choked up.

He does not know what to tell his brother's son, who is going off to war, and can think only of the words his own old man gave to him and his brother when they were children, getting picked on by the neighbors because they were the only Negroes on their all-white block. "When they want to fight," says Wallace, remembering Henry Rose, who did not care much for the emotions, and signed his name to his dying day with an "X" and his thumbprint, "fight brave." His father still spoke with the voice of another age in his accent, but his words fit into his son's mouth with uncanny ease tonight. "Whatever those bastards do, just remember you come down over them mountains, and ain't a thing jackass or government can show you ain't seen twice before you was ten, then tear their fucking hearts out."

Mather shakes his uncle's hand, and sees momentarily his father in Wallace's face. Wallace sees his brother, but he sees Mather as well.

He sees a son. He sees a Rose. Neither of them can stand to drag out this good-bye. They clench hands tighter, and nod. Mather goes inside to catch his train.

From his proving ground, four soldiers are sent to the same base overseas, with the elite Negro battalion. But as the year closes, they watch platoons of white soldiers come and go to the front lines, while they have yet to be assigned their duties. "Maybe they have some specialty," Mather reasons whenever he sees another group leave.

He knows better, but holds the benefit of the doubt out to the army to protect his own sanity.

"Nigger, the only thing they expert in is being white," says Blix coolly. Mather loves Bilkens's ability to curse, which he can never quite do. The one time he said "motherfucker," Gansley, another man in their unit, asked him if he was British or something, and "nigger" he refuses to say, because he finds it revolting, but also for fear it will sound the way it does in the mouth of Jack Jones—a rough sort who is also assigned to them, even though he was conscripted—like he means it.

"Nigger," Jones says when Mather asks him whether or not he is married, "all you need to know about me is that I'm from Minetta Street and I can kick any man's ass from Bed-Stuy to Harlem, and every mick, ginzo, and kike in between."

Mather does not especially like Jones, but Bilkens tells him they need cats like that around. "He come up fighting, and that's what this war is all about. You gone love him as soon as we get to the front."

"We'll see," Mather says.

In July, after Palermo has been won, their lieutenant comes to them and finally announces their assignment.

An excitement sweeps over the men. They are all pent up and eager to get there, wherever they may be sent. But this elation is deflated again when he announces the details of what they have been assigned to do. Even he, who is white, knows it is a waste of his men's talent.

There is no shame in support, the lieutenant tries to cheer them. Every job in this army is important. It does not go over. They are combat troops. They want to fight, and are edgy with it. They look at the lieutenant stoically and do not complain.

Mather and Jones find themselves on a detail loading and unloading supply planes, while Bilkens and Gansley are assigned to transport around the base.

On his first day in the warehouse, Mather looks at the pile of boxes before him as a file of fighting soldiers drills on the grounds. He looks at the faces around him. He begins lifting the boxes; he begins cursing them for keeping him out of the war. He knows with half a chance he could liberate Paris alone, but they are Axis and Allied, he thinks, hoisting two boxes onto his shoulders and walking them across the room. All acts of nefariousness, as well as honor, will belong to them. His own presence, his own life, is merely happenstance at the edges of what they do. That it has been disrupted does not matter to them. They do not want to acknowledge his stake in the outcome of what goes on between Them. Yet They have laid all of this at his doorstep. The men stare as he lifts more crates.

If he is to have any chance at all of regaining what has been lost to him, he knows, he must first give them this effort.

If he is to have any chance of seeing combat, he must first appease them with this collateral, which they seize from him. He knows more has been demanded of other men. But he will not be broken, nor lose his dignity. He lifts, as if lifting is the best job on earth. It is infectious, and the other men join him in this task, like beavers building their dam.

That evening, when they return to barracks, dog-tired under the grime of sweat and the grease of the warehouse, Bilkens stands up at the top of the aisle between the bunk beds and unused gear. "I want every man here to know there is an all-girl dance revue from Harlem at the USO tonight," he says as the men let out testosterone-laden cheers. None of them have seen a woman for months, let alone a whole troupe of them, and Bilkens's words conjure for them images of sweethearts, and women they have slept with before, as they half shut their eyes, trying to remember the feel of pussy nested waist-high around their pricks.

"I also want you to know, all of us are cordially not invited," Blix continues.

"How'd you find this out?" someone asks.

"Because I had to drive them from the bus station this morning," he says, shaking his head. "Fine, fine things."

The whole barracks begins to grumble "Howdoyalikethat?" "Ain't this some shit." "Plus the girls are from Harlem."

"Gentlemen, wait." Bilkens raises a finger. "There's more."

"More what?"

"Does not the Negro soldier enjoy his entertainment as much as the next man?" asks Blix.

"Damn right he does," someone calls up.

"Does not the Negro soldier have the right to some rest and re-laxation, to soothe the nerves frayed by present circumstances?"

"Indeed," they answer.

"Then, men, at eleven hundred hours," Blix carries on, "each and every last one of you, with the appropriate password and entrance fee, is invited to the grand opening of the Church Hill Casino."

Uncertain looks are passed back and forth among the troops. "What are you talking about, Bilkens?"

Blix ignores the naysayer and keeps talking. "Now, the password is top-secret, and if you learn it, I ask you to treat it as such. Divulging the info to squares will be regarded as an act of treason."

"What do they have at this thing?"

"Prizefighting, for starters," Bilkens grandstands.

"What else?" asks Gansley in his flat Nebraska twang.

"Gansley, do you know the password?"

"No."

"Then I am afraid I can't tell you, cowboy," Bilkens laments real sad-like as he walks back to his bunk. "Eleven hundred hours."

"I don't know about this, Blix," Mather says, as the two of them walk to mess hall under the voluptuous Italian sunset. "Can we be court-martialed for this if we get caught?"

"You got to be a fucking soldier to get court-martialed," Bilkens says, the vein in his temple throbbing and the flecks in his eyes jumping like they are about to pop from his head at any minute. "All the somumabitches can bring *us* up on is tax evasion."

"What if it goes wrong?" Mather asks, still unwilling to believe he has let himself get pulled into this.

"Tell you what," Blix says, "I'll raise your cut to twenty percent of the house take."

"You'd do that for me?" Mather asks. "Eighty percent of the risk and twenty percent of the take. You're a swell fellow, you know that?"

"Thirty percent," says Bilkens, and adds, before Mather can speak, "not a dime less and not a dime more. You may be my star attraction, but I have overhead to cover."

"Ah, Negro," says Mather, "you know we're going to the gallows."

"Don't get chicken on me now," says Blix.

"Cut me in forty, funny guy."

"Can't do it."

"The casino's gonna lose an act."

"Okay, but you know you're breaking me."

When the men begin filing into the tent that has been set up in the woods a little ways off base, they find the music in full swing and the bar open for business. Gansley and Jones sit behind the roulette wheel and craps table, under pictures of pinup girls, as Fats Waller fills every empty space between them.

"Where the hell did you get this stuff?" one of the soldiers asks, looking around the tent.

"Nobody knows, my friend," Blix says, taking entry fees and ushering a line of soldiers inside, "but the Shadow.

"Welcome to the Church Hill Casino," he barks. "I think you should find the evening's festivities more than satisfying."

"Is this all you got, some craps and a roulette wheel?" asks one of the troops, who was hoping for something more out of the ordinary.

"The night is young, friends," says Blix, who has handled tougher crowds in his day. But they are still tense with unused masculine energy as the place begins to fill with the curious and drunken around midnight, and Gansley and Jones clean them out of their wages at the tables.

"This joint is a scam," explodes one of the latecomers, who isn't quite drunk yet but is behind odds all the same. "Is anyone winning in here besides these jokers?" He points a finger at Blix's chest.

A murmur of anticipation rumbles through the crowd as they wait to see how Blix will respond.

"Is this the thanks I get?" he asks, turning away from his challenger, then walking to the middle of the room and hopping onto a chair. "So you're not satisfied with cards and liquor?"

"We can do that anytime," they complain.

"You said this was going to be better than the show they're having at the USO."

"You promised prizefighting."

"Soldiers," Blix says, as Gansley drums the tabletop, "prizefighting there will be."

A klieg light bursts on outside the tent as he speaks, to reveal three rows of chairs cordoned off around a ring.

A few of the men shrug, but the others rush forward to grab seats. "I don't know what these turkeys are up to," one of the soldiers says to his buddy, "but just about anything is better than not seeing that show."

"Did you see them when we left mess?"

"No, but I saw a bunch of legs wearing skirts up to here." He makes a line below his chin.

"What's he gonna do to top that?"

"Hear ye, hear ye," Blix announces, taking the middle of the ring. "The Church Hill Casino is proud to present, for your evening's entertainment, not one, not two, but a triple-card title bout!"

The men all cheer and peer around, looking for the fighters, and, "oh no he didn't," then whistle and stomp, rising to their feet. "God save you, Bilkens."

"For the title of best fighting cock in the United States Armed Services," Blix bellows on, feeding from the energy of the men. "The action will proceed as follows: The winners of the first and second bouts will meet to determine the World Champion, not tomorrow, not next week, but tonight, right here at the Church Hill Casino."

"Who's fighting?" the crowd yells.

"I'm glad you asked," Blix answers archly. "Representing the navy is none other than former Heavyweight Champion of the World, and the first Negro man to hold the title. GIs, a round of applause, if you will, for Mister, Jack, Johnson!" The men look to the corner of the ring where Blix points to see Jack Jones holding a gigantic red rooster.

"Representing the army is none other than the current World Heavyweight Champion, Mister Joe, the Brown Bomber . . . Louis," he continues, to the eruption of another wave of cheers.

"On the second card, direct from the Signal Corps of these United States, GIs, put your hands together for Max Baer."

"Who's he fighting?" they yell.

"Fresh from the Coast Guard and his first Hollywood film, still caged, but the number-one contender, Kiiiid Galahad."

The joint is just about losing its mind. Money starts changing hands, and everyone bets on the size of the rooster, or the sentiment they bear each fighter.

Gans and Jones are ready to turn Baer and Galahad loose for the first fight when a voice from the back of the crowd pipes up, "Hey, can we get in on the action?"

Blix holds his hands up for silence and walks to the front of the ring. "Well, looka here, looka here. Look who got tired of all that goody-goody shit over at the USO. Don't be shy, show your faces, men."

"Don't let em in, Blix," the crowd yells.

"This is a segregated army."

"Aw, boys," Blix says, "these are fellow soldiers. They ain't with the War Department, and they learned the password same as anyone else. Am I right, boys?"

The band of white soldiers are no longer sure how they feel about this after all, but what the hell. "That's right."

"You heard the man. Make way," says Blix, as the white soldiers pick their way through the uneasy audience to find seats. "Somebody gotta bet on Baer and Galahad."

The men guffaw tensely, and a few beers are passed up the aisle for the late arrivals as Gans and Jones let loose Galahad and Baer, and the fighting begins to throb amid screams for blood.

"I did not plan it this way," says Blix, after the first two bouts have ended. "But you saw it, and you saw it here. Max Baer pecked the shit out of Kid Galahad, and, well, I guess Johnson was a little past his prime. So, once again, the World Heavyweight title comes down to Mister Joe Louis, and Airman Max Baer. Get your bets in. It's going to be a battle tonight."

The men double and triple down, looking for sides to hedge against those sentimental favorites they picked before the first fights.

Baer killed Galahad stone cold dead, they debate the odds for the title, but, I don't care what nobody say, that's Joe Louis for real. The bets keep coming in as Jack Jones prepares Baer and Gansley handles Joe Louis, until one of the Louis backers calls Max Baer "Max Schmeling."

Jack Jones is six feet five if he's an inch, and has never been closer to an animal in his life than kicking a stray in the street, but he holds that bird and looks in its eyes like he loves it, then checks the spurs with a lemon half, announcing, "I've changed his name to Just Max."

Gansley lifts Joe Louis's wings and checks under them, squeezes water from a cotton ball into his mouth, then stares his fighter in the eye as well.

The men look up at each other, and each shakes his bird. Blix announces from ringside, "Begin."

Gans and Jones drop the birds in the ring, and they bolt from the corners straight toward each other with all the instinct of warriors. Max lifts his wings to their full span, then crows out a cockadoodle-doo to curdle your blood. Joe Louis squawks back and pushes out his chest, his feathers rising into the air, standing on end.

Max announces himself again, but before the call is out good, Joe Louis leaps up, twists around, and stabs at Max's head with those spurs.

Jones flinches forward to go to his aid, but holds himself back and starts talking to him instead. "Come on, Just Max, you come up surrounded and fighting. You know this motherfucker can't kick your ass."

The crowd laughs, but Just Max obeys as if he understands the man, and lifts up off the ground with both spurs back, his unflying wings just holding him there for what seems like forever.

Louis is cut on both sides of the head, and smooths down his feathers, then takes off running around the ring. Max gives chase, slow as can be, stalking the other bird, as he waits for his chance to pounce.

The sun is coming up now, but neither bird calls. Joe Louis because he's scared. Just Max because he's winning, and the loser's blood feels better in his mouth than sunshine. He stops walking and stands there, staring his opponent down, as Joe Louis runs, dripping blood around the circle.

Louis goes to his corner to quit, but Gansley is there pumping him up and egging him on. "Mr. Joe, Max making you look like a sissy," he says. "Get back out there and show him what you made of." Gans is open-faced and soft-spoken, but starts screaming at the top of his lungs, smashing his fists into the wooden boards. "Fight or die, goddamnit. Fight or die!"

Max waits, and Louis lifts his head just in time to get a good look at the beak that comes to peck out his eyes.

All he can do now is cut his way out, or never leave that corner again. Louis's feathers thrust out. He bleeds, and cackles loud as he can, digging deep to come up with a roundabout blow to Max's head.

Feathers fly from both those birds as the turbine spurs flash and gleam out blood, and the dust kicks up fierce as any storm.

"Cockadoodle-doo!"

"Goddamn."

Joe Louis hits the ring floor, dead.

Just Max starts walking back to his corner, and Jones is there cooing. The bird staggers forward, dripping blood from his chest, his wings, and the comb that has been cut from his head. His feathers lie down, and if a bird could cry or swear, Just Max would.

Jones climbs over the wall and gathers his bird from the ring. Just Max, scalped and bleeding, clucks one more time and dies.

Jones clutches him around the neck and holds him aloft before the crowd. "Pay your debts, motherfuckers," is all he says.

Joe Louis's backers pay up, feeling low-down, not just to be out of the dough, but also because they dubbed the bird Schmeling and lost to him. They wonder if this is an omen of how the war will go.

Some of Max's boosters are feeling the same, and keep saying it was Just Max, not Baer, or Schmeling, as one of the white boys cracks wise, "Harry, you think they're gonna start rioting?"

"Just games, just games," Blix says. "The bar's still open, and Church Hill Casino has one more treat for you. But I will need the bravest man out here tonight as volunteer."

"What's he got now?" the crowd asks, but they're pumped up for whatever is in store.

"Will you get a load of that."

The sun cuts orange and almost full over the edge of the horizon, as the sky around it refracts the diffuse blue light, sharp and clear as an angel's unconsoled weeping. Fifty feet from the cockpit, a man walks toward them, dressed in a full-face mask. At thirty feet, he stops and tosses up his empty hand, causing the men to startle as a shot rings out. From the top of the tent, a red flag comes sliding down to earth.

"What the hell . . ."

He rolls back his sleeve to reveal the derringer strapped to his wrist, and stands out there in the field like a phantom.

"My fellow GIs," says Blix, who lives for a show and is having the time of his life tonight, "may I present to you the best shot in the armed services. No one knows his name, or which branch he comes from.

"In fact, his very existence is classified intelligence, but, as a bonus for the patrons of the casino, we wish to present the finest display of marksmanship any of you will never see again.

"Remember where you saw it, but loose lips sink ships, boys, so we ask that you don't tell a friend." He leads them out closer to the guy in the getup, and arranges six bottles on a stand.

"Marksman, are you ready?"

The masked guy nods, and Blix moves aside.

Six shots, and six bottles are shattered.

"Now, who here is the bravest man?"

Everyone has caught on, but no one moves.

"Bravest or stupidest?" somebody asks, but nobody else says a thing. Blix has challenged their manhood, but they don't want to die like this. "I think it's you, big Blix," somebody yells, and the others all agree.

"I am afraid, gentlemen, that, as your host for the evening, I'm forced to refrain," Blix explains with that energy people get when they're trying to sell you something that's a better bargain for them than for you. "But don't tell me I'm in an army of cowards. What about you fighting soldiers?"

"I'll do it." Jones raises his hand.

"How about me?" says one of the late arrivals.

"What's your name, friend?" Blix asks, passing over Jones.

"Harold Boyle."

"Harry Boyle? It's going to be a long tour with a name like yours."

The guys laugh appreciatively, but it's nervous laughter. That's live ammo he's using.

"GIs, a round of applause for Technician Harry Boyle, the bravest of the brave."

The men applaud Boyle as Blix leads him to the mark and places a Coca-Cola bottle on top of his head.

"I think this shot is too easy for the best shot in the services," says Blix to the marksman. "Why don't you take another five paces back."

The Ghost Soldier turns on point and counts five steps, then turns again to face the target. "Anytime you're ready," Blix signals, moving aside.

Mather lowers his gun and looks down the sight at the man in front of him. Something feels off. As he lines up his shot, all he can think about are his parents, and he keeps moving the barrel between the bottle and a point above Harry Boyle's tight-shut eyes. He squeezes off the shot, barely aiming.

Boyle's fucking knees are knocking as he waits for the report from the pistol. "I came here in good faith, but this is stupid," is all he can think. "You're about to get yourself killed in a nigger carnival, Boyle. This ain't a game." He shuts his eyes tighter. "It's a twisted revenge, like Amos 'n' Andy with real darkies and real guns." As the glass rains down over his head, his testes descend again. He lets out his breath and opens his eyes.

Everyone in the casino is applauding for him, but the masked man has disappeared.

When he gets back to the barracks later that morning, Blix finds Mather retching in the latrine, with his head halfway down the hole.

"That was brilliant," Blix says. "I've seen a lot of shows, but that was near the best. And, to top it all off, we just made three months' wages."

"Blix," says Mather, "I could have shot that man."

"No, my friend, you could not have," says Blix. "You can't miss, man. I don't know what the hell it is, but it's like shooters you hear about from back when."

"You don't understand," Mather says, unable to explain to himself what happened to him out there, because his parents had instilled in him what he thought was a hereditary respect for life. "I could have shot that man and not given a fuck, Blix."

He has not been to the lines, but he understands how much larger this war is than he had grasped before its violent blood-lust worked its way into him. It is larger than his rage, larger than his will to avenge his parents, larger even than Nazis and Fascists. It is a machine of gods who shit and laugh at any man's effort to do right, or have justice. He understands, no matter what the outcome in Europe, he will die before the war is over. The gods have called for a sacrifice. They will receive it. But his own body, he will make it bitter as bile to their altar.

SIX

Mather's face is harder now. The six stripes of master sergeant grip his shoulders and set him apart. He has lifted more boxes than he can count. Though he knows it has been a contribution to the war, he thinks of it not as work done, but as that much more he has to get back. When he surfaces from these places, Mather knows he can lift all the boxes on earth, until the very mass of the planet has been shifted. When he writes home to his wife, he does not tell her this, but is all kisses to their children, love to her, and calm words in the face of the Zoot Suit Riots she has told him about.

The only person he bellyaches to is Blix. Blix alone understands what his stripes have cost, or knows what Mather has gone through in the warehouse, lifting boxes, while others are sent off to fight. "But if it is in you, does it matter whether or not it is seen?" Blix asks as they counsel one another to be patient, trying to push away the slights they have daily received. There are still moments, though, when they wonder if the problem is with themselves.

As he rides in the back of the truck to Bastogne in early winter, Mather barely remembers why he volunteered to begin with. But he knows by the hollowness of interior spaces that were once full, that he has a whole planet of things to get back. His face is a little bleaker than before. He has a Mather's worth of things to retrieve from this war.

The closer they get to the front lines, the faster his brain burns, as he feels the ground shift with each jolt from the Luftwaffe and B-29s above. They drop bombs Mather has loaded, and tear apart a world he has loved. He wants all of it back—the earth, the bombs, the effort. He wants his youth and his parents back from this thing; to be able to see without cynicism, and live again as he once did, not innocent, but unruled by hatred or fear. He smokes his cigarette without hands as they move toward the front line, and watches villagers flee, and small children wave to them, calling out blessing in French. What is at stake for him is no longer states, or ideas, or his parents' death, but his very self. If his motivation extends beyond this, it only goes as far as his family, who were forced to run as these villagers do now, and the men here to whom he has grown as close as family.

If he fights in a country's uniform, let that country win. But he would as well face battle wearing a zoot suit.

As the front line looms and he thinks these things, his face gains the concentration it had nearly four years ago, when he enlisted. He knows the only thing that will prevent them from doing it again is to fight with more courage than other men; to exterminate them if it costs his life. This means more to him than anyone may know, and he has volunteered for the riskiest assignment. When they demanded it, he gladly traded in his stripes for the chance to go into combat, to kill that he might live in a just world.

A million of them pledged as much, including the one Mather replaces as their ranks are culled and reaped from.

When he finally does get to the front, it is not the porous formation of men he thought it would be, but a solid tunnel, whose sides are formed of bullets and fire. A hundred trainloads of ammunition are spent here, and they divide the air like walls. He moves and lives in the small, ever-moving subdivisions between them. The only constant in this murderous forest is the snow and rocky mud at the intersection of these four countries. The boundaries of the countries themselves are as movable as the bullets and bombs. As they advance, so too do the borders of France and Belgium; when they retreat, Germany grows larger, and freedom shrinks to the size of a machine gun's chamber.

He spends the month like this, living between bullets, fighting to gain another tree or rock, here in permanent winter. If he has a family, he seldom thinks of them. If he has a self, then it is without borders, but absorbed into the selves of those million, whose only purpose on earth is to fight.

They flinch and kill whatever they see. They close their eyes and do not look, but keep pulling the trigger, hoping it is not the last thing they do.

And they die. They die in all kinds of ways. They burn. They are stabbed. Their skulls are smashed. They are ripped apart, body from limb from life in fire and bombblasts. Inside the sieged city, they starve. They die who are not in the war. They who have already surrendered. They die at night; in their sleep. They die only half awake, like zombies, from seeing so much death and cold. They freeze.

These images of men, literally frozen in death, stay trapped inside his mind. He does his best to avoid looking at them, but they are mowed down with such merciless speed and are everywhere he looks. He swears if he gets out of here he will appreciate every day life gives to him, knowing how brief any of them might prove to be. But here he must cast himself into the killing and death, whose aggregate causes are too far removed for even Mather to think about. It has been reduced to homeland, way of life, history, race, and supremacy. It is only a shorthand, and some of it even the slowest of them know is soberly absurd, but it does its work. They die for it. Until they are drunk with dying and killing.

The mountains fill with shit, piss, and trash. Sniper fire follows their every move, and the bombs, the bombs plague their dreams.

He no longer begrudges moving boxes. It is an effort for the war well done and worth it. It helped move us this far, he tells himself, as machine-gun fire pins him down in the abyss of destruction. He knows he must go farther. He wants to grow old, so gives himself completely to that machine of killing and death. He fights to go home again, but does not care about glory.

As his unit advances through the Ardennes, the tide of battle begins to turn, until the Negro squadron he leads is as legendary on the fields as the Ghost Soldier is on the rumor circuit. Even on the German side of the line word has spread, and they are proud when they learn the enemy fears them more than any other unit in the entire Second Army, and its veterans think they are in it with the legendary Hell Fighters again.

A propaganda plane flies overhead one morning, and a shell races toward it, before arcing over the horizon, missing. The men hug the earth and hold their breath, waiting to be strafed by merciless metal or the fiery hell of dynamite exploding through them. Instead of a bomb, though, when the plane passes overhead, a thousand leaflets came fluttering down over their heads.

Blix picks one up and opens it, then starts reading aloud:

Hello boys, welcome back! What are you doing here? Fighting the Germans? Again? Have they ever done you any harm? Of course some white folks and lying English and Americans told you the Germans ought to be wiped out for the sake of humanity and democracy. What is democracy? Do you enjoy the same rights as the white people in America? Or are you rather not treated like second class citizens. And how about the law? Now all of this is may not be as well in Germany. We invite you to come join us to see. For example did you know there are Negro Germans? We tell you there are. We even maverickly predict for one to be Führer before they terminate Negro maltreatment in the U.S. To carry a gun in this service is not an honor but a shame. Throw it away and come meet with us. You will find friends here over the German lines who will help you.

Signed,

General der Panzertruppe und Kommandeur der Panzerhops von Rheinland und Sudwest

Second Panzers of Southwest and First Panzers Provisional of Rhineland

"I wonder what they'd help us to?" Blix asks, balling the pamphlet up and tossing it back into the snow.

"Hey, Sarge, you ever been to Germany?" Gans asks, making a point of using Mather's rank.

"I lived in Berlin for a year when I was a kid," Mather says.

"They really got Negro Germans?" Gans continues.

"Gans, they got everything everywhere, and every last one of them is out somewhere in these hills trying to get a bead on your country ass."

"Do you really think they're going to have a Negro Führer one day?" Gans presses on.

"They will," Blix answers him, "if you don't close your mouth and start shooting."

"Ah, Gans," says Jones, "you make it too easy for him."

They go back to war, pressing on through the forests.

As the weather finally begins to clear, the tide of battle turns decisively in their favor, and the Allies chase the retreating enemy, launching a full-out counteroffensive.

Mather, Blix, Gans, and Jones all fall in with their division and begin the long march south. It is the second-longest Mather will ever make. They walk through red and ashen snow, their feet freezing inside their boots and their clothes lined with old newspaper, looking to anyone like orphans of war. They carry their bundled homes on their backs, through the trees, over the spiny ridge of earth. Ice forms on their whiskers, and no one is above pissing his pants for temporary warmth. All have known winter, Mather in France, Jones in New York, Blix in Missouri, and Gans on the plains of Nebraska, but none of them has ever known a coldness this bitter before. It creeps up their fingers and follows them to bed at night. Their words decrease, because when they open their mouths winter enters into them. It licks around their feet and shoots into their bones, like shells piercing a tank's skin. Their own skin grows ashen, and some of their hearts also begin to freeze. They march through a winter so cold, one day there will be monuments to it. This is the permanent winter. For a month they march, die, and freeze, chasing Nazis through the bloody woods.

Mather's face is placid now, numb with no more determination than to survive the winter. "Is this the best they got?" he asks, reaching that point when he must decide either to stop right there, or that he can walk forever. Mather can walk to the end of the earth. He picks up a handful of snow and washes his frozen face with it, licking away the ice crystals that cling to his mustache. He holds the remainder in his hand and looks at the sky it fell from and laughs a challenge to winter.

Winter laughs back at him.

"Bring it," he says under his breath. Bring everything you got. "You will not take us." He shouts for his men to march in double-time, as the other units stare at them in disbelief. "See you in Germany," his men cry, waving, literally running toward the last days of the war.

It is midnight on the fifth day of the counteroffensive, and nothing stands between the Second Army and the Rhine except a stubborn nest of snipers they have been unable to dislodge. Mather and his men are digging in, preparing for what promises to be a drawn-out battle, when the order comes down for them to attack the nest of Germans the next morning.

It is an impossible task, but when he receives it, Mather does not flinch. He knows he and his men are capable. They will be first to cross the Rhine. They will win the war, or else they will die in the attempt.

Regardless of death or victory, he also knows he will lose some of them the next day, and as he digs his foxhole to turn in for the night, it does not escape him that perhaps it is his own time that has come. If so, he is ready for it. To die in this battle.

When he finishes the foxhole, he climbs in to prepare for sleep. Before he does, he takes out his kit knife and begins carefully cleaning his fingernails. He knows it is absurd, and imagines how it should look if he died in this position. But he is not preparing for death. He is preparing to live. He cleans his nails because he knows how little keeps men from losing their dignity and becoming animals. Less than animals, men who no longer know the difference.

When he finishes, and is about to lie down, he hears Blix, Gans, and Jones outside calling his name.

"Happy New Year, Sarge," they say when he emerges. Blix gives him a cup, then produces a bottle of whiskey. It is the last bottle from the old Church Hill Casino.

The four of them all hold their cups and could cry to see that handle of bourbon. As he receives it, Mather clasps the neck of the bottle and takes a slow, careful draft. He wants this drink to last until the end of time. It is whiskey he will one day tell his children about:

"I once had a bottle of black-market bourbon, sitting high on top of the earth. Snow stood as high as my hand. It was dark from smoke, and red with blood. New Year's Eve, 1945, and I shared that drink with the only friends I had in the world. When the war ended, I named you after one of the men who drank from that bottle.

"It is a blessed name, because there were four of us that night, but not all would live to the end of the next morning."

He knows he wants another child. If he should lose one of these men, he knows he will name it after him.

Before they turn in, the men ask him to sing again the song he used to when they first met four years ago, which they recognize now as "La Marseillaise."

He whistles it still to himself when he wakes up next morning.

Allons enfants de la Patrie
Le jour de gloire est arrivé
Contre nous de la tyrannie . . .

A carpet of snow has settled over the battlefield during the night, and they break the first tracks in the blank stillness, walking in the iron-green light of half-morning darkness through the forest. The wind nettles their faces and escapes from their mouths like a phantom, as the sun splits over the tree line. They are silent as the morning itself. Mather feels a love for these men as deep as he has ever felt for anyone, because they follow him on this suicide they have been put to.

Across the forest, the German soldiers watch the same sunrise, knowing they do not have much time left. The no-man's-land between them seems now like even less than it did the day before, but they summon their own will to murder for it.

Mather leads his men across the line to the position on the map, and begins looking for the enemy. They come across an abandoned airstrip and think momentarily the Germans have already turned tail, until the skies above them darken and shadow the ground. The air around them crackles with the sound of thousands of airplanes approaching.

They look up and realize they are being carpet-bombed, but it happens with such speed, by the time they know what is happening the space they move in is lit up like an inferno at the end of time.

Mather tells his body to move, but all he sees, feels, tastes is fire.

It laps against his skin, circles his tongue, enters his lungs, and singes the lashes from his eyes. It yanks the hair at the top of his head, and lifts him from the ground. He fires randomly into a void of yellow and orange that moves toward him in massive waves edged in black. It is the Reich's last grasp at victory, and his eardrums vibrate from the force of its will, as the shelling keeps lifting him higher off his feet, suspending him in air and time.

When he looks around again, instead of men, all he sees are skeletons outlined in fleshy red, strung together on the long metallic line of a single, infinite bullet.

Mather hits the earth again and stares up from the explosion into the eyes of a dead man, staring back at him. He wonders briefly whether it is himself he looks at, as two wings grow from the corpse's back. The Luftwaffe drop another bomb. He is kicked from the ground again, with such destructive force he knows this time he will not survive.

Miraculously, when his eyes reopen, he hears voices, speaking in German, coming from behind a stand of trees just yards away. He looks around for his men, and doesn't see anyone but a wounded Jack Jones. He pulls himself up, then goes to Jones and drags him through the snow from harm's immediate path.

When they are behind the tree line, Mather fashions a sling for

Jack's shattered arm. Jack winces, then holds his scream in as Mather points out into the forest, motioning for him to keep quiet. But it is too late. They have been discovered, and shots rupture through the leaves and air around them.

Mather helps Jack to his feet, and the two of them make a desperate dash to hide behind a boulder. The bullets increase, gaining greater and greater surety, as they crouch there, until they know they will be pulverized if they do not move. There is no road through the bullets chipping at the rocks as the Germans advance behind their shield. They hold their breath, trying to figure out what to do. In either direction is a notarized death; the only way more certain is doing nothing at all. They look at each other for what may be the last time, and nod; then Mather takes off in one direction, and Jones goes sprinting in the other.

Mather is hit by one of the bullets as he dashes deeper into the woods, but keeps running until the din of gunfire grows dim and he finds himself alone, creeping through the silent forest. When he is safe, he does not go on to his base; instead, something in him turns his feet back toward the source of the fire.

He tries to breathe evenly as he pulls his damaged leg along, calming his nerves when the trees shake from each unknown breeze that passes through them.

He will not turn back, but keeps moving through the woods to finish his mission. To get across the Rhine, even if his entire unit is gone.

When he comes behind the German position, he calls for the six men in front of him to put their hands up.

One of the Germans turns around but moves too quickly, and falls to the ground, dead, as Mather pulls the trigger of his pistol reflexively. "Put your hands up," Mather commands again. "We have the woods surrounded." The Germans see him alone, and let loose three precise rounds in his direction.

He knows he cannot, but swears he sees the moment the first bullet cuts into his skin and the blood begins to spurt. He finds presence of mind to return fire anyway, and his aim proves more accurate than the other men's. One after another, three more Germans die.

When the woods fall still again, he searches around for the rest of the enemy, who he knows are somewhere right on top of him. He cannot find them, until the two remaining soldiers rush from either side, and he finds himself in a hand-to-hand struggle for life. He manages to get his outstretched fingers around one of the Germans' throat in the babel of fear and instinct, but the other circles his hands around Mather's.

Mather tightens his hold and tenses the muscles of his neck, gasping for breath, and fights, refusing to let go, until he hears a click of bone. The man in his hands falls to the earth without last words. He does not have time to enjoy this respite from death, but feels himself growing weaker as well, on the short edge of blacking out, beneath that other set of hands. He looks to the ground, and looks to the sky, still feeling the dead man's invisible throat in his hands, and the air inside his own body lodged, unable to find a way out. He tries, but is too weak to escape this grasp.

As he looks up again, he knows it is the last time.

Instead, he sees Jack Jones advancing, from the corner of his eyes, and has never been so happy to see any man. Still he does not know whether Jones will arrive before he loses this fight, until Jones crushes the barrel of his pistol into the other man's laboring face.

Mather puts his hands on his knees when the German soldier's hands fly from his throat, and works to recover his breath, but knows he might yet lose it again.

"*Jetzt bin ich Kriegsgefangene,*" the German says, looking at the two of them with fear. "I am now a prisoner of war."

"Not that fast," Jones yells, still cocking his pistol. "Where the hell did you come from?"

The German looks about dumbly as sniper fire buzzes them again. "*Wo sind die anderen?*" Mather asks, slapping the man hard in the face.

"Over there," Jones yells, pointing. "Behind that tree." But it seems to come from all around, as if there is a sniper perched on each particle of air.

Mather aims into the trees, holding the trigger like his wedding ring, as he releases everything in the clip, and the bone-rattling percussion thunders through all of them. He had thought at the beginning of the war he would feel vindicated when he killed those who took life from his parents. But all he feels now, still holding the trigger, even after the shooter has fallen to earth, is the terror of the moment.

He wills himself toward calmness, but knows how easily any of the dead in those woods could be him. He repeats his oath to himself that if he leaves this pine forest he will cherish life as never before.

"Where's the rest of the master race?" Jones screams with bloodshot eyes and blood streaking his face. "*Wo sind die* bastards?"

When he sees the last sniper fall, the German prisoner realizes they are beat, even before Jones lifts his pistol to pound his face again. He no longer resists, but leads the Americans to the German encampment.

"Tell them to come out," Mather says as they take position around the warren.

"With their hands up, and slow," adds Jones.

"Kommt 'raus, alles in Ordnung," he calls, repeating Mather's directions, giving him a strange, vacant look even under these circumstances, when he realizes how well the American speaks German.

From the ground, a dozen boys hear him and emerge, shaken as leaves.

Mather and Jones keep their guns trained on them, secure their hands with belts, then command all thirteen to march.

"Wir, wir sind das Schwarze Kommando," Jones mutters, his eyes waxed glassy with war.

They march now, almost with relief, through the eerie woods, over the snow hills of death, their pants slipping around their waists, and some down to their feet. But there are rules for treating war prisoners. They cannot be shot. They must be fed, and they can't be left outside in that cold.

As they make their way through the trees, it is hard to tell who is more afraid, but for those ten, there is the relief of knowing that now the war has ended.

When they arrive back at camp with the prisoners, Captain Smith looks at the ragtag mess in astonishment. "Damn good work, Rose," he says, assigning a group of men to take the enemy soldiers.

"It was mostly Jones," says Mather. "I just kept him company."

"Well, I'll be damned," the officer says, looking at Jones. He looks back at Mather. "Somebody find Rose a medic."

Mather had not felt it before, running on pure adrenaline, but feels now the skin around his wounds begin to bubble, and a terrible itching deep in the openings. "I'm fine. Just send me back to the front," he says, growing lightheaded, before falling crumpled against the ground.

When he wakes up, it is in a military hospital. He is as surprised to find himself there as the doctors are to see him wake up at all. They tell him the fight is nearly over, but that he must remain in the hospital until his wounds have healed completely.

He stays only until he feels they have healed enough, then goes AWOL. He makes his way back to his unit, where he is thankful to see the boys again, but is even more ready to get back to action. He wants this war to be over, and allows himself to think perhaps it will end in his lifetime after all.

"How were the nurses, Sarge?" Blix wants to know, even before he asks after Mather.

"Ah, forget that, Blix," Mather says, counting the men left in his unit. "Where's Gans?"

Jones and Blix look at each other.

"Gans went back to Nebraska on the 1 'n 5," says Jack.

Mather does not get it, and wonders what else has happened while he was in the hospital. "They built a train across the ocean?"

"The 1 'n 5 only ran from the Bulge," Blix answers him. "And it carried a lot of heroes home."

SEVEN

Few better things have happened to man, woman, or speechless GI than to be kissed by the Queen of the City.

Mather rejoins his company in February, but the two months he spends marching through the streets of Germany into the heart of the defeated seem half as long as the month he spent in those mountains.

When they are discharged, it is in May, and he is laden with medals—silver, bronze, gold, and palmed. When he returns Stateside, his captain tells him, there will be a special ceremony in Washington where he will receive the Medal of Honor. The platoon applauds something wild when they hear about it. He is their hero, and to know he will be honored makes all of them feel the war they have just fought may have changed things after all. For once, no one can deny they are the victors.

Mather downplays the medal. What he is excited about is returning to Paris after so long. It is early in the morning when he gets on the train leaving Berlin, with Blix and Jones, and as he promises, they arrive in the French capital by sundown. He was a teenager when he left. He is fully grown now.

The train pulls into Gare de L'Est, and all around the station is a rainbow of men in uniform and bandaged wounds. His friends stare up at the great cathedral ceiling and look around themselves in wonder, to be in Paris.

Mather searches the crowd distractedly, looking for faces he knows. He does not see any.

When they leave the station, he leads them to a mid-range hotel just off the city center.

"Ah, Rose," says Blix, dropping his rank. They are free men again. "Can't we do any better than this?"

"Blix," says Mather, "there's nothing wrong with this joint; besides, we're on a budget." "Budget" for him is "broke," because he has sent all of his pay home to Mercedes.

"Are you kidding?" Blix asks, opening his musette bag to reveal bricks upon bricks of cash. "My friend, the war has made us rich."

Mather looks at the cash and nods. The three of them leave the lobby of the mid-range hotel and walk into the center of the city, where they take four sets of lavish rooms at the Ritz. It is extravagant, and sentimental, but the fourth room is for Gans.

"Now, this," says Blix when they leave the elevator and the bellboy opens the door on the first suite, "is what I'm talking about."

"Yeah," says Jones, beaming, "this must be how generals live."

They make plans to meet up at ten, and Mather goes to his own room, where he lies down for a long nap, trying to adjust to the monumental change between army life and being a civilian again.

When he opens his door later that night, Blix and Jones are also exiting their rooms into the hall, and all three of them are A-dress clean, but Blix is in civvies, and damnit if they're not bespoke.

"Where the hell did you get those?" asks Mather, eyeing Blix's new suit.

"Brother, if you got twenty," Blix says, "I can get you a submarine." The entire world is up for grabs. As they take the elevator back down to the lobby and leave the hotel, the three of them are floating in their small piece of it, which they have gambled their lives to seize.

They hail a taxi in the middle of the street, as Mather points up and down at the sights he has not seen for years.

It is a good re-entrance, but he cannot yet bring himself to make the journey home, and is thankful to have his friends with him as he musters up his resolve.

They get out of the taxi in front of a club, and the doorman tips his hat, opening the door onto a room that glows and pulses with jazz.

"Welcome to Bricktop's," says Mather, when they have taken their table and ordered bottles of champagne. It arrives, and the friends make a toast to the end of the war. Blix reclines in his seat and lets the champagne drip down his throat one dry note at a time, basking in the comfort at the end of their long campaign.

"Is this where you grew up, Mather?" asks Jones, who is not as comfortable in fancy-pants-type joints.

"It's a part of it," says Mather, happy to show off his city.

"This is great," says Blix, taking another stroke of champagne, "except ain't no colored girls here."

"When in France . . ."

"Find some Germans to give your house keys to?" Blix asks.

"Come on," Mather says, a little sad, as he touches his friend on the arm. He knows Blix was just being funny, but somehow feels that comment includes him, and he just wants to have a good time tonight. To push everything else aside.

"Well, she looks like she could be from Missouri," Blix says, looking over at a table of girls when one of them leaves for the ladies' room. "Cause she's switching that thing like a conductor."

The girls at the table smile at them bashfully. Mather and Blix are mellow, but Jones looks at a girl with curly auburn hair and apple-kissed cheeks and feels a flame that crushes him, as she looks back just as goo-goo-eyed as he. "In that case," says Mather, beckoning the waiter to send a bottle of champagne to their table.

When they receive it, the girls lift a toast to their admirers and send an emissary to greet them. She thanks them in a halting English, but Mather invites them to join their table in French. Blix calls for yet another bottle to be brought to the gathering.

When the women come over, the men stand, and the waiter pushes more chairs up to the table. Blix and Jones introduce themselves in that slow pantomime of people who do not speak the same language, and the conversation moves in bursts of hand signals and slow speech, stopping every sentence or so for Mather to translate.

Jones and his girl barely need Mather's services, but are positively lost as they look at each other. And Blix keeps asking Mather to translate the most absurd lines he can think of, until the entire table has grown fluent in grapes.

"Mather, tell her," says Jones, who's been scrambling through the Italian he picked up their first year in Europe but not getting across what he means. "*Lo parlo poco. Capisco un po'. Puo aiutarmi, per favore? Tell her.*" His mind works, trying to think of any metaphor it knows for not wounded or scar tissue. He can think of nothing.

"Ah, Jack," says Mather, "you like her?"

"I do," says Jones.

"Well, go slow," Mather advises. Blix, he knows, has one of those lover's hearts that could get him laid even at the South Pole—or a plate of ribs, for that matter—but big Jack Jones, war hero from Greenwich Village, does not have a clue how to talk to a woman. A genius at fighting, and not the first idea about the dialogue of love.

"What should I say?" Jack asks, worried he has already screwed things up.

"Let's see." Mather thinks, turning to her. "*Il voudrais savoir votre nom,*" he says simply, at last.

"Annette," she answers, with a smile up to Jack Jones.

"What's she saying?" Jack asks nervously. "What did you say to her?"

"I told her you'd like to know her name."

Jack Jones nods in understanding. "Jack," he says, extending his hand as the lights go down in the house and focus again on stage. "How does it go again, Mather?"

"*Je m'appelle?*"

"That's it. *Je m'appelle* Jack Jones, enchanted to meet you."

It is simple sometimes, Mather thinks, pensive and wistful as the master of ceremonies introduces the night's performer. All around him the postwar crowd stands, but he sits there in his thoughts of comings and goings and all his crossroads in between.

The Queen of Paris is sedate as well tonight, when she takes the stage, walking with slower-than-usual steps. She has not given them a show in a long time. The footlights feel different somehow to her. It is a changed crowd from the ones before the war.

She pulls her white Dior stole up a little closer on her shoulders and looks out at them, contemplating the faces looking back at her.

"How many service people here tonight?" she asks, to a thunder of applause from GIs and WACS, and Resistance fighters from all around the world, cheering because they are not out there but in here. And because they know she has been out there with them, not just onstage like an actor, but behind the lines in the Resistance.

"Which one of you brave people was the bravest out there?" she wants to know, and it is not rhetorical playacting before the crowd. She wants to know what they have been through, and soak all of it from their brow.

She will take what they have seen and turn it into something different, because she has been through it as well, and knows its need for transformation.

The audience is too modest for any of them to claim the distinction for themselves. "Because I know I see a lot of brave faces in here." She ambles from the stage, and they all look around the room at the people sitting there in the dimmed lights with them, and wonder what the others did in the war. Each feels a sudden spark that someone else has been where they have. They are not alone tonight.

The band starts up softly as she moves through the room under the midnight-blue light, languorous notes from the pianist, full as Blix's tongue under champagne.

"Right here," cries Blix, standing and pointing down at Mather Rose. "This is the bravest man I ever met. He is a hero."

Blix is just wild for her, and nearly jumps from his skin when she comes over to the table. Boy-oh-boy, wait till they hear about this back in Missouri.

"Where are you men from?" she asks, and she's still not performing, just talking to them, having a conversation like it's her own living room. They are not here just to be entertained. She is not here just to sing and dance.

"Kansas City," Blix says.

"All right, Missouri," someone calls from across the room.

"What about you?" She turns her attention to Jack Jones.

"Minetta Street," Jack says.

"What's your name?"

"Jack Jones, ma'am," he says, awestruck as any of them.

"Welcome to Paris, Mr. Jones," the Queen of the City says to him, with a wink to his date. "Looks like you've already met. . . . What about you, sugar?" She looks down at Mather. "Where are you from?"

Mather looks at her up close tonight. He saw her perform seven years before, when he was still eighteen, and had not thought of her as having an age, but sees now the lines of time, and laughter, and thought in her face. He figures she looks in her mid-thirties, though he knows she must be a couple of years older, because when he was growing up she was already grown. She had embodied for him then all that was right in the world. She was not just famous, but a star that shone over the place he first loved, making that time and space electric with the sense they were all living in a special, more hopeful age.

At other times he has wondered, in a young expatriate's or immigrant's way, how he must answer that question. Tonight he looks at her and he knows. *"Je suis de Paris,"* he says, "by way of Los Angeles."

She looks down at him in his crisp walking-out uniform, and she sees the scar on his temple that has been left by one of the bullets. She looks at his chest and sees all those gleaming medals that cannot heal his wounds. She sees the thought on his enigmatic face, the wistfulness, and a beautiful boy grown older. She sees herself a hero even without those medals. She knows exactly what he is, what he means, and leans to him. *"Nous sommes tous de Paris, mon frère."* And for the benefit of the non–French-speakers in the crowd, she asks him what street he grew up on. The piano is still playing, but she has half sat down in an empty seat at their table. She knows this man, and a thousand others like him, as cocksure as one of her husbands, as fragile as one of her children. She traces the scar on the side of his face. She rests her finger beneath his chin.

He is not certain, until it happens, what kissing her will be like. She had been his childhood heroine, but he knows fame in and of itself is a condition more grotesque than anything else P. T. Barnum ever found to display. He has driven by and been beside it a thousand times in Los Angeles, or seen it in magazines, and always sensed some extra organ of wanting, as an extra hand devoted only to manipulation. Fame, he has always thought, is frightening. He glimpses in it an endless hole of emptiness. But she is more than fame and celebrity. She is pure starlight and, like any furnace in heaven, generates her own energy, heat.

She radiates it out to him, and sends it through the room like a present bestowed, not a giftless pulling in. It is the heat of a fire already received. She pulls him into the warmth and energy stars exude, as he realizes, with an increase of gravity the nearer he gets to her face, that the humming molecules belong not to the celebrity but to the woman. She is a magnet of human depth and charisma.

An omnisexual love. As their lips touch, he realizes she would be a star even if her picture were not plastered all around Europe. Even if no one except those who knew her had any idea what her name was. She would be the beloved of some small town, because her existence was a reminder that the universe's true gifts are equally distributed, and be proud that this one had been born to them. She would be the waitress who, night after night, picks up the most gold from her table, or the washerwoman who sings to herself on the street as she walks home from work, making every passerby's day the better for it. She would be the legend of only her husband's eye, or the eccentric, favorite aunt of all her nieces and nephews, because she lived in a rare world of the possible instead of an arbitrariness of ifs and must. The Queen of the City knows what she has, as any magician knows magic to be real, and possesses her gifts fully enough that they no longer belong to her, but to all the room, and to Mather's own cells. The closer he gets, the more he hears them buzzing inside of himself, as some small portion of misery flees. The war is really over.

He has the added delight of knowing how Blix's and Jones's faces must look, because everyone knows her name. No single person since the end of the monarchy loomed as large over the city as she did, and no one ever would again. She is Josephine, their last queen.

She kisses him deeply as a lover, innocent as blessing. He is a giant who kept the world from tumbling down. Only yesterday he was a little baby boy.

When their kiss is over, all the room cheers as she makes her way back to the stage, because she has kissed not just Mather but each and all of them.

The band is going full-throttle now, and she has that mood

tonight, so sings "St. Louis Blues," just for herself and the three men at the table. She sings it the way she sang it to herself when alone in her room.

When the song ends, the audience is stilled for a full thirty seconds before they can break its spell enough to applaud. Blix leans in to Mather under the clapping, with his eyes lit as Mather's father's must have been years earlier, when a prophet once sat at their table for dinner, and demands a full report.

"Tell me every last detail."

Mather does not want to be disrespectful of his wife, nor does he want the gift of energy he has been given to depart so quickly, but nonetheless he understands he owes them the pleasure of knowing, and maybe telling them will make it last even longer, so reaches for words to describe what they have missed, the secret she has shared with him. "Man-oh-man," he says, grinning, "Blix, that was really something. Come to think of it, it was just like kissing a bighearted woman from Missouri." Blix knows what he means, and Jones feels it even now. It is like nothing else he has ever known.

They spend a week wrapped in this mood as they go sightseeing, and Mather tries to look at the city through their eyes. He delivers them to those monuments that impart to them the oldness, the grandeur, the continuous soul of the city. He shows them the heights of Mont Saint Michel, the black madonnas of Myans and Puy, and he takes them to Fontainebleau.

He does not know it, but he is showing them all that, besides the Parisians, made his father decide to stay in the city, as they visit the tombs of the great and, because they used to be soldiers themselves, salute, in seriousness and in jest, when they arrive at those of

Napoleon and Lafayette. When they leave, they go pay their respects to the sarcophagus at the Chapel of the Invalides.

Because they are not immune to the charms of love, they also visit the tombs of the great lovers buried in Père Lachaise, and that same evening, Mather shows them the houses where rich men, or men who are rich for an evening, go to meet girls who are lavish and poor.

They are among the first customers at a new restaurant called Haynes, and they walk through the gardens at Versailles and the Tuileries. On their second-to-last day, Mather shepherds them across the Pont de la Tournelle, and on across Pont-Marie to visit L'Île Saint-Louis. Once on the island, they walk down a cobblestone alley whose walls are so narrow one would barely be able to squeeze a bicycle through, to emerge in a great outdoor room.

In a corner they sit at tables, as he shows off his favorite café. It is a place Parisians go to be alone. No one tells anyone else where it is—either one finds it or one does not.

After lunch, the three walk across the bridges again, and he feels as enchanted as he did when he was a child walking them for the first time, until they come to L'Île de la Cité, as he tells them of the denseness of its past.

When they reach the portal of Notre Dame, he looks with them, as if for the first time, pointing up to the Rose Windows that could be a map of all that had been learned about either life, beauty, or obsession not up until the twelfth century, or in the two hundred years it took to build, but in all the time people had lived here. "You know up close the worst," he says, "but these are the best facets of Europe."

Blix poses his friends and snaps an entire roll of film with his new Russian camera. "Have you ever seen such a thing, Jack Jones?" he asks, reloading and handing the camera to a passerby to take a shot of all three together, as he will always remember them.

"No," says Jack, who, with an open ear for languages, has picked up a surprising amount of French in the few days he's been here. "*Mais je désirais la connaître.*" No one tells them here they are less than men.

Mather smiles for the camera, and also at Jack's neologism. "You know, Jack," he beams, "you said that just right."

"Now, don't take this the wrong way," says Blix, hugging his comrades near, "but I'm in Paris with both of you."

"Well," says Mather, after the photograph has been shot, "I'll leave you to her, because I have some errands to run."

"Should we come with you?"

"No," he says, turning away from them. "We'll meet up in the lobby before the ship sails tomorrow morning."

"You were a good tour guide, Sergeant Rose."

As he leaves them, he turns back for one last look at his friends in front of the cathedral, and smiles, looking up to the steeple. When he was a child, it had always seemed so stable and certain that he thought it the sturdiest place in the world. Now he sees in its reach the fear that at any moment it could all tumble and be reduced again to the bottom of the river. But he smiles on, thinking it reminiscent of nothing so much as a self-conscious and overserious vision of the Watts Towers.

He walks again over the slow lapping of the Seine, and stops to ponder the river from the Quai d'Orléans. He takes off his jacket as the day heats up and feels briefly serene again as he walks over the arches spanning the river.

He draws a deep breath and goes back to shore.

He walks for hours. Through the pure light, and through squares that have been bombed out, and those whose genius had been ruined by tourism even before the war. He goes through those working-class neighborhoods no visitor would care to know about, and on past the international school, looking at the lawns he walked over as a child, watching the children who roam there now.

He walks through gardens, past memories, and through Place Pigalle. He walks down Rue Fontain, and he goes slowly down Clichy, rolling his eyes at Moulin Rouge, and climbs the stone stairs to Sacré Coeur—heart of the revolution—a rage growing with each movement of his feet, until he finally reaches its summit. He stares out over the city and waves his fist, all but screaming. When this surfeit of emotion has waned, he walks down the other side, past the sweet point, and walks on through the narrow, winding streets. He walks home.

He sees beauty and details he had not noticed before. He sees how shabby and dim it has become, but also why his parents must have chosen to settle there, even as he walks past a beggar boy who sees Mather's uniform approaching and does a grinning tap dance, then extends his hand expectantly for a centime or two.

Mather frowns at the child with disapproval, but the little beggar mimics him, forcing Mather to smile. He does not know what minstrel dance he is doing, Mather thinks, or perhaps he does.

We are all Negroes in Paris, he sings with his shoes. We all see conspiracy everywhere we look. We trade an art for existence for the currency of the realm, then barter it for bread, and pray there is more art to be gotten from the air, that the bread will last until the next dance. We pray the dance will always be free. We are theoreticians of anarchy but practicing conservatives; too put upon; less free than we pretend. We are all worshippers of idle aesthetics. We are masters of the knowing look. We all wish to live on a human scale, and wish at once for more space to move in. We all want to get out of here, out of our minds. We must all eventually return. We are all Gypsies. We are all beggars. All fools and clowns. All lovers. All ache and fight an endless war. But mostly we are all Negroes in Paris. Mather gives the child a coin and makes his way on through the old Negro quarter.

He walks up the grand staircase of an opulent eighteenth-century home whose original owners had lost their fortune, as fortunes are lost and found daily, and divided it into apartments. It is his former home. It is lightless in the entranceway, and the elevator man has also gone. He lets himself into the cage of the lift, and when he gets to his floor, steps out into the dark hall.

He opens the door on the first apartment and walks into the rooms where they once lived. The carpets are filthy and ruined, and the staircase to the second floor barely holds to its moorings. He steps through the litter and looks around what remains of his parents' furniture, and the shreds that have been made of his father's books and letters.

He weeps for his parents, then opens the cupboard where he used to hide as a child whenever he was in trouble, and discovers a marble he once left there. He goes to the window and pushes aside the tattered curtains to look out on the park he played in as a boy. He feels that, because he was not there sooner, he has let his city down. He failed Paris when she needed him, and even if his life there had not been the utopia his father liked to pretend—because, if they did not know it when he settled here with his new bride, the French learned quickly enough, or drew from memory, the words for "nigger." Still, Paris had sheltered them from something in America that Mather knows well now, but still has no proper noun for. It is more complex than hatred, running both closer to the surface and far, far deeper, fantastically so.

He does not know how much weight one place-noun can support, or what it may feel for a single family, let alone a single man, but he knows his own history is tied unalterably to this city, and it to his.

He knows, even if he never lives here again, that without it he would not be himself. He would be less. He hopes, if a city may remember anything as small as their clan here was, it may remember them and what they tried to give to her. He asks this of Paris, but also that she may forgive him.

As it grows dark, Mather leaves their old rooms, without souvenir, and steps back out into the abandoned corridor.

Before leaving, he knocks on the door of the old woman who lived across from them. Everyone knew her by reputation and that when she was younger she had been a great prodigy, but no one in the building had any idea what she was living on by then. The students she took in could not possibly have afforded her her lifestyle. Even at sixty, though, she was still one of the most fashionable women in the city. The only pieces of jewelry she ever wore were huge and gaudy glass beads from Prague and Bohemia made a century earlier, and even when he was a boy she spoke to him as if he were a grown-up. What his father could only explain in clinical or philosophical terms, she always managed with the directness of a wisdom that knew better than to hope.

"Mather," she instructs, when he tells her his parents are going to allow him a pet, "men, dogs, and diamonds must always be large. If you cannot have a large dog, then you must ask for a fish."

He has loved that woman since he was a boy, and although he did not bother very much with such things, and knew less about them than he should, to him she was not just mischief and grace; she was art. He has tried to fight for her as well.

She had given to him not only his first champagne, and the taste for caviar, but also Beethoven and, when he was still young, a glimpse that the world was a thing to be thought about, and life a thing to be made any way one's daring would allow. She taught him what strength is.

He is eight, and has bullied another student. "Mather," she scolds, "I see you are a very strong boy, but would a boy who was really strong do such a thing? So you have hit Henri because you did not learn your Bach." He has spent six years learning again what he learned in these halls, before they filled with ghosts, but knows them better than he did before.

He pushes open the door on the dark, musty rooms, but they have destroyed her piano as well. They have tried to make war their art. Because they cannot speak to Him, they will annihilate God. He enters the flat and calls to her. There is no answer.

He leaves, and as he does, knows somehow he will never come to Europe again. Because without his parents, and without Mrs. Lebenovitz, the entire continent feels empty. More aggressive than that. It is emptiness defined. He will go back to America, where definitions are more fluid, and there is space enough to build other emotions. The war is over, but he will take his own fight with him.

He knows they are not avenged. He realizes he holds a place that has been held before, but the war has been pushing against its walls for so long, perhaps he will never be able to avenge them, perhaps no one will ever avenge him. That medal he is to receive in Washington is only for holding a portion of it at bay. It is not because he has kept the dream that sparked and flickered in these rooms. It is only because he helped keep it from dying out entirely.

He closes the door and walks back down the darkened stairs. He loves and tries to cling to the Paris he knew. It did not pretend to innocence, but it was the Paris of light. In the street he hails a taxi, and rides back to his hotel.

He hums to himself now an aria he had thought long since forgotten.

EIGHT

One by one, he has lost his friends from the last four years, and when they meet in the hotel lobby their last morning in Paris, Jack Jones comes down without his suitcase to wish them a *bon voyage*.

"Aren't you coming with us?" Blix asks.

Jack shakes his head, but Mather sees the look in his eyes that is more than the euphoria of peacetime. He is not surprised when Jones tells them he will stay in Paris awhile.

"How long?" Blix asks.

"For as long as they will have me." Jack shrugs.

They leave him in front of the Ritz and hurry to catch their boat. Jones goes back to his room, where he prepares to approach the world with more hopeful eyes. He has energy enough and dreams enough. He will become Parisian.

When Mather and Blix arrive in New York, their ship is greeted by an excited crowd of brown faces along the waterfront, who have come out to welcome the most decorated Negro battalion home from the war.

The men wave from deck and allow themselves to be swept up in the mass of people when they come ashore. For the first time, Mather permits himself to taste the full sweetness of what they have accomplished, and poses willingly as Blix shouts to them that they are standing next to a Medal of Honor nominee.

In his hotel the next morning, he receives a telegram from Uncle Wallace, who has seen his photo in the *California Eagle,* welcoming him back and asking what his career plans are. There is a place for him.

When he has finished reading his uncle's letter, the bellhop rings again, this time with a yellow note from Mercedes. Mather holds it in his hands, as he imagines holding her in his arms. His mouth waters as he thinks of the taste of her beneath his tongue, and he decides to leave the very next day for California.

He had been looking forward to crossing the country with Blix, but since he cuts his trip short, the two of them go only as far as Eighth Avenue together.

"Mather Rose is married," Blix says, with a slow nod of his head, as they approach Penn Station. "Jack Jones is in France. But Roy Bilkens has a pocketful of money, and just saw a sign for the A train.

"If you ever find yourself in Missouri, though, look me up and make sure I made it back down from Harlem."

In a twinkling as fleet as that, Blix goes down the stairs into the subway, and his friends are gone. He looks after him, then continues to the station, where he boards the 20th Century Limited to make his way out to the Pacific.

As the train backs out of the station, he looks at the snarl of tracks glistening like metallic veins in the noon sun, and wonders if he will ever see them again.

By the time he reaches Chicago and changes trains, though, the images in his mind have begun to change from the army and friends to those only of home. He looks forward to his wife, his children, his kin. He craves the comfort of his own bed, and lying in a tub with hot sudsy water. He will spend his first day back removing the grime of travel and of war.

He reclines and watches the countryside's acute changes, from the trees and rivers of the East Coast, to Midwestern flatlands, and finally undulating desert sand. When he goes to sleep that night, he imagines the lights of Los Angeles, and when he wakes in the morning, he finds the landscape outside his window the same as the one of which he dreamed.

He leaves the terminal and stretches under the Los Angeles sky, then searches about until he finds a taxicab. He sits straight in his seat, absorbing the surroundings, as the landmarks begin to grow vaguely familiar again.

He has the driver let him out at the end of his block, and comes to a house where a five-pointed star still hangs in the window. It is late June.

They know he will be there soon, but the day itself is a surprise. He walks around to the back door of the little house he and Mercedes had rented. He lets himself in with a key he has held with him throughout the war years. He is twenty-five years old. He is home.

When he enters, two small children play on the floor in the kitchen, each of them as old as a tour of duty. He bends and picks them up. They are his.

"Remember me?" he asks, pulling one of them near to him again, and touching the other for the first time.

Hector, the oldest, gives his father a kiss, while his daughter, Jocelyn, looks at the strange man and scrunches her face in bewilderment. He laughs and comforts her.

When Mercedes comes out back to see what the commotion is, he holds all of them, tightly, sadly, greedily, until they feel to him again as they should, as part of him, breath and bones.

They gather that evening at the West Adams house, and Wallace looks at Mather in his uniform and salutes him. "Welcome home, Sergeant," he says. He is proud.

As the house fills up, there are kisses and hugs all around, and Mather is amazed when both Lydia and Eunice come in with children. The cousins are grown, and a new generation plays together noisily on the floor, as they themselves never did.

His grandmother Vidia smiles on the gathering, and will barely believe what is before her. "You're home, but are you home for good?" she asks.

"Yes, ma'am," Mather answers. She is glad, and beams with the abundance she has been given at the end of a life that has also taken much away.

Mather returns to work with Wallace, taking up where Eunice had filled in. He performs his duties well, and enjoys working side by side with his uncle, but has a difficult time mustering the enthusiasm he had before. Butter and eggs bore him. As the civilian days march along, everything else begins to as well.

When he goes home at night, he finds himself listless, moving from a single martini before dinner to three and sometimes four.

"Mather," Mercedes says to her husband when they are alone in their room at night. "You do not have to keep fighting that war."

He does not answer her, but finally confides to Wallace what has been bothering him these last months. "I never received my medal," he says as they eat lunch together one afternoon.

"The Medal of Honor?" Wallace asks, looking at him thoughtfully. He does not know what else to say.

"Yes," Mather answers him. "I never heard anything else about it."

"It will come," Wallace says at last, without believing, for one of the few times in his life, the words on his own tongue. It is a soothing lie, but Mather does not believe in it either. Still, it lends him the strength of good faith when he begins a letter-writing campaign.

The replies are all evasive, or frank in the statement there is nothing that might be done about it.

"They're all a bunch of no-good bastards," Wallace says, feeling his nephew's anguish, and himself helpless to do anything to alleviate it.

"I'm going to Washington," Mather says at last in an impulsive surge of speech, but knows as soon as he says it that this is what he will do. "I'm going to get an answer."

"Don't," Wallace says sharply, withdrawing his empathy like a warning. "Ain't nothing out there but trouble." But he is his father's son, Wallace knows, he will go anyway.

When Mather packs his things into the back of the car for the drive out east, his wife is uncertain of his mission, and his children want to know why their father is leaving again.

"Daddy is just going away for a little while," he tells them, looking into their fat, sweet faces. "I'll be back by the end of the month." The children try to figure out how long that is as he kisses the three of them good-bye in turn.

He is rock-steady before them, but as he drives away, he does not know what this trip will hold. When Sunset gives way to desert, though, his inner heart begins to shine, to know what he does is the right thing. He would not have his children inhabit any other kind of world. He would not have himself either.

Mather's face is older now, and he drives past the October-morning fields of Missouri feeling his anxiety evaporate, and himself hopeful as he has been before. He knows he could spend the rest of his life traveling the world as he has for the past six years, but as he looks at the houses, he thinks of his own family. He fights for them, and vows, no matter how his business in Washington goes, he will put the war behind him. This will be the last trip he takes alone.

But before he can fulfill this vow, he wants from them his medal. After what he has been through, he is as obsessed with its sign as a gentleman from another century.

He sits that afternoon with Blix in the stands of a stadium, watching his very first baseball game, and trying to get into the action. But he is tense with his secret, and knows he must tell his friend the true reason for his trip to the coast.

"You ain't never gone see it," Blix says with a look of concern when Mather has told him. "What you need to do is turn around, go home, and fuck your wife like a hero, then start building back up your granddaddy's business."

"But you were the one making such a big deal out of it when we first came back," Mather says, not understanding what has come over Bilkens that he should be so bitter.

"That was yesterday. Today all I care is, we made it out of there. Everything else, including honor, is as bullshit as integrating baseball."

"I'm still going to get my medal," says Mather, trying to keep his temper under control. This is not what he stopped here to hear. "I won it. We won it."

"We got it already," Blix says, his eyes bulging the way they always do when he gets riled up. "You see that Puerto Rican out there on the pitcher's mound for Newark?"

"The guy throwing?"

"Well, that's Leon Day, and he spends half the year barnstorming, and sleeping in segregated hotel rooms, and the other half throwing down in Mexico."

"What does that have to do with anything?" Mather asks, looking to the field below.

"I'm telling you," Blix says.

"Well, tell it a little quieter, buddy," calls another fan in the stands, because the game is scoreless and they've already gone through ten innings.

"Leon Day is the best pitcher in baseball, and he fought in the war just like we did, but you don't see him on the cover of *Look,* or even that *Ebony.* Do you? That's cause nobody knows who that man is except real baseball fans."

"So?"

"So—that's honor. You think Leon Day give a damn about the Dodgers?"

"Blix," says Mather, "I don't know what that man feels, and neither do you."

"Well, do you think all these people sitting up here in these stands care who Leon Day pitches for? All they care is that he's the real thing, and I don't care what any man says about desegregation."

"You're just being contrary," Mather says. "Everything is supposed to be different now. Hell, it was supposed to be different before."

"Ain't nothing changed," Blix says, pointing a finger at Mather's lapel. "It's all a trap. Look at those people in that magazine, happy as hell to be having tea with Eleanor Roosevelt, like everything was just a misunderstanding. And there goes old Eleanor, pleased as hell to show the world she ain't a racist."

"Well, Blix," Mather says, losing patience, "she's not supposed to be a racist."

"That's the whole motherfucking point." Blix's finger starts wagging. "It ain't something you should be getting congratulated for. But tell me one good reason why integration means nanolining, and playing white baseball, but not being just as black as Africa and the first African—the first man anywhere—must be, or running a little nightclub in Kansas City, not giving a natural fuck whether or not somebody invite you to their next party?"

"What the hell are you talking about?" asks Mather, turning from the game.

"I'm saying, if you let them, this country will turn everything into smaller and lesser versions of us, and I don't just mean black people—they want to integrate the whole motherfucking world with Spam and Nanoline. All those people sitting in Ebbets Field or at the Polo Grounds yelling, I'm white, baseball is white, just mean without whiteness around to protect them they wouldn't be nobody at all. But with it wrapped around them, they'll stand up and tell you, Mather Rose got to stay in the warehouse three motherfucking years, Satchel Paige can't throw a baseball. But the first time they see

Ruth or DiMaggio strike out, then all those white people sitting out there would have little bits of white falling off them every time the ball whizzes over the plate.

"That's why the Germans lost the goddamn war, because they had to make up some shit about who they were and go through a whole lot of trouble and evil trying to keep up with it, all the way to the point, and see ain't this shit crazy, of driving Albert Einstein away. But Einstein come over here, and he say, 'Okay, so I am not vrom Europe no more. Vell, is all right. It does not matter, cause the little mustache don't tell me who I am. Goddamnit, I'm the Satchel Paige, I'm the Harry Houdini, and I have got some real shit to blow all your little make-believe the fuck up.'" Blix's eyes are bulging, and that vein in his temple is throbbing like it never has before, as Buck O'Neil sends a shot that heads toward the Alaga sign on the right-field fence, waves hello at the wall, and keeps going, going, going into space. Mather makes a visor with his hand to watch the long ball leaving the park.

"I love this game," he says as they jump to their feet.

"You better." Blix pumps his fist, getting back into the action on the field. "Because you're Mather Rose, and you been playing it all your life, because baseball is like blackness. It can contain the entire world."

"Is that so?" Mather asks, happy for a moment of levity, as his first game goes to the bottom of the twelfth.

"That is so," Blix says, waving to the vendor for another bag of peanuts and a couple more beers, "nothing more and nothing less. And that, my friend, is all the love and honor you will ever need."

Try as he might, though, in the end Mather can only see baseball as a game with too much invested in it, and he refuses to be as cynical as Blix. He will not believe, cannot allow himself to believe, it is an evil country, because that bitterness is too easy. He is less concerned with the thing itself than the struggle it is a sign of.

But in the stillness of the empty highway, he knows he cares about that medal more than he will admit. It is the sign he has been treated once with fairness. He dreams of what it will be like to stand at the dais, and what it will mean to be a Negro man on that stage. How proud his parents would be. But he also wants simply to drink, however briefly, from the cup of glory, no matter how shallow it should prove to be. He knows it is forged from the same fire as the war he has been through. It is the holy face to the hell of that which makes it possible and necessary, and that it cannot exist without. If he who has been through this hell and carries these ravages can touch that chalice with his lips, he hopes they might cancel each other out, and allow him the quietude of being just a man again. He wants to be released from the anonymous churning of history and power that takes up any man and spits him back out unrecognizable. He will have his medal if it is the last thing he does.

He knows how naïve he has been when he shows up at the offices of the War Department. He is in full uniform, and the medals already on his chest command the respect of every passerby except the attendants of those who have given them. He knows then the worst of what he has held at bay so long is true. It is an endless, permanent war.

"I fought at the Bulge. I helped capture a platoon of Germans. I have lifted boxes. When I got my medals, they forgot to put in the one for honor. If the War Department won't do anything about it, then I wish to speak to Truman. My name is Mather Henry Rose."

They are on the verge of laughing at him, and he is on the verge of becoming deranged.

He goes back to the office every day, though, until the secretary no longer acknowledges his presence. When Mather stands before his desk, the man simply looks through him. When he cannot take it anymore, he loses his temper and must be escorted out by armed guards.

He should go home. He should give up, but that is not in him. Instead, he takes a room in a Northwest hotel. He vows he will leave with an answer. He calls the senators from his state, and when they refuse him, he goes to his representative. It is a mad trail of paper and carbons and silence.

The representative is not a bad person, and the weight of seeing this man so crushed compels him to see what he can do about it. "I will look into it for you," he says. He makes no promises.

Mather sits drinking a beer in his hotel room, where he has waited a full three weeks, when a letter is slid under the door. He has been granted a meeting with an attaché to the secretary of the Secretary of War.

His heart races faster, because he knows all he needs is a face-to-face opportunity to present his case. They are civilized men and only need to be spoken to with reason.

He takes his uniform out of the closet and presses it carefully, dabbing the knees and seat with water where they have become shiny with wear. He affixes his medals and he combs his hair carefully, then dons his cap and is ready.

He walks, because he has been here almost a month longer than he planned and is over budget, so careful with gas. He will not call home for help, but will face this alone. He will tell them when he is victorious. He walks. Through the wide Washington streets to the Pentagon. Passersby nod at him and salute to the medals on his chest.

He is escorted into a small room within the mammoth building, and sits down in front of a desk behind which sits a man whose face is nearly obscured by the stacks of folders piled in front of him.

"What can I do for you?" the civil servant asks.

Mather wants to laugh, he damn well should know, then realizes the paper jockey is serious and grows dumbfounded.

"I've only come to see you about my Medal of Honor," Mather says at last.

"It did not go through. There is nothing I can do about it."

"Who can do something about it?"

"Nobody."

It is a useless fight, and when he leaves, Mather is shaken to see how far down it goes. But he gets into his car, and as he drives westward, he tries to shake it off, contemplating his life and his country. The history around him that shot through his skin and life.

It is the one made up of his family and friends. It is made up of the men he has fought with, those beside him as well as the ones he killed and captured because he had to. It is Mercedes, and Eunice. It is his uncle Wallace, his grandmother Vidia, his aunt Sorra. It is his mother and father, his daughter Jocelyn and son Hector. It is the isolation of Jack Jones, the Nebraska of Clarence Gansley, and the bulging eyes of Roy Bilkens. It is Watts and West Adams in Los Angeles, and the table they shared in Paris. It is Mrs. Lebenovitz smoking her cigars and telling scandalous stories about Vienna at the turn of the century as she plays her piano. It is the café where he brunches in Santa Barbara. It is Harlem. It is the languages he speaks, and the ones he dreams in. It is a country between oceans, without end, and as he drives through Mississippi, he thinks of his namesake and grandfather, Henry.

Meridian is the same distance east of Shreveport as Oakland is north of L.A., and he resets his odometer, so that, when the cousins tell their children the story of Henry Warren Rose, distance will not be an abstraction but an actual number of miles. He calls to the Queen of Angels to take him back to them.

When he returns, they will go for a swim in the generous warmth of the Pacific. He will hold his son above the surf. He will press his breast against his wife's again. They will help him remember himself, and lay aside all the false things he has believed. He has no gifts for them this time, but himself.

He is proud of the journey he has taken, but when he returns to the City of the Queen of the Angels, he will be home, and will never leave them again. The war is over, and he will go forward with the fight that is his own. He will not have the medal, but honor enough for any man.

He is a man because he has broken his back to pay for his way in the world. He is a hero because he has done so without having what he believes in destroyed; there is still something in his heart larger than self.

Mather's face is bleaker now, but as late November brushes the blacktop with a light dusting of snow, and he drives past the autumn fields and rough-hewn fences of the countryside, he wills himself to be strong.

He turns his radio on and does not cry, but a single tear slips and hisses down his face before evaporating under the motion of his hand. The black ribbon of highway pulls him home to California, like an epic song.

He gasses the Zephyr and drives over the newly connected highways of America, then, as it grows late, pulls into a service station just west of Meridian. There, a hungry-looking boy attends to him.

The child stares up at those shiny medals on Mather's chest. The medals start telling him a story, and he asks the hero where he got them all. He does not think he can ever remember being this close to a real live hero before.

When he finishes filling the tank, the soldier flips the boy a new silver dollar, telling him someday he will win medals too.

Asks where he might find a room for the night.

II

A STRANGER COMES TO TOWN

PROLOGUE

He is your firstborn child, heroic. You tremble and must steady yourself to hold him, knowing nothing stands between his safety and harm except the certainty of your fingers.

As he rests in your hands, you know you will not drop him; he will not fall. And your pride grows to even more exaggerated heights. In turn, the spirit level takes hold of you, and you remember your own father. Beyond him—to Adam's ancient awakening from God.

He will be a better son. You will be better as well. You will do all you can to make an Eden for him that will hold as steady as your arms, until he can stand and hold it up for himself. Still, you give to him the name your own old man gave.

Your wife adds to it one she has carried a dozen years away from her first opera.

He will lift every burden you give.

It takes him a while to find his feet, but once he does, there is no limit to who he might be. He, you say, will grow into a great man. Higher. He will be a great Southerner.

When he joins the war, you warn him, after the local manner, "This is Roosevelt's fight."

He replies to you in your tongue: "It is America's, and no one ever called a Mississippian coward."

He is your oldest, and will be as large as any hope a father ever held for his son.

His younger brother is more worrisome. He has niggerish ways, like your sister's children in Arkansas. But you admit to yourself, late at night, the younger boy is far more like you as a young man than his brother. He will need a while longer, and perhaps never achieve great things; however, you know he has it in him to find happiness.

But when a draft card comes to him, the younger son makes no secret of the fact: "I paid a nigger fifty dollars to go in for me."

You tell him to watch his language. "That is not the way we talk in this house."

Perhaps, he says, he should not live in it.

Your wife becomes distraught. She says she is going to march right back down to the Woolworth's and exchange the window banner she bought for one with a solitary star.

"No, ma'am," her firstborn says. "I think you should hang the two."

She is proud of him at this moment, and even if he did not see so with her eyes, would do anything for him. He will be a great Southerner.

He will lift every burden you give.

ONE

He—Lewis Hampton—returns from Europe wearing the braid of a second lieutenant, and is nonchalant when neighbors make a great deal of his Silver Star. Everyone knows, if he had not gotten sick and spent three months in the redeployment depot, he would have won even better.

He is not from a wealthy family, but every home in the state is suddenly open to him, and employment offers come pouring in. Young ladies vie for his attention as well, but it takes him a while to find one who satisfies his mother. One is too obviously ambitious; then there is another who is not ambitious enough; a third is too much, "just nervousness"; and yet another is too brash. Others are also dismissed. "Marry *her* if you want to be mayor of Meridian, but *her* if you want to be president."

He actually has no interest in politics, but has developed a taste for thought, and he finds himself most taken with a girl named

Dolores Parker, whom he meets at the end of his first summer home. She is less beautiful, or shrewd, than simply good. They seem well matched, and wed in a perfect ceremony. His life then will have found its arc. This is in the future.

When he first comes home, he still does not know what he plans to or should do, so takes back the job he worked during college summers, buying space on railway cars to sell to the merchants on the coast moving their products inland, or to landlocked folk shipping their goods to other markets.

His father has never understood the job, and is dubious that it is actually honest work. "I just do not understand," he says, "how you can buy and sell train space when the trains do not belong to you." His mother tells her husband it is called logistics.

It is not what he will do forever, but it is good enough for now. Still, everyone thinks his eventual lot must be politics, because not only is he a war hero, but he also has such a way with people, even beyond a Southerner's natural charisma. "Well, if I did go into politics," he tells them, "it would be less the baby-kissing kind than diplomacy." Because, besides a taste for thought, being away from home has also given him an interest in the affairs of nations.

This fascination began during the war, when he learned the British and Germans are really the same people, and the queen of England is a German.

"Even the name 'England' is German," his friend George Mason, an erudite Bostonian, tells him. "It means 'Land of the Angles.' And the Angles invaded them from Jutland. What is more," George continues, "English is a German language."

Lewis barely understands what he means and believes him even less until, one day, as they hang out in the recreational area of their camp in Cheltenham, England, waiting for their mission to begin, George shows him a book written in Middle English. "You'd understand it better," George triumphs, as Lewis puzzles over the odd words, "if you spoke modern German."

"What is the use of that?" Lewis asks.

"Because this war goes back as far as the forests," he is answered. "As far back as the Vikings and Romans. We are like Graeae, sharing one eye and one tooth, which, by the way, is why Americans are so obsessed with blondness."

"Well, what is wrong with blonds?" Lewis asks.

"Nothing, except we give to it a power it does not have, but comes from a primeval memory of Nordic forests, or else from Rome—of armies that could not be dismissed or vanquished."

"George, if I didn't know better I would call you a sympathizer," Lewis says.

"I'm just telling you how it all started." George shrugs.

"Maybe for you, wiseguy," Tom Flaugherty yells from the pool table on the other side of the room. "I happen to be an Irishman."

"And I'm Italian," someone else butts in from the table next to them.

"You're all Americans," a captain corrects them. "That's all we allow in this army."

"Maybe so," Flaugherty calls back, to the sound of Gaelic laughter, "but I'll be an Irishman when I die."

In his own town there are Catholics and Negroes, and a handful of Jews, but nothing so varied as the what-alls they have in the army. Lewis is at first hesitant about fitting in, but soon grows comfortable in that hodgepodge, seeing they are not so different from him, and that he holds his own against any man there. His only real discomfort comes on the rainy nights they spend debating their favorite topic, the war between North and South, as they try to kill the stagnant time before the journey to France.

After these rows, the Northerners are always quick to add, "Of course, it doesn't matter"; "We're all countrymen"; and "To these British, a Yank is a Yank." Lewis is not the type to dwell on the past, but to many of the other Southern fellows, this was as much as rubbing their noses in it.

"Well, then," Lewis says, speaking on their behalf, "why don't we just say all of us are Rebels."

"You mean reactionary?" George Mason responds, relishing the argument. "That's just yous-alls from the South."

"What do you mean by that?" one of the men from Kentucky wants to know.

"He means reacting contrary to civilization and contrary to Negroes," a lieutenant from Delaware explains, not wanting to put the subject down once they have started on it.

"See, that just shows you have never seen it. White and dark have been living amongst each other for a thousand years in the South."

"That and the lack of art is exactly what's wrong with it."

"Well, the North doesn't know much about living."

"And the South will rise again."

"Too bad nobody knows when."

They can go on for hours.

When the war is put aside, though, Lewis has no problem talking to Northerners and actually becomes friends with a few others besides George Mason as well.

When left alone, he thinks he understands the flaws of his homeland in their eyes, and does not take it personally. The Negro, to his mind, is a problem for the whole country. Of course, he would never concede even this ground to a Northerner, and during the rows is always one of his homeland's fiercest defenders. In all-Southern company, though, away from Northern aggression, he frequently argues the other point.

"That's just what they think of us," Clark, the Kentuckian, says after one of the debates grows especially delirious.

"Aw, Clark, they're good boys," Lewis calls out. "Besides, they're not talking about us, but what they have received."

"I don't see a difference."

"One is real," Lewis says. "The other is just recirculated currency."

"Whatever you say. I still don't think they have the respect for us you would a nigger."

With his friends from outside the South, he tries to talk mostly about girls, or movies, or international things. Never American history beyond the Mexican-American war, or sports. When he makes a point of this, the arguments decrease.

He has deprived them of a great topic, but they respect him for his intelligence and determination.

Above that, everyone respects his ability as a soldier.

"Well, Lewis," their commanding officer says, turning the attention of the table on him as they sit at mess the night before crossing the channel for Le Havre. "Tomorrow, France."

"With all due respect, sir?" Lewis answers with steady nerves, not even bothering to lift his head from the tepid split-pea soup. "I'm on my way to the Reichstag. I'm only going through France to get there."

He never makes it to the Reichstag itself, but he does make it to Germany.

When he does, he sees things there, he knows, he is not supposed to. "No, George Mason," he declares, looking at, breathing in, and exhaling holocaust all around, "I do not care what your books say, all I am is an American."

In time, years from here, he will revisit, and wonder in shattering, briefest flashes of epiphany, and remembrance, whether Germany was not only a giver of American language, but also its twin.

TWO

When the *Queen Elizabeth* exits the open sea for New York Bay, it is the first time Lewis Hampton has entered port without sweat or fear of submarine fire.

He stands on the crowded deck, without his life jacket, fighting for space along the rail of the ship to get a glimpse of the Statue of Liberty, which he had failed to see on the crossing to England. Around him, soldiers hang every which way from the sides, like summer fruit, heady with the skies of home.

He bids a boisterous farewell to most of the men he has shared the last two years with, as his destination becomes his own again to decide. He and George Mason take their leave of the others and walk east from the Hudson to check into a midtown hotel, which is to serve as their base for the five days they spend in the city.

They walk around, marveling at the height of the Empire State Building but find the Chrysler even more impressive. They stroll the streets of lower Manhattan, whispering the names of its former in-habitants in hushed, reverential tones, then walk across the board-walk of the Brooklyn Bridge with a thrill like spanning the world. At night, they listen to the jazz music they found a taste for in the army, in small basement clubs, and slur down Broadway in the early hours, carefree, and enthralled by its glamour.

It is a tourist's view of the city, but they do not care, because for five days they are suspended in its everness, and the welcome they receive, as they reintegrate with peacetime society.

At the end of the week, the friends part at Port Authority, where George catches a bus back to Boston, and Lewis begins the eight-hundred-mile ride home to Mississippi. Both are anxious about the readjustment still ahead of them, suspecting it will not be as simple as coming home.

Their minds move faster now than they did before, worrying about how they will fit into their old lives, or into the new role ex-pected of them. They wonder in this anxiety whether they are equal to it, but have great hopes for what they will build, after years of nothing but killing. They salute, telling each other without words that they have changed the world for the better, and each catches his Greyhound home.

Lewis is proud of the way his mind has opened during his time away, but he has been judged ignorant or barbaric on occasion, by those who did not know him, simply because of his soft Southern speech. And when the bus dips and rises from the rough furnace of the Mid-Atlantic summer to the sweet, sultry air of Virginia moun-tains, besides elation he also feels a measure of relief to be down south, in his homeland, in Dixie, again.

He realizes, though, he has changed in some ways that might be thought too modern and radical, as he strips down to shirtsleeves and opens the paperback he bought in New York. It is a best-seller, and he wants to know what people are talking about, even if some of it is things unpleasant about where he is from. He can only read a short while before pausing to look out the window, to check the scene outside against the book, and his own remembrance.

"That thing sure has you caught up," his seatmate says, during one of Lewis's breaks from reading to check reality against words. "Mind if I ask you what it is?"

"Not at all," Lewis says cordially. "It's called *Black Boy.*" And as a show of politeness, he then asks the stranger whether he has read it.

"Can't say that I have," the man answers, taking the book from Lewis's outstretched hand, and giving it just as quickly back after reading the cover. "Personally, you won't catch me dead reading a book by a negra, telling lies about what we're like down south."

"Well, he is from Mississippi," Lewis protests, before reconsidering. He knows he has begun to think in ways that might be regarded as out of place, and does not see the sense in stirring up an argument. "Well, like you said, you have not read it." He is just a poor dirt farmer, Lewis thinks to himself, looking at the man's grimy hands. It is not worth getting into. War, on the other hand, has made him an officer, and a man of the world. He craves to be like the poets George introduced him to, and go on a spirit journey.

He goes back to his book, arguing with it, but confident that its mere existence is the sign of some less slantwise movement than the ones he was accustomed to before the war. He feels strange, but also released and free. His own ears do not have to burn with the shame of what Wright speaks of, because, as the bus moves through the brilliant blue mountain light of Virginia, he knows everything is different now. Didn't they just stamp evil out of the world?

He is young, and ready to help lead it.

When the Greyhound finally pulls into Meridian, his chest is still swollen with this thought as he greets his parents. But he cannot help noticing the conspicuous absence of his brother.

"How is Nathan?" he asks, riding in the car back to the house where he grew up.

When his mother answers, he feels the tension his question has stirred, and knows to drop the subject.

Later, when he finally does see his brother, there is a coolness in their transaction that Lewis knows he is not responsible for. His parents watch the two brothers together and trade uneasy looks between themselves, without their sons' knowing, and without even actually having to make eye contact. They are crestfallen, they say to each other with this look.

Lewis brings it up again with his father that evening, as the two of them porch-sit, drinking cold beers and watching the lightning bugs play over the summer lawn. He wants to know why his brother had to be so short with him.

"Be sensitive with him. Nathan has always felt a little in your shadow," Lewis's father answers thoughtfully, "and since you come back, I knew it was bound to get worse."

"Why is that?" Lewis asks. "He was never like this with me before."

"Well," the older man nods, taking a sip of his sweating beer, "you remember Mabel Clark's boy he gave those fifty dollars to?"

"Yessir," Lewis says.

"Well, he never come home but it was in a coffin. Ever since, Nathan's been acting crazier and stranger every day. It got so bad for a while there, I thought it was going to give your mother a breakdown." Lewis thinks and promises to reach out to his younger brother.

He means it too, but the two of them do not interact much in the days that follow. Lewis knows it is not purposeful on his part, he just never gets the chance to try to make peace, since Nathan keeps an apartment in town and is always busy with work or his own friends.

When Nathan does come home, it is to borrow money from their parents, and Lewis does not want to shame him then with his presence. He wishes their relationship was different, but accepts that it has never been one of particular closeness.

One morning, the two of them do happen to sit alone in the kitchen together, Lewis having risen late for breakfast, and Nathan just coming over to see what is in the icebox. Lewis tries to make conversation, but it ends with them getting into it again, after he asks Nathan his plans for the future.

"By the way," Nathan says finally, looking up from the free food, "how long are you going to wear that damn uniform around? You know you look just like a natural-born idiot."

"It is mine to wear," Lewis says, not wanting a fight, but not intending to take an insult either. "It's not my fault if some people don't have any more uniform than that of filling-station attendant."

"Working at a gas station," Nathan counters, "is better than being a grown man still living at home with his parents."

They go on, circling around each other with words, until they find themselves standing chest to chest.

This is how their mother finds them when she enters the room:

staring at each other, waiting to see who will strike first. They are not like little boys fighting over a red wagon or a Daisy gun either, but like grown men fighting over something they would kill each other for in an instant.

She, Abigail, is nearly a full foot shorter than these two tall men she has raised, but steps between them and spreads her hands as they tower above her.

When Lewis and Nathan notice their mother, they calm themselves and part—Lewis with embarrassment, Nathan feeling deprived of the fight he knows would restore to him a sense of parity.

"Boy," he says, stepping away but still speaking to Lewis, like they were standing somewhere out in the streets instead of in their mother's kitchen, with her right there. "You don't know what you messin' with."

Lewis does not answer him. He does not think the challenge is one that needs speaking to. Still, he shudders at the arbitrariness in his brother's eyes.

Even though he is younger, Lewis has never managed to whip him in a fight, and Nathan is willing to bet he still can't, uniform or no. Of course, Nathan had a reputation around town as willing to bet on anything. But fighting was different.

Lewis might be a war veteran, but King Nathan was once the best high-school wrestler between Mobile and Jackson, and he is willing to bet anything you name, his brother still can't lick him. Can't no one. It takes all of them together.

Maybe he has spent the war years the same way he did the first few out of high school, roaming around town looking for something to entertain himself with while his friends all drifted off, or were drafted off to war. But in their absence he has held the same status he had before, even if his friends were now slightly younger than himself. Because of this age discrepancy, he is the first to initiate them to drinking, and to the houses of ill repute spread around the small city. He loved as well to see the frightened, blustering look on their faces when he took them to Darktown for the first time.

"Are you sure this is safe?" they ask.

"As long as you stay with me," he always assures them, because, while his brother might have been a war hero, everyone knows King Nathan is the baddest man for a long way around. On especially good nights, he has even been known to stretch it further. He is then not only King Nathan, but King Nathan Sho Nuff. Every time he wins a fight, or a hand of poker, or his luck otherwise comes up showing sevens, he does a little nigger dance, like the colored boys do, that cracks you up and breaks your heart. On these nights, if only in his mind, King Nathan is so large, he is married not only to Rita Hayworth but also to Lena Horne.

They blow on his dice and do the little nigger dance with him as he commands the table. Sho Nuff King Nathan, sho nuff. It cracks you up and melts your heart. Eventually, he will find the way he is looking for.

"Nathan, you gone just fight and gamble your whole life?"

"Nope. I'm gone drink another beer too."

It works well enough during the war years, but does nothing for his reputation afterward, and he has begun to worry. During the war, when men were scarce, he had a fine time with women of all sort, and preached to any who would listen the special charms of the recently widowed.

As the world has returned to normal, though, he has felt sometimes that a pox has fallen on his luck. He tells himself it is less his indiscretions than his being indiscreet, and hopes that in time all will be forgiven as Nathan's being "just wild in his youth." Still, he worries. He hopes he hasn't gotten caught in the crossing of those scissor blades.

He may not be a goddamned war veteran, he tells Lewis, but neither has he ever run from a fight.

Lewis's temperament is more reserved, and he does not respond. He has bigger things to worry about than his maladjusted brother. Like Nathan's reputation, he knows, his new status as a war hero will gradually pass if he does not parlay it into something more tangible.

When the fight in the kitchen breaks up, he leaves his breakfast uneaten and goes upstairs to pack for an overnight trip he has been invited on down in Ocean Springs. He does not place much store in what Nathan the Coward thinks, but as he decides what to take with him, passes over his uniform in favor of a white linen suit he is almost as proud of.

He regrets fighting with Nathan that morning—it is not how brothers are supposed to behave—but he is concerned for his brother's future, and, like his parents, he has the niggling worry that the way Nathan behaves reflects poorly on all of them.

He does not mention these concerns as he rides down the highway in the back seat of his friend Connie's car, on the way down to the coast, but thinks and watches silently the earth change from red ochre, to alluvial black, to wet. He is not Cain, Lewis tells himself, holding his hand in the slipstream out the window, and refuting the obvious Bible verse. I am not Abel. We're just two brothers who happen to be made of different stuff.

He is still thinking about it that evening, staring out from the balcony of a handsome old house on the coast, past the magnolia trees and out into the water, absorbed and oblivious, when a young woman joins him out in the lilting night breeze.

"A dollar for your thoughts," she says, studying the stranger's pensive face.

"I was just thinking, I've never seen a finer sight than the Gulf of Mexico," Lewis says, turning around. "Well, I now eat my words." She is not his usual type, he thinks, looking at her. He has always tended to pursue women whose sex appeal was obvious, but he finds her comely in a wholesome way that stirs him up all the same.

Lewis is six feet one and a half inches, and the woman on the balcony, he guesses, is five foot six, max, but she carries herself with such assurance, he cannot help thinking about a giantess he once knew in the Netherlands.

They introduce themselves, and she points out over the water. "If you look close, on a summer night," she says, "you can see all the way to New Orleans."

"I see." Lewis peers where Dolores Parker points. "You say it has to be a summer night?"

"Of course," she answers. "What kind of fool would stand out here in winter?"

"A romantic one, I suppose," says Lewis. "A fool for love."

"Oh, I would do just anything." Dolores yucks it up with him, singing from a pop tune. "Anything for love." Lewis joins in as she completes the bar, and feels with her the spark of kindredness that flies between strangers who have just discovered a shared taste.

He is not always good with women, but "Dance with me," he says when they finish singing.

Dolores is usually ambivalent about these parties, with their endless rotation of the same people, telling the same stories and expressing the same opinions, but tonight she smiles, knowing the point of any party is to have a shock of this feeling that flows through her now. She will, she answers him.

They go back inside to rejoin the party, where the band is playing a cover of Lena Horne's "Fine Romance" as they make their way out onto the floor, certain and expectant. They dance together until the end of their song, then continue on, pressing closer, as the musicians play another tune.

As they grace the wooden floor, overlooking the Gulf of Mexico, Lewis in his linen suit, Dolores in a simple and elegant summer dress, they each enjoy the heat from the other's body that wafts and bounces back and forth in the narrow space between them. Each of them wonders whether this dance they share has a future.

In the movement of their touching bodies, sharing this moment tonight, there is no future. But neither is there a past.

They twirl through the room and the early-September breeze that blows in from the windows, each as enchanted by the evening as ever they were by anything.

Those who watch them from the sides of the room, or who dance but are less enthralled with their partners, feel almost as much pleasure to look at them as Dolores and Lewis themselves.

There dances the pride of the South. If anyone were to ask them tonight what that is, they would tell them: It is Lewis Hampton, just home from the war, dancing with Dolores Parker. In September. High up over the Gulf of Mexico.

At the end of the night, Lewis soft-shoes over the lawn with his friends, back to the hotel. His tie is loosened, and his shirt unbuttoned at the neck. Grass scuffs his new white bucks, and the condensation grays the tips, but he does not notice under the rambunctious fragrance of gin that spreads through the late air. It will be morning soon; this walk over the lawn will hold him long after sunrise.

He necked with Dolores in a pantry the night before, and smiles when he wakes up thinking about it. He does not want to be presumptuous, or jinx his chance, but neither does he want to end up back in the repple depple again. He showers, then leaves the hotel in search of a pharmacy.

Inside the small family store, he lowers his voice to ask the old man behind the counter for a package of prophylactics. He is twenty-six, but it is a sleepy village, and he feels a powerful sense of embarrassment as he tries to make the request sound as officious as possible.

"You mean rubbers?" the old guy says in a normal voice, as Lewis reddens. The pharmacist sees his blush, then begins to whisper as well. "Down the last aisle," he points, "top shelf, behind those ointments."

Lewis pays for the condoms in an effort of nonchalance, but can't help feeling the old guy is smirking at him, or otherwise disapproving. It makes him angry and sheepish as he leaves the store, feeling he has done something naughty.

He is walking down Washington Avenue having this conversation with himself when he sees Dolores and a group of her girlfriends coming up the other side of the street. The girls giggle at Dolores as Lewis crosses over to greet them. "Good morning," he says, his cheeks still burning from his mission.

Dolores's friends recede and withdraw a pace while the two of them speak awkwardly on the sidewalk, conscious of being on display. As he talks to her, Lewis sees the shyness and shelteredness in her green eyes, and begins to feel more and more guilty about those rubbers he just bought.

The more he thinks about them, the redder his face grows, until he notices his blush has spread to her as well and Dolores is as flush as he is. The world may have sped up for him, he thinks, but Dolores Parker is still near to innocent.

He walks back to his hotel alone, and the girls proceed to Sunday brunch. He is even redder than before, ashamed of those rubbers in his pocket, and reminding himself he is not in the army anymore. "You can't just go around thinking every girl who gives you a kiss is gonna let you go all the way, pal."

He is comforted to know that while he was at war, watching the most dreadful things, and learning exactly what he, as well as other men, was capable of and would do, there were still girls like Dolores Parker and her friends—who did not know these things, and perhaps would never have to. Dolores Parker, who was sheltered enough to blush simply because someone else did.

She is not the kind of girl you were thinking, he reproaches himself again, who will just up and let you score the second night. She can give him back, he thinks, not his religion, which is gone forever, but better faith in the world. She is a gal to marry.

He has never thought about why people get married, just knew it was what you were supposed to do around his age and point in life. He is surprised by how quickly it has come over him. But he has, he thinks, a reason as good as anyone has ever had to want anything. It is Dolores Parker.

There are things he does not want to remember, and as he climbs the stairs back to his room thinking of her, he is thankful there is a girl in Mississippi who has, for a moment, brought him to a state as blissful as not knowing, if not never having seen. It takes further and further possession of him, and he luxuriates in it the rest of the morning.

He feels his state increase throughout the afternoon, when old man Parker, Dolores's father, takes them all out on his boat. Lewis has crossed the ocean twice, and been once over the rough waters of the English Channel, but he has never known the sea as a place of simple joy. He did not know it could calm the extreme emotions, or make a woman more beautiful. Nor has he ever known a vessel could be such an ode to man's better relationship with the oceans as was Mr. Parker's ketch.

They sit out under the open sky, drinking cocktails and floating their laughter across the waves, as the captain looks on them, wishing he had had it half so easy when he was young, but proud to be providing this time.

Lewis watches Dolores as she asks her father whether she might steer for a bit, then takes over expertly at tiller. He stares at the hypnotic effect of her green eyes reflecting the blue Gulf waters as she pulls her curly hair back to frame her face. The wind plays with what stray strands it can, and he feels as relaxed as the calm in her face at that moment, and hopes briefly she is taking the sloop all the way out into the Caribbean Sea.

He feels this calm, but, swift beneath it, her possession of him prompts a stronger and stronger wanting. What he wants, he thinks, looking at her unlikely beauty—or, rather, her spirit, which lifts her ordinary looks to something rarer than beauty—is to be born again. She sees him from the corner of her eye and smiles.

Lewis Hampton is in love for the first time. He knows now why that feeling is so central to other people's imagining of life, and cannot believe he has never known it before. But even this makes him happy, that he has not known it until now, as if his heart knew itself better than he did and has been waiting for her.

Captain Parker watches the young upstart looking at his daughter and comes to sit next to him, beckoning Mrs. Parker to freshen their drinks.

"So," Parker says, scrutinizing Lewis's unseasoned skin, "Dolores tells me you were quite something in the war."

"I had some luck," Lewis tells the older man, downplaying what he did. He does not like talking about the war.

"That's all well and good," says Parker, as they both look at Dolores. "I have nothing except respect for what you boys did over there. Now what are you going to do with the rest of your life?"

Lewis has respect for all his elders, as properly trained Mississippians invariably do, but he also knows old Parker made a fortune in the rails, and Lewis has in himself just the smallest bit of the toady.

"Captain," he says, dodging the intended pressure of the question, and looking Parker in the eye, "I can't think of anything better to become than a great Southerner such as yourself."

If there is anything Parker cannot stand, even more than a young man with too brash an eye for his daughter, it's a bootlick. He does have, though, the robust self-regard and recognition of an intelligent man, and he feels a respect, greater than the one he has for soldiering, for any man who can look him direct in the eye and say something as ass-kissy as that. "You will go far, boy," he says, expressing both his sentiments toward Lewis. "Sounds to me like all you need to do is go out there and start collecting the money." He combs his tuft of white hair back into place with the flat of his hand.

"He ain't got no idea what it costs yet," Parker thinks to himself as Lewis sits, trying to unravel insult from compliment in his remark. "Don't hold it against him, Emile." He keeps trying to cool himself, looking at the arrogance in the younger man's face. "He just don't know."

Lewis knows he is off to a bad start with Parker, but cannot find a way out of the old man's treacherous attention as the two of them sip at their drinks and settle into the uneasy silence of two men in love with the same woman.

Dolores watches the exchange, steering the boat into the natural harbor of an offshore island, where she asks her father if they can anchor awhile.

He agrees, and the craft rests still in the water, letting the young people slip overboard, one by one, like flying fish, for a swim in the warm, late-season sun.

Lewis is grateful to be out of Parker's clutches as they make their way to the island to lie out on the baking sand, until they are hot with sun and their own youth, then splash back into the brackish water to cool down.

When Mrs. Parker sees them in the water again, goofing around, she rings her triangle to announce lunch.

"Race you," one of the guys yells, responding to the sound, and they all take off furiously toward the boat.

Old Parker has kept an eye on Lewis the entire while, and watches now as the young man cuts through the water like a sylph, to win the contest. After touching the side of the ketch, Lewis swims back out, as if it has cost him no effort at all, to see the ladies safely in.

In spite of himself, Parker is impressed by the display of athleticism and gallantry, as well as by how at home Lewis seems in the water. "Maybe," he thinks, "he does reminds you a little of yourself at that age."

When the young people climb back on board, Mrs. Parker finishes laying out the noontime meal, and they eat, as old Parker tries to engage Lewis in talk of railroads and ships, both showing off, and trying to ascertain what kind of head the young man has on his shoulders.

Dolores shushes her father and smiles at Lewis, then comes over to take him away. He is grateful again for her sensitivity in rescuing him.

They lounge in the sun, on the water.

After lunch, Parker lifts anchor to head back to shore, his passengers more subdued than they had been on the trip out. They are in the lull of their stomachs, and the pull land exerts on their trip as the sun sinks below the horizon. They laze there happily, no one on board especially eager to get back to port—or, for that matter, ever to be anywhere else again.

At the end of the weekend, Lewis still has not opened those condoms. In fact, he has not even thought of them again. But he finds himself red-cheeked all the same when he asks Dolores if he might write to her down in New Orleans.

Dolores Parker has admirers enough among the Old Confederacy's eligible beaux, but none of them are six feet one and a half inches, according to their army physical; none could outswim her, not to mention all of his friends; nor was any so valorous, so charming, so thoughtful. Maybe some of them were some of these things, but no one else made her feel like that, danced like that, or ever looked her father in the eye to disagree with him—as Lewis had after Parker said the South had not seen a truly great man since Huey P. Long sat in the governor's mansion—or was so unafraid to rise up by his own bootstraps. As she tells him yes, all she knows is that there is not another man in the world who captivates her as does Lewis Marcel Hampton.

Perhaps he does not know all there is to know about the business world, but Lewis does know a thing or two about chains of command. He wants to help his cause, so, before writing her, first writes to her mother and father thanking them for a lovely weekend. Only when he is certain his note has been received does he venture to write directly to Dolores. His notations are at first cautious, but grow with each back-and-forth passing, to letters of youthful earnestness, and as he gets to know her better, become an unbridled emptying of all that is in his heart—until one day she finds herself touching his letters with the sensation of feeling the contours of his soul.

Dolores takes this most recent letter and places it, along with the others, in a lovely box tied with a yellow ribbon, as her grandmother used to with her grandfather's letters in the last century. When she closes the box that night, she realizes it also weighs as much as the one from her grandparents she had found in the attic.

In his next love letter, Lewis carefully intimates he might come to New Orleans for a visit, since he has relations there he has not seen for some time. As long as I am in town, he asks, might we not see each other? When she writes back to tell him she would like nothing better, Lewis then mentions to his parents his plans to go visit their relatives in New Orleans. His father does not think anything of it, but his mother, being better attuned to the ways of her son, and having noticed the feminine stationery that arrived for him every fourth day, asks immediately what this sudden interest in Aunt Charlotte is really about.

Lewis shifts up and tries to tell her he simply wants to travel a bit, for the sake of self-improvement. His mother counters that she knows that city, and it strikes her as a strange notion: "What in the world is improving about New Orleans?" So, in the end, because he cannot out-and-out lie to her, he confesses he sort of has a sweetheart there.

Abigail immediately begins to badger her son with the questions he feared she would. He suffers through to the end of this conversation, when she offers him a bit of unsolicited courting advice. "Interested, but not overeager. Neither the first one at the party, nor the last to leave." Lewis thanks her, but, for what he feels, there is no need for counsel. He will heed nothing but this feast of emotions. He will stay at the table until he is offered a room for the night, or thrown out on his ear.

He knows he has entered a space where there is no penalty for eagerness, and no rules but the ones of their own invention, because, he thinks, if all those theories people had on the subject amounted to anything at all, then the entire world would be successful in love.

Lewis has worked three college summers, and six of the months since he has been home, in the logistics business, and lived in a railroad town all his life. He has traveled in England, as well as Italy, France, and Germany, and he has gone back and forth to New York. But he has never before looked forward so much to a trip.

When he was younger, he might have fretted about what might happen to him in the city, or how he should behave, but he has gained confidence enough to feel at ease anywhere in the world.

New Orleans, he tells himself, will be like New York but smaller, or like Paris but less French. It will be a city of love.

On the way down, he finds himself newly impressed by the train, having always looked at it as a means of moving troops or mundane things like produce, but never as an instrument of romance. He eases now into his seat, feeling he is on a great adventure no one else can know.

As the locomotive crosses Lake Pontchartrain, he focuses all of his thoughts on Dolores, remembering the weekend he spent dancing and sailing on the Gulf of Mexico, and what she felt like when he kissed her.

He closes his eyes and dreams again of this green-eyed girl.

He feels impressive as the train pulls into the station, and he takes his suitcase from the overhead, then walks out into the terminal. He rents a car from the Hertz counter and follows the directions to his aunt's house. Knowing he is the luckiest fellow alive, he begins, as he loses his fears of becoming lost, to notice the city around him. He feels then his luck has doubled.

No better thing ever happened to man, woman, or overawed Mississippian, Lewis gushes, than to love a girl here in New Orleans. He is ready for anything else that might be offered him on this, his great journey, to stake and claim his portion of the treasure that is happiness, which she has made him feel.

He spends his daytime hours exploring the town, and his nights with Dolores in pursuit of music and passion. After waking in the morning, he goes first thing to the arcade of the French Market to start the day with chicory coffee and beignets, until he is all but ill. For lunch, he knows he should not but can't help it, he grows an addiction to oyster po'boys and muffulettas. In the evenings, his aunt Charlotte always makes a wonderful dinner, but he finds himself looking, late at night, for still-open bars that will feed him gumbos and fresh crawfish.

After dinner, he calls on Dolores to take walks in the Garden District and the French Quarter, where he marvels at the wrought-iron work, which is art to rival any Venetian glass, or stroll in City Park, and grow rapturous under the bearded lace spell of Spanish moss that turns the stern old oaks into retiring white-haired willows.

He fills himself with the smell of late-blooming crape myrtle, which he finds even more intoxicating than magnolias and Cherokee roses, as they give off a perfume all of New Orleans seems wrapped in. He learns to dodge the streetcars, and the horse-drawn carriages a certain kind of man still uses to drive to work. He wishes to see himself in one someday, and tells himself he will, as he listens to the washerwomen going to work on Monday. He felt magic in New York, and has nothing but the highest regard for Atlanta and Charleston, but he tells himself New Orleans should be the country's capital.

It is the greatest city in the world, he thinks. It is American, even in ways he did not realize before, and he sees nothing but its grandeur, turning an eye away from the dilapidation and violent undertowing there.

He is careful of its Negroes, but thinks early on they must be geniuses too, because even the street names in New Orleans are brilliant. Prytania, Melpommenne, Terpsicore, Thalia, and Calliope. Mystery, Elysian Fields, Desire. Chartres, Decatur, Bourbon, Basin, Royal, Cabilldo, Paris. Rampart, Magazine, Simon Bolivar, Washington, Jefferson, Davis, Race. General Robert E. Lee.

He loves a girl here. He is drunk on New Orleans and falls into

the bad habit New Orleanians have of always thinking they are living inside a story, and continuously telling that story to themselves.
When his own story is over, Lewis tells himself, toward the end of his
week with Dolores, I hope to die right here in New Orleans. Bury
me in New Orleans, and give to Lewis Hampton one of those loud
funerals in the street, such as they give to what must be the great
New Orleanians.

Just as he had not known before meeting Dolores what feeling a
woman may inspire in a man, he had not known before coming here
what it was to feel truly at home in a place—no small matter at all—
as he sees the kind of cosmopolitan life he knows he cannot have in
Meridian. He has been told as well that this swampy town overflows
with angels and spirits, but becomes convinced there also exists one
there who watches over Lewis Hampton when he discovers Louis
Armstrong is performing his second-to-last night before leaving.

He drives his rental car to Dolores's house and waits in the foyer
for her to come down the stairs. She trails her slight hand across the
mahogany banister as she descends, under the watchful eye of her
father, and stops near enough for Lewis to kiss her. He does not, but
feels, looking through cineascopic eyes, that it is a good place to be.
It is good to be home. He restrains himself from kissing her.

When they arrive at the banquet hall, they take their table, feeling
the energy of both the crowd inside and the colored people on the
lawn across the street, waiting for Louis to take to the stage. A
combo comes out to warm them up and prepare the place, because,
as he tells Dolores, you can't just sit down and start listening to
Armstrong cold, it would be like emerging too fast from the bottom
of the ocean.

The crowds indulge the warm-up group, as it brings them slowly to the surface of their skin, because they know when Louis comes out they will be taken to new heights.

Lewis Hampton touches Dolores Parker's hand, remembering to her the first time he heard jazz music broadcast on Armed Services Radio, and the Negro clubs he visited in Paris and New York afterward. Dolores one-ups him by telling how, when she was ten, her mother took her and her sisters to see a movie with a funny colored man standing in soap bubbles playing just to them.

On the lawn outside, the colored people pass cold pieces of fried chicken back and forth, waiting to hear Louis out in the open, and remember when Mary Albert's kinda sloe-eyed bad boy first come marching through the Battlefield with his peewee band. Or when one of them steamboats used to come down the river and you heard a horn flying over the muddy waters that sounded like it came straight out of the mouth of the Mississippi itself.

He is theirs.

They wait for him to take them places they all want to go, or have not been in too long a time.

Armstrong slips into the light onstage, wishing them all a good evening, as they rise to their feet to applaud the little colored boy who made good and rose New Orleans up with him.

Louis is a long way from Basin Street tonight, but he begins a scat that bridges the distance from the banquet hall to the Battlefield, and everyone in and around the hall goes into a lightheaded trance. Presses a little closer to who they know, or who they are trying to.

He starts off slow and melancholy, because, he knows, even with the warm-up act, they still ain't quite ready to come up all the way.

Lewis feels something deep and invincible pulling him in closer to Dolores as they stand on the lip of that horn riding the surf of notes. Armstrong lifts them up a little higher, and they go shim-shim-shimmering out there on the lawn, and inside the hall. He pauses and rests them there. Lewis moves closer to Dolores, closer than he has been since the night of their last dance, as the colored man gives them another slow song, and the band pulls out of them everything they feel and want to feel tonight.

When they are exhausted and can't go anywhere else with him, Louis gives to them an elegy to take with them, so they will know how to talk about this evening later, then mops his brow and wishes them all a very pleasant evening. They are worn out, tired, up here on top of the world.

Louis returns to his dressing room, where he tries to figure out what he is going to do with the rest of the night. He loves to work a crowd like that, and likes nothing better than the love everyone sends back to him, but he knows a spot where musicians, hustlers, and tap-dancing boys go after hours. There is a cathouse upstairs, and if you know the owner, you can still get a bottle of moonshine better than anything they make since Prohibition. He knows he ain't got no business going over there, but wonders whether there's some-one out there he might share a couple of riffs with, because one day it will be gone but tonight there is still music in him. Tonight there is in all of them.

Dolores and Lewis leave and walk through the mass of dark bod-ies to the car to make their way back to the city. Dolores rests her head in the crook of Lewis's shoulder, feeling a poetry beyond the natural senses, as he wraps an arm around her. Neither is ready yet to call it an evening.

"Why don't we drive out to the levee," she suggests.

Lewis knows that look. He wants to wait until they are married, but right now he will do anything she bids. He follows her directions to the waterfront, and parks. She slips in closer to him. He kisses her, and kisses her again to make up for the one he did not get in the living room. He wants to wait, but also to devour her, and be replenished, as by a long sip of water on a tropical day. He begins. They will give and have whatever they will. He lifts and pushes her skirt up over her legs, his fingers humming the music they still hear, then pulls the bra from her cloistered breasts and takes one of her nipples in his mouth. He frees himself and guides her hands. She holds him, not certain what to do, as he helps her along, then takes her other high nipple in his mouth, following the curvature of her breasts. He holds her hips and she trembles. It is a hurried, decadent love they make tonight.

When it is over, instead of feeling as he feared he might, Lewis finds himself wanting her again. He will make love to her slowly this time.

When they finally drive back to Dolores's house, she is thoughtful; he is worried.

"A dollar for your thoughts," he says.

"Don't you think it was just awful that all the Negroes had to listen to the concert from outside?" she asks.

Lewis does not want to talk about Negroes right now. He doesn't want to talk about anything. "I don't know," he says, "seems like he could do another show somewhere they might come in. Is that all that's got you so bothered?"

Dolores shrugs, and slides back into the crook of his shoulder. She does not know what you are supposed to talk about after doing *it*, but knows the night has turned her thoughts serious. "You think black and white should always be segregated?"

"There's nothing white or black about jazz," Lewis says. "As far as the rest of it, I personally wouldn't have minded, but that doesn't mean you can just force it on everyone. It just wouldn't be right."

"You think the Negro is less than the white?" she asks.

He is irritated by this questioning but tries to indulge her. "Jeez, Dolores, I didn't say that, but I don't think that guy is Louis Armstrong," he says, pointing to a hobo loitering on the corner. Dolores nods and settles back into him a little less easy, upset that he does not consider her opinions more, especially after they just did it. When he stops in front of her house, she does not kiss him good night.

The following evening, Lewis is at the Parker home for a dinner party he had already been invited to when the conversation turns again to race, after someone mentions a string of break-ins they have had in the Garden District.

"That's all they're good for is stealing," one of the guests at the table remarks.

"I don't know," Lewis replies, when he is asked his opinion. He is learning to be more careful, but tonight cannot hold his tongue. "I wish we had black people in Mississippi like the ones you-all have here in New Orleans. I'm starting to think all of them are just geniuses."

"Well, if you want, you can take some home with you," one of the men counters.

"Geniuses at ripping you off," another man says, as Mrs. Parker tries to steer the conversation to a more genial topic.

"Geniuses for making music, building houses, and ironworking too," Lewis argues, causing a small titter at the table. Half the guests grow instantly to hate his guts, and the other half to admire Dolores's young man for being so full of spunk and grit.

"Well, I'll be," old Parker says contrarily, the top of his weathered scalp darkening like a Choctaw's. "Damnit, son, if I didn't know better, I'd say the army had made themselves a Yankee out of you."

"No, sir," Lewis replies, "I'm a Mississippian in every way that hasn't been smitten by New Orleans. I guess that just makes me a Rebel unto my very bones."

The table laughs and applauds. Parker laughs especially loud. "Don't kill this jackass, Emile," he tells himself. "He still don't know what the damn thing costs."

"You'll think different about it when you have an investment in property or business," another man at the table says, tempering the laughter.

No one can disagree with him, but neither can they fault Lewis for being bested in the argument, especially since he is still young.

Dolores is happy to hear him speak her own opinions, and Lewis glows to know men such as Parker's friends find him a worthy conversationalist, and also that they think he is the kind of man who will someday have investments in common stocks and property.

THREE

From merely imagining it, Lewis finds he has become a frequent passenger on the road between Meridian and New Orleans, until the frequency of these trips compels him to buy a car of his own.

His mind on these voyages always shifts into dream mode as he speeds over Lake Ponchartrain, picturing and telling to himself the story of Lewis Hampton, as it has been in the past, and as it will be told by others in the future—after he has built the bridge from his particular crossing of youth, idealism, and ambition to the storied life he will someday achieve. He was a hero, tall, think for hisself, from Mississippi, they will say then whenever his name should be mentioned, who became a great man in New Orleans.

Not that the present, he tells himself, is anything to complain about. But he hopes his courage may win for him in peacetime even more than it did during war, where what it got him was a ticket home. He wants now a ticket to achieve the world.

Whereas he read before to know something about culture, or the play of life and human ideas, he reads now to keep up with what is going on in the larger world, and especially the ones of politics and business. Today, though, when he checks into his hotel, he has with him a book of verse he sips from for other purposes entirely. He turns to it for an inkling of how to express what it is he wants to say to Dolores Parker.

They had met in early September, and as winter ends, it seems to him like time enough, especially since he has been certain since nearly the beginning.

He reads verse and agonizes through the night in his rented room over the proper way to proceed—whether he should ask of her directly, or first petition the father. He still has not slept as it turns to morning, and he decides at last on the latter, because he knows he has raised old Parker's ire once or twice in the past, and wants to do what is correct, but also to keep away from the man's bad side.

He dresses and calls on the house that afternoon as young men in pursuit of marriage have always called, with his black hair carefully brillianted, his best suit on, and a gift for the house instead of the daughter. He has prepared his case carefully.

He walks up the steep wooden stairs and rings the bell, feeling the small trepidation he always feels before the doors of the grand house, awaiting an audience. When the Creole maid, Melinda, opens it and sees him standing there, she tells the caller Miss Dolores is not expecting him for another hour.

"I was actually wondering whether I might speak to Mr. Parker," Lewis says nervously.

That Creole girl, bless her heart, she can't keep from grinning. "Lola, bring Mr. Hampton a drink," she calls into the house, looking at the trail of sweat creeping from behind Lewis's ear as she bids him come in.

He enters, and sits in the parlor, rehearsing his lines in his mind, until Mr. Parker comes up and catches him unawares. Lewis startles when he hears the man's voice. "So you've come to see me, have you?" the old man asks, toying with the younger one a bit. "And I see you brought me a pretty vase to keep my flowers in."

Lewis nods, stutters the slightest bit.

"Well, come on into my study and let's have us a chat," Parker says, ushering him through the bright halls of the house into his sanctuary.

Parker closes the door, then sits down before offering Lewis a seat. When he does sit, Lewis tries to keep calm but finds himself sweating more profusely as Parker appraises him.

He is a fine-looking boy, and there's even something irrepressible about him. But he doesn't seem to give enough of a damn about moving against the wind, or going faster than he should, Parker thinks. He is not sure this is what he wants for his daughter.

"Well, sir, what can I do for you this fine evening?" the old man asks, half hoping the boy wants a job, or a sponsor, and not what he thinks he does.

Lewis clears his throat and takes a sip from his water glass. "To get right to the point, Mr. Parker, I would like your permission to marry Dolores."

"I see," Parker says. "You certainly ain't one to waste words, boy. So—have you and Dolores talked about this yet?"

"Not directly," says Lewis, his clear voice less certain than usual. "I thought I might talk to you first, as proof of my good intentions." Lewis does not know anymore what the words coming out of his mouth mean, but he has thought about this so much they pour forth from him like machine-gun fire, he hopes eloquently, until Parker cuts him off.

"You don't think you're rushing it?" The old man shakes his head slowly. "A man meets a woman, and before you know it without knowing anything more about each other, everything is forever and ever after."

"Truth be told, sir," Lewis says, "I've been thinking about it since we first met."

"I forgot," Parker says, meaner than he needs to be, "you do get your mind around a thing."

Lewis begins to wonder whether his cause has drifted off course, or whether this is some time-honored humiliation he must suffer through before being allowed into the fraternity of married men.

"Do you have anything to recommend yourself other than your own good intentions, or am I to understand you're one of those young men with a great future ahead of him?" Parker asks.

"That's about the size of it," Lewis says straightforwardly, refusing to be bullied. He either gives his blessing or he does not, he tells himself, but I'm not going to jump hoops all day.

"It's just gonna come to you?" Parker asks.

"I will work for it," Lewis answers, as he remembers what a general told him before a great battle, after forcing him to admit he was afraid: It is not shameful to fear it, he was told then, it is whether you face the thing or turn tail and run.

Lewis is fearful of what Parker will say, and tells himself in a moment of doubt that perhaps he will not be great, but neither will he fail. As for happiness, all he needs is Dolores Parker, who makes him know with her presence that the world is not all darkness, as it has been some days in the past.

"In a small company in Meridian?"

"Wherever they do honest business and allow me a fair chance," Lewis answers, with a growing awareness of where Parker is leading the talk.

"And you would not see any shame in any work so long as it was honest and you had the chance to prove yourself?" Parker asks, puffing away at his cigar, and doing a better job of masking his own nervousness than Lewis. He knows it is time for his daughter to marry, but he also does not want her to go away.

"No, sir, I would not," Lewis says.

"Good." Parker nods, picking at his fingernails. "But what is it you want, son? Why does the hero engine need to climb the great big mountain other than thinking it can?"

Lewis is thankful for a question he can answer without having to think about at all. "Because," he says, looking the old man in the eye, "Dolores Parker is up there. It is the only reason I know for anything anymore."

Parker has hoped in the past he might use his money to buy up some old family name, as the bourgeois of another era would have purchased titles and coats of arms. He sees now, though, that all of his daughters will be marrying down, instead of making matches that might aid him in business or society. But he is thankful, at least, Dolores has not chosen someone frivolous or useless. "If my daughter will have you, so will I," he says. "And if you work with me, Lewis, we will see to it that she never has to know anything but that pedestal you got her up on."

When the interview is concluded, both men are satisfied enough, Parker to know Lewis is not just a wild ex-soldier full of ideas and unable to get the army out of him; Lewis because he has survived

the interview and received the permission he sought, but also because, in less than an hour, his entire future suddenly seems clearer.
He feels this bounding elation, but is surprised to find new kinds of
worries already there with it.

By the time he retired, and his son-in-law was running his business, Parker would claim he knew from the very beginning that a
single Lewis Hampton was as good as an army of all the old names
in the city. As he leaves the office, though, the old man is not without a few misgivings about the union. He has respect enough for the
ladder he himself scaled to hold the social ordering in great esteem,
and knows the difficulties of climbing out of one's given place. But
he also once had even less to recommend himself than Lewis, and
when he thought he had finally made it, had been rebuked the first
time he asked for a young woman's hand in marriage. He, who had
raised himself up from the swamps of Biloxi to the might of the railroads, thought he would look forward to the day when he was in the
position to grant yea or nay to others. Instead, he has found age
turning him into a romantic. "So he is not who you would have chosen," Parker thinks, as he has after each of these interviews when it
has come time for one of his daughters to wed. "But who are you to
deny them?"

When Lewis bends down before Dolores on the front porch that
evening, he finds that all the fine words of verse he has memorized
fly away. He has now only enough presence of mind to speak in the
tradition that has been performed by billions before him. They are
simple words. As they leave his mouth and hang in the air, though,
he feels as if he is first ever to walk this limb and humble himself before emotion and the thought of a shared life.

When Dolores says yes, he hears this reply as if that word too has never before been uttered, and she has only now invented it on her susurrous voice to communicate her willingness to be his wife.

They wed, in May, at great costs to her father, under the high ceiling of St. Louis Cathedral. When they exit the church into Jackson Square, Lewis feels the world glowing before him with hope. He knows there is nothing he cannot achieve with her by his side. He is whole again.

They honeymoon in Cuba, and move into a modest newlywed home uptown when they return. Lewis goes to work for his father-in-law, as he agreed. He has much to learn, and is treated without special favor, but nonetheless earns his first promotion before the end of summer.

The war seems ancient to him now, and he settles into married life, trying his best to become a good husband and provider. This is what he has fought for. And if from time to time he expresses an outrageous opinion, no one holds it against him. He is one of them now, and is growing into his potential more fully.

When strangers meet him now, the first thing they notice is seriousness and devotion. He is not only well related, you think, but has something in him that will someday make his name loom large in its own right as any man to walk these streets and soil, American. He will lift every burden you give.

FOUR

One touch is enough for Lewis to know she loves him. He assumes there is honor between them, because she has never shown him dishonor, and even brags about him on occasion to her friends. But Dolores Hampton has not yet quite gotten the gist of marital obedience as he understands it to mean. Nor—as the headiness of romance and platonic notions of love, which, Lewis has begun to suspect, need nothing more than a steady surface that will allow them to rest still upon, begin to give way to the compromises of shared meals, unmended socks, and occupying a house with a finite number of rooms, and a not very large yard—can he seem to figure out how to master his new wife, as everyone, and the very Bible itself, says he should.

It begins with the steak. He is determined that they live within the means of his salary, and they have only enough money for occasional domestic help. When he complains, though, that his dinner is still bleeding, his wife replies, "Lewis, it is Kansas prime. Don't you think it would be heathen to have it any other way?"

Lewis looks at her mutely. He can remember nights during the Depression, when he was young, and there was barely enough to eat. "Dolores, we simply cannot afford to have prime steak and chicken every day," he tells her, trying to keep control of his temper. "There are still shortages, and people all over this country eating horsemeat."

"Which seems to me like a very good reason to be happy with your steak," she retorts. "If you are worried about money, then you should just ask for a raise."

"I cannot do that," Lewis says, putting his food down, and trying to keep from screaming. "I am paid fairly, and I have not been there long enough. Besides all of which, there is also a railroad strike." He also knows his father-in-law has higher expectations for him than for his other employees. He is determined to meet those expectations, and to rise further than her sisters' husbands, who also work at Parker's firm. If he cannot even manage his own home, he knows, he will never be given buck-stopping power or last say-so over anything else.

"Then I will just have to ask for you," Dolores volunteers innocently.

"You cannot do that," Lewis cries. "It would humiliate me."

Sure enough, though, he finds in his next paycheck an increase over the last one, large enough to make up for any sentiment of lost pride, as he now earns almost ten thousand dollars a year.

He does not mention it to his immediate superior, and is, in fact, nearly ashamed of it, for he suspects he earns more than his own boss, and is certain he makes more than his father, who has slaved twenty years to become supervisor of a foundry.

He is upset to find that Dolores uses this extra money for things that do not seem appropriate to her husband's Protestant mind. He finds, for instance, a new suit and hat, from the city's best tailor and milliner, respectively, laid out on his bed one day when he gets out of the shower to dress for work. It is a nice gesture, he knows, but he cannot wear these things, which smack so much of dandyism. "Don't start acting nigger-rich," he tells her.

"Suit yourself." Dolores shrugs her shoulders and leaves the room.

Lewis dons the new clothes, only to find, to his chagrin, he enjoys the way he moves in them, and the figure he cuts in the office that day.

Instead of reproaching him, his colleagues bestow an additional respect, as men in the army would increase their level of attention and correctness according to the rank they read on the braid of an officer's uniform, and when he walks down Canal on his lunch break, he finds he is dressed impeccably like a New Orleanian.

He eventually gives in completely to the campaign of Lewis-improving she has set out upon. His acquiescence, though, is accompanied by the suspicion that she did not find him good enough before. He starts wondering in whose image she is trying to remake him.

"I am trying to help you be the best version of yourself," Dolores says to her ungrateful husband. "Don't you like my taste?"

His father-in-law is a man of only the roughest polish, who indeed took pleasure in the coarseness he had been able to retain from the swamps of Biloxi as he rose in the world. The other men in the company followed Parker's example, and Lewis is determined to do likewise. Not to behave like a college boy, or go in any way against the culture Parker had determined for the office. He even sees the value in this, since the men they do business with tended to be as rough-and-tumble as Parker himself.

Lewis tries to tell his wife theirs is not a commercial landscape that has found the leisure time and self-satisfaction to scrape the grease of the rails from their fingers and retire to a place that does not stink so much of striving.

"But why should hard work have to look ugly?" she wants to know.

He cannot answer her, so, while he tries to cultivate hardiness, his wife keeps attempting to turn him into one of those men he knows her father would have chosen for her to marry but would never hire to work for him.

What image, Lewis keeps asking himself, is she trying to metamorph me into? In these dark moments, his brain burns over other fears, which do not allow him to rest. He stays awake late into the night, as he looks over her motionless form for signs of guilt or spoilage. His thoughts turn then to the levee. Who was it who first took her there? he questions. How often? And am I the usurper of his bed, while he sleeps in sheets of greater purity and whiteness? He tortures himself until sunrise. He knows if he lets them these thoughts will tear him down, and he resists the urge to wake her and demand answers to them. In the morning, though, he is sullen, and refuses to give cause. He knows it would be evil to cast such aspersions out loud on his own wife, and finds instead other ways of coping. There pass whole weeks like this, when he will not touch her.

It begins with his thinking about the levee and staring at her in the dark, then grows as he wonders why, after six months of marriage, even his father-in-law asks why they have not started a family. He worries at these times that perhaps she is barren, so erects even greater distance between them.

All his worries put together give growth to his first gray hairs. When Dolores sees them, she comments that they give him dignity.

He asks if, on top of everything else, he was also not dignified enough before. She is miserable. They both are.

"So you are learning," Parker says one evening when he sees Lewis still at his desk, bent over a pile of work, as he himself is leaving the office.

"Sir?" asks Lewis.

"What it all costs," his father-in-law says.

Lewis thought he had learned that during the war. He paid there a horrible price. What more do they want from me? he asks himself. I have killed for them. But on those nights, he knows, he was able to sleep soundly, if only for a few hours, as a child in the life-giving womb. His sleep now has become arbitrary. It is harder, he thinks, to build a decent life than to defend a country or ideal.

Besides the tribulations of marriage, he is also haunted and hunted some nights by warthoughts he would give anything to forget. Is this what it fucking costs? he screams in his head, unable to sleep. What does he think he knows that I do not? He suspects that familiarity with the currency he does know has brought a caul over him. It has done violence to the boy he was and the man he thought he would become. He struggles to control it, in the same way he resists crawling closer to her and waking his wife, or screaming after one of his nightmares has brought him to horrible wakefulness. When she touches him on these nights, he recoils from her.

He wonders if he experiences this alone, and wants to talk about it in a manly way. When he cannot bear it any longer, he writes his old friend George Mason a light letter, whose only signs of discombobulation is a quoted line from the *Aeneid*. If George does not get his drift, he thinks, it is just as well. He will deal with it as he has been doing.

But George, bless him, writes back a good honest letter from Detroit, where he has taken a job in the automotive industry. He confesses he has been wondering of late whether the best of their generation were not the ones who died. In spartan moments, George goes on, he thinks of a boy he grew up with, and had competed with throughout college, who went missing in action. Whether he is buried in French, or German, or Luxembourgian soil, no one can say, or for that matter that he is buried at all and not picked apart by birds of prey and other wild animals, instead of proper, slow-moving worms. George does not speak so directly, but leaves Lewis to figure that he wonders whether he lives in that man's place.

What George does say is that he wonders whether, if he still had him to compete with, he might not be urged toward greater heights, for he knows there are some he would not have passed without being pushed on in that former contest.

Lewis is unnerved by George's letter. He had easily outplaced most boys in Meridian, but now feels in a cutthroat race with his brothers-in-law. He agrees it has made him a better worker, but he knows power is not a thing to be shared in the world of business, and all else is weakness. There is but to get it, or to be something less than him who does. He hopes that when he has it it may count for something in other spaces as well, perhaps even in his own home. He does not want to think about the dead.

He moves from being embarrassed about making more than his father, and probably even his own boss, to enjoying the extra income and the confidence it lends him in the city. He is still careful of Negroes, but for regular white men feels no one has anything over him. He even begins to believe, as his mother has always told him, that he will be a great Southerner someday. He knows without being told that to be great in the South is to be the equal of any man in the world. That much is still true.

He tells himself the story of his future greatness as he walks through that great city. He grasps now all the foresight that went into its construction and sees it is the imprimatur and lyric of a powerful civilization, the sum of all civilizations before it. If he wills, it exists for him.

He works toward that goal, becoming comfortable in his new life as in his new clothes. He will grow into it and better, he tells himself. He will have tailors in New York, Chicago, and Charleston who know his measurements by heart. Lewis will. He will not think anymore of war. If there was something else he once wanted, he forgets it with the dead. He knows any other way would yield incapacitation.

Parker senses this change in Lewis, and there begins the inkling of a favoritism that makes the other brothers jealous. Lewis in turn is careful to cultivate allies, and keep a tight rein on his underlings. He gains power in the office as he did in the army, but knows now to consolidate it.

He writes—or, rather, dictates—to George a short letter suggesting that, if he ever has the time, he would like to show him the South up close, since George always seemed most interested in it during those debates they used to have. His postscript this time is of his own devising, as florid quotations have little place on company stationery, but belong more to the dinner table.

George senses the coolness his last letter has brought, and replies to tell Lewis how much he appreciates the invitation and looks forward to someday seeing the Southern states; however, it will have to wait until sometime in the future, because he cannot yet get away from his duties at work. He then proffers a little investment advice and wishes his friend, and his friend's new bride, all the best in their endeavors.

Lewis takes the news in stride, and the financial advice for what it is worth. He even sends George back a few tips of his own, but does not mention the bet he is making on this new thing called television. War friends, he tells himself, belong back there with the war.

He copes with the pressures of his new life by spending greater amounts of time relaxing at his club after work instead of heading immediately home, as he did in their first months of marriage.

The club not only allows him time for relaxation, but also proves a boon to his career. He has discovered that leisure time spent with his colleagues strengthens their trust and bonds, and that work is something one may do all the time, even in the parlor of a bordello.

The only way we will get the war behind us is to put our energy in the building of America, the army told him when he came home, and Lewis is much admired when he repeats it. He keeps his political opinions to himself, and never invokes God except piously, as he suspects pragmatic atheism is not going to win him many admirers.

This respect he wins from his colleagues, and the time he spends away from home, have the unexpected benefit of improving his domestic life as well. He does not even raise a fuss when he arrives home one evening and notices for the first time that his wife has redecorated their house in what she calls the new Art Deco style.

"Do you like it?" Dolores asks his approval.

He is beginning to trust her taste in such things. "I think it is wonderful," he says, as he tries to calculate mentally how much all of this has cost them. It adds up to something awful, but he dismisses it as an investment in their future. "We might even throw our first dinner party soon."

"What about Thanksgiving?" Dolores suggests.

Lewis tells her his mother would be terribly offended if they did not have it at *her* house. He has already promised. He does not mention how much he misses her cooking.

"Why didn't you tell me sooner?" Dolores protests. "It is only two weeks away."

"Well, I am telling you now," Lewis answers.

"I'll have to ask my doctor whether it is okay for me to travel."

"Why?" Lewis wants to know. "We're only going up to Meridian."

When she tells him she is with child, Lewis is overjoyed. He hugs her, feeling as though he himself has grown larger. She is not barren, as he feared.

When they sit down to dinner that night, though, he finds yet new worries pounding around in his head. He trusts they are ready to bring children into the world, but muses aloud whether they shouldn't move out to the suburbs.

"What is wrong with the city?" Dolores asks. "It is where I grew up."

"Well, the city is changing," Lewis says, unloading all of his arguments. "Besides, I grew up with open spaces, and don't think my child should have less. It will also save us money." Lewis worries less about money than he once did; he knows now he will always be able to provide, even if the market should crash. Still, he remembers nights during the Depression when there was barely enough to eat. He plans now not merely on providing but on assuring the future, and knows there is too much danger for a child, and too many temptations and idle time for her in the city.

Dolores does not believe a man is something you obey just because he is your husband; however, she is not only wife now, but also expectant mother. "I suppose," she says. "There is time to talk about it."

Lewis does not want to shatter the aura of happiness her news has brought to them. As he cuts his meat, he says only, "Just think about the idea, Dolores." He knows he will have to buy a house soon, and is not sure the city is the place to make that investment. "But ask your doctor about Thanksgiving. My mother would love to see you."

When Dolores tells him, the next day, that the doctor has advised against her traveling, he begins to suspect subterfuge.

"Well, I am your husband. I don't care what any doctor says," he confronts her, giving vent to his frustrations. "Do you have something against my family?"

"I thought *I* was your family," she counters, hurt by his distrust and look of malice. "Is seeing them more important to you than protecting your child?"

"Dolores," Lewis says, "I have not seen them in half a year, and we see your family all the time." He is surrounded by her family. Besides seeing old man Parker and his brothers-in-law at the office, they also visit each Sunday for brunch with a clan that includes not only her parents, sisters, and their husbands, but also close friends and whoever else just happens to stop by and get pulled in by the gravity of Parkers. He feels suffocated by Parkers, and knows this is not what the chain of command is supposed to look like. She is a Hampton now. He is her husband. He will do anything for her, and even more for the child she is with, but they owe his mother Thanksgiving.

"Lewis," Dolores says, "why don't you go alone?"

"Because, Dolores, they want to see you too."

"But I cannot travel."

They circle like this the entire weekend, him wondering that she does not respect him, or else has something against his family; her suspecting he does not value her health, and is too much a boy to make the decision he ought.

When she turns her lamp off Sunday night, she is sallow with crying and falls asleep on waves of sobs. He stays awake, figuring numbers and power and past life and futures in his head.

The next morning, he is at his desk when the old man comes in and closes the door. Parker stretches out across the leather sofa in Lewis's office, and looks up at the ceiling for a good long while before shutting his eyes.

"Lewis, you don't know nothing about women, and even less about your wife, so let me start from the beginning and tell you something," he says, under the shade and meditation of his own eyelids, "and this is something I have had to tell all of my son-in-laws eventually, so don't take it personal."

"Okay," Lewis agrees.

"Son," Parker continues, "men and women ain't got nothing in common. Why, the average man has more in common with the boy who gives him his shoeshine in the morning, or the dog that chews them up at night, than he does with his own wife, who comes from his rib. That's why we have jobs, and offices, is not just to do business but to get out of the house.

"I'll tell you something else. Dolores is not like most women, because she is good and cause she got understanding. Her sisters have given me every heartache a rich man ever received from his children, but Dolores is different. She has been since she was a little girl. She's the closest thing I ever had to a son, but she's still a woman, and you have to live with her, hard as it may seem right now, and you don't even know half of what you will go through with nobody else but her.

"Why, I remember when me and her mother first got married. You know what I thought that first year? It wasn't, Thank God for sending me such a good woman, but: Emile, how in the hell did you get yourself into this trickery?

"I imagine there was not a table I wouldn't rather be eating off of, or a bed I wouldn't rather be climbing into, than my wife's." Parker looks over at Lewis and watches as he turns bright red.

"Ah, hell, boy, don't get embarrassed. Just because she come running to her mamma and daddy every time you two have a little fight ain't no reason to get concerned. What you need to be concerned about is that day she ain't got nobody to turn to but you, and that little child she carrying ain't got nowhere else to turn either.

"Now, never mind her for a minute, the baby gonna say, 'Daddy, why is this and why is that?' And you know more, so will try to answer it rational, until you get yourself a question that can't be reasoned out, and you will look down and say, 'Cause I'm the daddy, is why.' You see the child nod and take that as just as good as if it were gold, and you realize it is supposed to be so. That don't nothing come between them and eating horsemeat or living in open air or slave quarters, or being otherwise dispossessed, than you going out there and being the daddy with the whole weight God give Adam to hold."

"The whole weight?" Lewis asks, not knowing if Parker is just bulling him and testing his gullibility.

"Every goddamn ounce of it," he is answered. "And sacrifice to hold it, and to keep even your wife from knowing the full burden of what Adam done passed down to you, with nothing in line between you and God, or your family and the kind of things you see in war, except your word being good as gold and your back being strong enough to keep Adam's raggedy-assed covenant.

"Now, I have not been in the army, but I imagine it must be like knowing ain't nothing between the men around you and death except one another. Imagine being in there alone."

Lewis imagines whether that is true.

"See, when a man builds, he got to build for more than hisself. When he suffers, it is for an equal number," Parker goes on under his closed lids in the sparse office. "Just think about that Japanese emperor, Hirohito. When he went to war, he was God. When he lost, they take him and make him say he is just a man. For a someone who was God, that's worse than killing him.

"Now, what about all them Japanese people? How do you think they feel, knowing who they thought was God is not? How can they believe in any kind of god at all after that?"

"I don't know," Lewis says, not certain where this is leading.

"I'll tell you how they gonna believe, they gone think ain't no God but the A-bomb, and take that into their hearts. That is why little four-eyed Harry Truman shamed Hirohito so. Because he was a bad big daddy, and when the Japanese children first come to him and say, 'Big Yellow Daddy, will you fight the A-bomb for us?,' he gone sit up there and say, 'I will give you the whole world,' instead of being just a man and telling them, 'Maybe next Christmas,' or 'I don't know. Why don't you go ask your yellow mamma?' When Truman done already called him up and said, 'Listen here, Hirohito, we both understand by now what war is, but, big daddy to big daddy, I need you to know the boys over here done cooked something up, I do not know how, but it has got the power of the sun. And I don't want to use it, no more than you want to see it, because after it fall ain't nobody gone believe nothing else for a long, long time, let alone in no big daddies.'

"But Big Yellow Daddy couldn't acknowledge no limitations, and turned around to screw it up for every father on the planet, just like those other two jackasses."

Lewis has begun to think his father-in-law is as wacky as General MacArthur was rumored to be in private, and hearing the Axis called simple jackasses makes him shudder, but he has also been around enough to suspect there is something wacky about most large characters, and listens to Parker until he finds his words beginning to make a kind of sense.

"See, don't nobody know what being a man costs until they have had to lift up that whole burden and then come to find out they did not have to do it so quickly or so alone. Because, son, there are other men engaged in the holding up of the sky. To keep our God from falling." He looks over at Lewis again. "It is a real thing, that, boy.

"Now, what does this have to do with what is going on between you and Dolores? Nothing except this: Men and women ain't got nothing in common, so God give to them the co-promises of love, and children, and time apart. I ask you as her husband to let her stay here with us for Thanksgiving, while you go up to see your people in Mississippi, and see if, when you come home, things don't be a little bit easier between you."

"Okay, Dad," says Lewis, who until then has used all invention to avoid addressing Parker directly, because he did not know yet what to call him. "I will do that. I will do all of it."

"You don't know how glad you have just made me," Parker says, sitting up again on the sofa. "Because I remember the way you looked at her and she looked at you when you-all first met, and it would break me to pieces to have to give you the speech I just gave to Mary's husband."

"What's that?" Lewis asks nervously; he has seen the Parkers rotate affection between the sons-in-law in the cruelest fashion, even to the point of taking away the names of those, grown men all, who had fallen out of favor, and rebaptize them like heathens. "Take this here to Sandra'shusbandwhowashe," or "Tell Mary'shusbandwhatdotheycallhim the father wants to see him." Lewis does not want to be known as "Dolores'shusbandwhateverthehellhisname."

"Spare the rod and spoil the child." Parker shakes his head conspiratorially.

Lewis is not sure whether the old man is still serious or not, but he feels the balance of power shifting in his favor.

When he goes home that night, he takes roses to his wife. In turn, he sees her open an invitation in her green eyes that he is prepared that evening to receive without suspicion.

I will give thanks for these things this year, he tells himself that night lying in his bed, and no more bring war or evil thinking into this home, nor let my mind go wandering, to and fro, and up and down, either in its own unknowable pathways, or else revisiting the dark places it has known before. Because he has realized that, if the things he has taken as sacred are fallible, then there is that much more reason for him to carry well and protect his share of their burden. Thus speaks Lewis in his heart, and all is right in his house, as it is in the world. He will no longer be an atheist, or idealist worrying, thinking too much, but a man with understanding of where faith and strength come from, and the purpose to which they owe thanksgiving.

FIVE

It is Tuesday when George Mason phones to tell Lewis he is in town on business. Lewis is busy trying to close up his office before Thanksgiving, and looking forward to just half a day more of work before the long weekend in Mississippi. He has vowed to be more understanding of his brother, Nathan, and reach out to him more earnestly on this trip than perhaps he has done in the past. He is not especially in the mood for visiting with an army buddy.

"Do you have time to get together for a drink this evening?" George asks.

"Of course," Lewis tells him, praying to himself they will have things to talk about besides the war. He gives George directions to his club and asks him to wait in the lobby.

When he arrives, he is shocked to see how much younger George looks than he remembers, as if days for him had not only refused to pass but moved backward. He has until then been almost proud of the paunch he has grown in his first year of marriage, but seeing George makes him feel old and self-conscious.

"I see married life is treating you well," George greets him warmly.

"Couldn't be better," Lewis replies, as they sit down at the bar and order late-afternoon whiskies. "So what brings you here on such short notice?"

Lewis does not intend to be gruff or seem unhappy to see his old friend, but the question just comes out that way, prompting him to try and make up for it when their drinks arrive.

"I am the only one in the office who is not married, so it fell to me," George says. "Sorry to call so out of the blue, but I figured, since you lived here, well, why not look up old Lewis Hampton."

"Have you had a chance yet to see much of the city?" Lewis asks, still with faux hospitality he is ashamed of.

"The usual, I suspect." George swills his drink. "It is not what I expected the South to be like."

"What were you expecting?" Lewis wants to know.

"I'm not sure," George confesses, looking at Lewis, who seems so robust, and feeling wan and sickly by comparison.

"Well, of course, New Orleans is not really the South," Lewis explains, "so much as its the northernmost point of the Caribbean."

They exchange niceties and small talk, each remarking how strange it is to see the other in grown-up clothes and grown-up civilian life. "Well, as a wise man said," Lewis recalls, "what else is there to do now but build America up?"

"It is all happening so fast," George Mason says, sensing his friend's discomfort, as he himself remembers the last time they saw each other.

They talk instead about wild nights smuggled, or bought for cheap, from the fallen rubble of the great capitals. They sit in silent contemplation. They do not talk about the war.

"So are you liking Detroit?"

"Oh, it is fine," George answers. The bond that had grown between them is slipping, but as they try to readjust it, each grows happy in his unspoken way for the other's company, if only to know for a moment that all of it was real and beside him sits a witness.

Because of this, because he feels their tie fading, and because seeing George, and seeing him doing so well, makes Lewis remember not only that those things happened but also that he too will do as he has been charged by his country, as they get drunker, he finds himself inviting his old friend to come with him to Mississippi for Thanksgiving.

"I could not," George answers. "It would be too much of an imposition."

"Nonesuch," Lewis argues. "It will be like old times, and you will get to see a sight you have never seen before."

"What is that?" George asks.

"Football," Lewis answers.

"Ridiculous," George says, having gotten a bit tighter than he should. "We had football in New England, and we have it in the Midwest."

"You might have seen football *games* before," Lewis extols, becoming again the boy he used to be, "but until you have been to an Egg Bowl you have never seen football the religion."

"What else you got there?" George asks, as he would ask on nights long ago when they stayed awake in their foxholes trading stories of home.

"Well," Lewis says, "if you had come a few months earlier, you would have seen the magnolias in bloom, and the camellias, and pink-and-white Cherokee roses. But since it is getting cold, you will smell the fresh pine, and I will show you the bald-cypress, sweet-gum, and tupelo trees. And have you ever known a better sound to the female voice than we have right here in the South?"

"It comes from the Scottish," says George.

"Good old George Mason." Lewis lifts his glass in nostalgia. "You will also taste a thing better than you have ever tasted in all your life."

"Which is what?" George prods.

"Wild turkey," Lewis answers, "and even you cannot argue with that, because I almost lost my wife to one." He laughs in his drink.

"Well, if you are certain it won't be an imposition," George agrees, still not entirely certain. Lewis, though, is insistent. It will be a wonderful weekend.

"Unless you would rather spend the holidays by yourself, or doing whatever it is the unmarried do."

"That settles it, then. I'll come with you," George says, because he does not want to spend the day alone in his hotel room.

When they part, Lewis reminds George again that he will pick him up at his hotel the next evening. George tells Lewis he can't wait, but in his mind is also prepared for a note or phone call next morning telling him the plans have changed. He will not hold it against Lewis, but will know he had only the best of intentions.

When Lewis arrives home later that evening, Dolores asks what has caused him to be in such a good mood. She does not ask why he is late getting home.

"I ran into an old friend from the army," he tells her.

"Why didn't you invite him by for dinner?" she asks.

It simply slipped his mind, he says. He does not tell her he had forgotten momentarily he was married. "But he's going up to Meridian with me for Thanksgiving." Lewis stops and says no more about it, as he thinks he might be picking at a fresh wound. "We will be together for Christmas and every holiday after that, though," he hastens to add, to bring the segments of his life back into line with each other, "and we will celebrate it any way you like."

He means this. He will give his wife all his holidays from now on, and whatever else she wants that is within his means to provide. He will extend those means according to her wishes and good sense, but he has been severed from his former life with such abruptness, as he raced to embrace the future, he has had no time for reflection.

This will be a weekend of reflection, he tells himself, and when he returns, he will come back to her a true husband.

He cannot express all of these things, he hasn't the words, but she accepts what he does manage in good faith, biting her tongue to keep from saying she will be the only one of her sisters there at the great table without a husband. Her mother has counseled her to give him as much of a leash now, in the beginning, as he needs, and she follows this advice.

"Man is what they called the ego before there was a word for it," she said. "He will come back to you. You will see. He will always return to you in his need, or when he has done something he thinks is great, for approval, like a hunting dog returning to its master with bird in mouth. But he will always come home, dear. You must learn to accept your burdens without complaint, and build a home without him knowing that it is you who built it and not he, who is only your proxy out in the world. Then, you will see, one day he will come home and all will be forgotten. Hopefully, it will be before then, but as likely as anything, he will no longer have hair left, or his fine shape, but he will look around to say, 'I have built this. There is no longer anything else, or need for me to be, out in the streets of the world.' And you will have to suffer him around the house all day, but little by little he will become your husband no matter what else."

"I am sure it will be a lovely weekend," Dolores says as they settle down to dinner. Lewis tells her about his day at work, and asks her advice on how to handle an especially delicate situation with one of the brother-in-law colleagues.

She tenders her opinion carefully, because she is aware now how her rise is linked to his own. She knows some of her sisters have less, and is happy for this say-so over her fate. He will rise higher because of it. She will be a good wife to him, so that he may become the husband she wants. The man she saw that day in Ocean Springs.

They will dance together like that again. One day in their own home. She is with child. Advises him carefully.

Lewis leaves the office early, which for him is when the business day ends, and goes to pick George up from his hotel.

They drive across Lake Pontchartrain, no longer men who have been charged with the weight of carrying a Great Society, but as boys on holiday, carefree and full again of adventure, instead of the limited thoughts of office.

Lewis looks out across the water as they pass over the narrow bridge on the golden-warm November day. "Is it what you thought it would be?" he asks, trying to see his homeland through the eyes of an outsider.

"No," George answers, giving heed to the tendency to always compare new places to ones that are known. "It is more beautiful, and not as different as I was expecting. New Orleans actually reminds me of St. Louis."

"I have never been there," Lewis says of his namesake city.

"Well, if I lived in New Orleans, I can't imagine much that would make me leave," answers George, taking in the landscape as the traffic decreases and he settles into more relaxing cadences of thought.

They pass through a small fishing community, and he thinks of tragic towns on the coast of Maine. The pine forests seem to him like the Berkshires spread out over flat land. The swamps are their own, but "It really is all one country," he says to Lewis, who is happy that an outsider can see his region of the world with unprejudiced eyes.

"For us to build up, as far as we can see."

Lewis is proud of his life as they drive through Mississippi, and when they enter Meridian, it gives him special pleasure to watch how his friend reacts to it.

"So this is where the great Lewis Hampton is from." George looks around the pleasant streets of the town, with its kempt lawns, and the eurythmic ebb of life on the streets. He thinks how much town life surpasses living in the cities. Why, here even the little black lawn jockeys seem to extend genuine hospitality, instead of mere dissonance, as he had always found in them on the lawns of homes in the North. He notices the increase in the number of Negro faces as well, but they do not seem dangerous, like the ones he was careful to avoid in Detroit or other cities, especially since he was once mugged of his wallet.

"Tell me about the Negroes," George says, after seeing a group of young boys walking the street.

"There's nothing much to tell," Lewis answers. "They have their place here and we have ours, but even they will come up by and by."

"And you-all get along okay?"

"As okay as anywhere, I suppose. Meridian is not like one of those towns you-all hear about up north. It is peaceful," Lewis goes on, "and that does not make the papers."

When they get to the house Lewis grew up in, George notices the two stars still hanging on the flag in the window. "Did you have a brother in the service too?" he asks.

"Oh," Lewis tells a small lie, "it was for one of my cousins."

When they go inside, though, he is pleased to see how well George falls into the warmth of his family. It makes him happy to be back in his parents' home, amid the comfort that has not yet been achieved in his own.

He finds himself as close to his mother as ever, but as he looks at his father, standing there in the living room, he has new respect for him. Not only because he realizes he is king of his castle and governs with a mild hand, but also simply because he understands better now what all of it costs, and the coin with which it has been bought, even if it took Parker to explain it to him.

When they go out drinking that evening, Lewis invites his father to join them as well. His father declines, preferring, he says, to listen to his radio program, surrounded by the smell of his wife's cooking, at the end of a year that has been halfway between wartime and peace. He is happy for the invitation, though, pleased to see how well his son honors him.

If he had to go out alone this year to get the turkey, he does not mind. He has done it alone before, and done it well enough to see his boys are grown up. It is good now, he thinks, for a man to have some moments alone with himself and his thoughts out in the wilderness.

Lewis's mother is a little concerned that her daughter-in-law is not there, and hopes all is well in her son's home. She pushes it aside, though, because of the joy having Lewis there brings. She knows it has gotten toward the end of the time when she will share a feast with both her sons as well as her husband, all the life they have created and sustained in the world.

Lewis and George make their way to the bar. When he enters, Lewis is pleased to find the place has not changed, and wraps himself in the ghost life of fond nights spent there in the past. He looks around for familiar faces, but sees none. It is okay, he thinks; it is still early in the evening. His old friends will eventually show up.

He orders beers from Mr. Wallace, and introduces his friend George.

"George is down visiting us from Detroit," Lewis offers.

"You're a long way from home," is all Mr. Wallace says, not really caring much for Yankees.

"He's an odd bird," Lewis says to George, by way of explanation, when Mr. Wallace goes down the bar to wait on two men who just walked in. One whom he shoos away, and another who sits down and orders a beer. Lewis does not know him but waves nonetheless in one of those down-home gestures George is happy to be near.

He appreciates his friend's consideration in trying to explain away the bartender's coldness, but knows the hostility he senses is real. It is confirmed, half an hour later, when a group of Lewis's friends come into the bar and he is introduced again.

"Are you one of those liberal Yankees down here to poke your nose around for a minute or two, then go back up north to tell everyone how inferior the South is?" one of them asks.

"George isn't like that," Lewis says, intervening on his guest's behalf.

"It's okay, Lewis," George says, "I can stick up for myself."

"Well, any friend of Lewis Hampton's is a friend of mine," says Connie, who has known Lewis about as long as either of them has been alive. "Don't mind this miscreant."

Lewis is regarded by his old friends with a special admiration, not only for being the most decorated man from Meridian, but also for being an upstanding fellow before, and a successful businessman afterward. But more than those things, they admire him for being a friend whom they have not seen in months but who is still one of them.

"Are you coming up to Oxford with us tomorrow for the football game?" Connie asks George.

"I can't wait," George answers, his self-consciousness decreasing, and continuing to dwindle as the talk turns to current events. He is always good in debate, and finds Lewis's friends are his equal at it, unlike some of the Southerners he met in the army. Nor does he feel the need, as he sometimes did overseas, or even in his office, to mask his own intelligence.

He debates, and watches them, so well adjusted and in control of their lives after the war. It makes him feel it is only a matter of time before he will be his old self again. There is something great about these guys, he thinks, before realizing with pride that he, like them, is also a hero.

Connie in particular draws his admiration when talking about the world at large. Even if he does not always agree with Connie's opinions, he loves the certainty and flair with which he presents them. "Winston Churchill is high as the oracle at Delphi," says Connie, "if he thinks there will ever be a United States of Europe."

He also appreciates the compassion that they extend to each other, expressed in ways both large, and as small as Connie's offering them a ride to the game because he knows Lewis must be tired from driving all day. George feels with them the camaraderie he has missed, drawn back into the circle of brotherhood.

Lewis thinks distractedly of his wife at times, down in New Orleans without him. But as they reminisce, and challenge each other to games of darts and drinking, he is happy that all of his best friends are around him, until he finds he can think of no better time, or any other place he would wish to be.

If they have become a little too loud and drunken, no one else in the bar minds much: They are on holiday, among friends. Lewis is not even bothered by his role as the butt of their jokes, understanding it is the price one pays for introducing old friends who have never met one another.

When they go home later in the evening, he and George are careful not to make too much noise, or to eat anything from the icebox that might be reserved for the next day's dinner. They raid instead the leftovers from the evening meal, then go upstairs to sleep.

George is thankful his friend has invited him, and feels as comfortable as he has been in any home since the war.

They fall asleep with this feeling, happy, if only for a long weekend, to lay aside all the worries of their lives. Neither of them can remember enjoying such sound sleep in a very long time.

SIX

King Nathan drives the streets of Meridian, crossing and recrossing the tracks that divide the city, looking for something to get into. He has thought vaguely in the past that twenty-five is no longer young and he has maybe ruined his life. This evening, he feels endless. He dons his coronet and gives his jalopy a bit more gas. Meridian is worthy of being called city, and he asks its streets to hold up something new to him. He cruises through the early evening, not caring about any moment beyond the next.

In front of the liquor store he sees his friend Allister and asks him where the action is tonight. "There's a party out by Terrence's," Allister says, "but it won't be starting for at least another hour."

"How're you getting out there?" Nathan asks.

"Lem is supposed to pick me up."

"Come on, get in," Nathan offers, leaning over to open the door, because the outside handle is broken on the passenger side. "We'll ride around some."

Allister gets into the jalopy and starts immediately fiddling with the knob on the radio.

"Don't touch that," Nathan commands. "It's the only station I pick up." He used to be ashamed of the car, which was his father's, then his brother's, before it was his own. Now he no longer notices the rips in the fabric, or the wheezes and moans it makes, and has even gotten used to the loose steering. Just don't touch the damn radio.

"Nathan, how come you don't let somebody take a look at this thing?" Allister asks.

"Never got around to it," he replies. "I'll get a new one soon enough." They cruise the city in circles, counting the minutes until the party will begin.

It has started to rain by the time they reach Terrence's house, and the two of them dash from the car to the front porch, where they pause under the awning before running up the exposed stairs. They have already finished the beers Allister bought, and when they walk inside, they greet their host perfunctorily before heading straight to the kitchen to find some more to drink.

Nathan scans the rooms of the party, looking for a woman who might let him, but there aren't any around. There aren't any women here at all. "Hey, Terrence," he calls, "where're all the ladies?"

"I don't know," Terrence says, louder than he has to in the small apartment, when he finally looks up from the couch. "Lizza and her friends said they might stop by later, but she didn't say when." The two of them had fought earlier that day, as they had most days this whole last month running, but at the mention of her name Nathan feels a pang tickling at his heart and knows, if he does not put it down and lets it, it might have him bawling and sobbing like a female the whole night through.

A new card game starts, and Nathan joins in, playing for a distracted hour, and eyeing the door whenever it opens. He thought he had the touch tonight when he left home. But this night has become like any other. To top it off, besides losing at cards money he cannot afford, he just got scheduled to work the next night, as well as Thanksgiving.

He thinks he should have paid his bills before going out, but makes so little it is hard to make it stretch. He shunts the thought away and plays just one more hand. He calculates how much he will make with holiday pay, and puts another stack of chips on the table. The bills will be there. He has that feeling, but luck is not with him at the table tonight.

He folds on another cruddy hand, and asks when Lizza said she was coming again. He waits another hour. Still no women appear.

"I think I'll head back to town," he says, getting up from the table. "Anybody want to come with me?"

No one else in the room moves. Nathan tells them it is a losers' party. What do you want to do? they ask.

Anything is better than sitting around here all night losing money at cards. Lem finally agrees to ride with him.

They drive too fast over the roads, as Lem asks Nathan how work is going. "Couldn't be better," Nathan says offhandedly. "I got a little nigger boy does most of it."

"Where'd you find him?" Lem asks, nonplussed.

"I won him on a good night at cards."

Lem laughs too loud, trying to generate a better time than the one they are having. "Stop pulling my leg," he says, not entirely certain Nathan is joking, as the car punches through the rain. "By the way," he says, "where are we headed?"

King Nathan stares hard at the road, concentrating to compensate for the effect of the beer. "I don't know," he says with a shrug after a while. "If we can't find nothing else, I thought we might go over to Darktown."

"You must be nutty," Lem balks. "They been kinda jumpy over there lately."

Nathan knows he means ever since the election primaries back in the spring, when six Negroes got strung up around the state for voting. None of that, though, was here in Meridian. Still, it has spread the fear and agitated all of them, making for a year of tense relations between the colors.

"That was all the way back in spring," he answers. "I was over there a few weeks ago and everything seemed fine."

"Nate, I just don't think we should be fooling around back there too much."

"Well," Nathan snaps, "ain't nothing else going on, Lem. Unless you know something I don't."

"Why don't we drive around by the college?" Lem suggests. "There's bound to be something happening there."

Nathan is not crazy about the idea, but agrees reluctantly, and turns the car down the shaded streets, past kempt November lawns, until they reach a row of fraternity houses. He pulls in next to a hydrant, then checks his hair in the mirror for signs of loss around his widow's peak. He still has those looks his father says are a curse on any man. He smiles back at himself. He burnishes his crown.

Nathan and Lem walk up the stone walkway to one of the buildings and push open the heavy wooden door. Inside, a few of the younger brothers, who do not know them, come and ask what it is they want. Nathan is about to tell them just that when Allen Boyd makes his way over with a shout of Nathan's name.

Lem goes off to the keg and comes back with a couple of fresh beers, while Allen asks Nathan to tell them again the story of the state wrestling championships in 1940.

Nathan feels uneasy in the crowd that has gathered around, but tells the story anyway. As he relates it, though, he feels his former glory restored.

"What are you doing these days?" one of the younger brothers asks when he has finished and everyone is still applauding.

Nathan looks out at their faces reflecting in his crown. "I'll tell you what I ain't doing, I ain't giving away business advice for free."

They laugh louder.

"Kidding aside, at the moment I'm just weighing my options," he goes on. "But the oil industry is booming in Mississippi right now."

It is not a lie. The oil industry is booming, and he has thought tons about it. He is not ready just yet, though, to give up the freedom of his bachelor ways. Besides, you gotta wait for the right time to make your move, in life as in wrestling. When he is ready, there will be opportunity enough for him.

He grows bored with the party and ditches Lem, to go back to his car. He is still desirous of something, but cannot name what it is. As he walks, he pulls out his car keys, places one at the end of a shiny new Packard, then pulls a prankish line in the paint of the car, as well as the college-boy vehicles in front of it, until he arrives at his own.

Nathan gets in his unscratched jalopy and drives down Lizza's block slowly, looking up at her window to see if there is a light on. The house is dark, and the streets deserted. He stays there, he knows, for too long, just looking up, hoping for his queen. He honks his horn, wondering where she is. He does not work until late the next day, and is not ready to have the night end and go back to his solitary room.

As he crosses and recrosses the grid the train tracks divide the city into, the night is shattered by the strobes of a police car beckoning him pull his ass over.

"Good evening, Deputy," he says, rolling down the window.

"Damnit, Nathan," Richman asks, "how long has it been since I last told you to get this nigger car of yours fixed?"

"Aw, John, I been too busy," Nathan answers. "You know I'll get around to it."

"Well, get to it soon, man. You liable to run over somebody one of these days."

"I have a clean record," Nathan tells him. "Not a single ticket yet."

"Not until now," says Richman, taking out his pad, "and the next time I see you in this thing, I'm going to have to take you in."

"You writing me out a ticket?" Nathan asks, squeezing the steering wheel between his fists. There goes the electricity.

"I got to, Nathan," Richman says, scratching at the pad.

"Come on, John."

Deputy Richman looks at Nathan and considers it. "You swear you'll get that light fixed tomorrow?"

"Scout's honor."

"This is the last time, I swear before God." He puts the pad away.

"Thanks, John," Nathan says, a tiny fist of victory and reprieve pumping in his head.

"By the way, how's your brother doing? I hear he's turning into quite something."

"Fine, I suppose," Nathan answers. "We don't speak much since he got married."

"He still down in New Orleans?"

"I can't deny it."

"Well, next time you talk to him, give him my regards. Tell him John Richman from geometry class says hi. Here, this is yours."

"What is it?" Nathan asks, taking the slip of paper Richman has given him.

"It is a ticket," Richman smiles.

"You told me you were letting me go with a warning."

"So I did," Richman says, walking away. "I suppose I lied."

Nathan rolls his window up, churns the car back into gear, and turns the radio louder.

It is one o'clock, but he still has an energy to find something to get into. His brother might be a war hero, but he bets he can whup his ass. If he ever sees John Richman without that badge on, he's gonna whup his ass too.

He lets loose a climbing scream. He is King Nathan. He counts his money out in his head and figures, if he puts off paying the telephone for another month, he will be fine.

He drives over to the new diner they just opened off the highway and orders a plate of biscuits and gravy to blunt the edge of the liquor. Under the fluorescent lights, King Nathan eats in silence, watching the door for someone he might know. He sees no one, and wonders where all the action has gone. He wonders where Lizza is, and what she is doing. He worries slightly about getting old, and touches at his hairline.

As he finishes his meal, he sees pipsqueaky Sydney Harris, whom he has known since grade school, walking to a table. He sticks out his leg and trips the little guy, just like old days, watching as Sydney falls.

The thrill has worn off, though, and he does not feel either the glee he once did or the one he expected. When Sydney gets up from the ground, Nathan mutters a halfhearted apology, avoiding eye contact. He calls for his check. He is still filled with boozy wantings, but knows it is time to go home.

He has put his car in gear and is ready to call it quits when he sees Terrence and the guys from the party pull up. He idles the engine, waiting for them to park. "What are you all up to?" he asks, leaning out of his window in the light rain.

"Just getting a bite." Terrence points to the diner.

"Well, the food here is lousy," Nathan says. "Follow me. I have a better idea."

No one else wants to come, but Nathan leads and Terrence follows across the grid to Darktown. They park in front of a bright-painted building, set back in an overgrown lot, and enter to the sound of a guitar-player performing for a crowd of rough-looking characters, listening or ignoring according to their want.

The room shifts uneasily with their presence, but they continue making their way to the pool table in back. Nathan feels a great exhilaration as he picks up his cue, because at least here there are women around.

Terrence racks the balls in agitation, trying not to look at anyone too intently. Nathan nods at a couple of faces he recognizes in the reefer dim light, and breaks the triangle of solids and stripes, then does his little nigger dance as two of the balls go down.

Terrence looks over his back. He thinks maybe Nathan is crazy, but no one pays them any mind.

They finish the pool game and are pulled by the tight-packed mass out onto the dance floor. They do not dance, but Nathan eyes a girl a little harder than Terrence thinks he probably should. There was a time, King Nathan thinks, when a man could just walk right over to a woman like that and pull her back to his cave, or throne room.

"Mr. Nathan," a voice says from his side, as if it has read his thoughts. When he turns, he sees Jacob Walker, whom he has known since they were boys.

"Hey, Jake," says Nathan, slapping him on the back. "How you feeling tonight?"

"I'm fine, Mr. Nathan," Jacob says, then draws his voice nearer and lower. "I don't mean to be rude, but this might not be the place for you-all tonight."

"Boy, don't tell me where I'm supposed to be," says Nathan, nearly exploding at Jacob.

"All right, Mr. Nathan." Jacob backs off. "I'm just letting you know, things been kinda funny around lately. I don't want no trouble for nobody." He walks away, back to his own business.

Terrence feels the agitation Jacob spoke of, and wants even more to leave. He tells Nathan again he thinks it is time for them to go home.

"Nobody," says Nathan, "tells me what to do. Neither him nor you." He holds his ground until he thinks his point has been proved, then nods to Terrence. "I guess we might as well head on in."

It is three in the morning, and the night is ending as all of them do lately, in disappointment, but Nathan has enough liquor in him to feel a little less let down, a little less possessed by the hole in his chest that brims with more emotion than any single man can contain but is fed by some source other than his own body—rather, by an infinite, universal ache without proper expression, yet full of ancient starts and fits of inarticulation in the face of such pain. He has numbed it.

When they get back to their cars, Nathan is about to get in when he notices the jalopy seems a little more lopsided than usual. He looks down to see one of his tires has been punctured. "Goddamnit," he screams in the rain. Terrence looks up and turns his headlamps on to light the darkness around them, as Nathan gets down in the mud to change the tire.

"I told you we shouldn't have come out here," Terrence says, cursing, scanning the lot around the juke.

"Close your mouth," Nathan tells him, struggling to put the new tire on in the wet gutter. "Somebody is just playing a joke."

"Ain't nothing funny about fooling around with a man's vehicle," Terrence says, looking over his shoulder again, then tensing up when he sees a group of men standing in the doorway. He swears he hears them laughing.

"Y'all need some help?" one of the unseen faces calls.

"Don't say nothing," Terrence soothes when Nathan jerks up his shoulder. "Just get the tire on and let's get out of here."

They do so.

Nathan drives home relieved. But when he climbs into his bed, and the room stops spinning, he finds he cannot unwrap the blankets of despair and anger that keep him from sleeping.

The next day, he drives to Terrence's again, and all his running partners are there, sprawled across the cramped apartment as they have slept. Nathan is intent and tries to work them up, but no one else wants to be bothered with it.

"You should have enough of fooling round with coloreds," says Lem, trying to calm him down.

"Son of a gun," yells Nathan, "Terrence you saw what they did. Now, what have I ever done against them?"

"Nathan, this ain't something we should be monkeying with," Terrence reasons. "We ain't got no business going back there."

"Well, goddamnit," says Nathan, "since when don't I have the right to go anywhere I want in Meridian?"

"That's true," says Lem.

"True as the day is long," Nathan counters. "But if y'all too chicken to go with me, I guess I will just have to do it myself."

They look around the room at each other. "What the hell, ain't nothing else to do today," Terrence says. He knows he cannot let his friend go out there alone. He doesn't think Nathan will get hurt, but, hell, you never know. Besides, at least it sounds a little more exciting than sitting around inside all day on a long weekend.

When he was younger, a group of them had once come up on two black boys swimming in a creek under the bluffs. Silently they crept to its ledge and jumped, tucking their legs into their chests, so that they fell, one after another, like cannonballs, on top of the boys. The boys emerged from the creek bottom gasping, spurting out water, and generally trying to exchange liquid for air in their lungs, but they were unharmed. Other than such children's pranks, he had never done anything against the Negroes in town. But neither had they done anything against him.

Now is different. Something has broken this year, and they cannot just sit back and overlook it, at least Nathan cannot. No one will get hurt, he thinks, but neither will he let them mock and abuse him.

Three cars drive through the tumbledown streets of Darktown. Their occupants' pulses work to fever pitch.

When they get to the juke joint, the music still pours from its plastic-covered windows, but no one is in sight outside. Three windows roll down, and three shotguns appear.

A wild blasting begins, and the people inside scramble to find the floor. The windows roll up. The cars screech away down the road.

When they get back to the railroad tracks, King Nathan and his men raise up a bottle of whiskey. They can hardly believe they just did that in broad daylight, just like gangsters or cowboys.

It has been a good run for Nathan, because he knows they have gotten away. They will not be caught, and are avenged. They drive through the grid of Meridian, with a great pulse of energy, looking for something else to get into.

He is vindicated. He tells Rita and Lena to go bring him another glass, and does his little nigger dance, like the colored boys do, in the seat of the car. He smiles to himself triumphantly, sho nuff. He polishes his crown. He tells his friends he has to work that night, but will meet up with them again when he gets off, then parts to go pick up his little buddy.

He has wondered vaguely in the past whether twenty-five is no longer young, and felt that his life might be going nowhere. But today he knows that when he is ready there will be a place for him. He has worried at other times how quickly anyone might pass through the world, and how many bullets can have one man's name on them. As it falls to evening, he does not think beyond the next moment, and what the night might extend. He is Nathan Sho Nuff, wide is his dominion tonight.

He touches his coronet another time, and gives his car a bit more gas. He will be king a while longer.

SEVEN

It is the middle of the night when the phone begins to ring.

Lewis's father answers it and hangs up quietly, then goes upstairs to wake his only living son.

Lewis rises and dresses in the pallid half-darkness, and drives with his father to the morgue.

"Did you tell Mother yet?" he asks, as they head across town to death's quarters.

"Not until we are sure it is him."

They are silent next to each other, hoping it is not Nathan, but knowing better.

"He was a good boy," is the only other thing his father says. "He was a good boy who needed a little more time."

He needed a lot more. "Yes," Lewis answers, looking to see if his father will cry. He is relieved when he does not.

They get out of the car in front of the blank building, and walk through the cold halls in the hospital basement as through a hallucination. "You wait here, Dad," Lewis says when the attendant finally comes for them. "I will go." He can tell, because his father does not protest, that he is thankful for this.

When he enters the cold death-room, the body is pulled from its drawer on the dead metal slab. Lewis looks at the thinning hairline on the corpse and sees the stomach wound, expertly placed, as though inflicted by an executioner.

"Yes. It is him." He nods at the attendant, and tries to answer his questions in full. "Nathan Hampton." "Because he is born of the same union of man and woman as I." "He is my brother."

He was not bad, Lewis tells himself, leaving the frigid grasp of the room to rejoin his father in the hall, just too enamored of freedom.

Lewis's father leans part of his soul's weight on his only living child, and they leave the morgue to make their way back to the house.

When they arrive, the two men sit awake in the living room, debating in muted tones whether or not to wake Lewis's mother.

"She should get this night's sleep," Lewis says at last. "So should you."

Neither of them moves.

Mrs. Hampton comes downstairs of her own accord early in the morning to see her husband and son asleep in the armchairs in the living room. "What has happened?" she asks, waking her husband. "Where did you go to last night?"

Lewis is stirred by the sound of his parents' voices, and feels discomfited and helpless as he watches them, his father looking through his mother without communicating.

"Lewis Junior," she pleads unsteadily, turning to him, "what happened?"

"Sit down, Mamma," he says, rising to give her his place. She does not sit, but listens to the maternal alarm sounding in her head.

"Where on God's earth is my son Nathan?"

George is awakened by the pulse of sobs rising up to him through the floorboards of the house. He lies still and listens, trying to decipher what has brought such a pall over that home.

He feels uncomfortable being there, and pretends to be asleep when the door opens a short while later and a Negro maid, who has come to help this morning with the cooking, brings him his breakfast.

"What happened?" he asks, when he sees that it is the maid and not a family member, to whom he might cause embarrassment or ill ease.

"There was a death in the family," she says, not wanting to be in these people's business right now any more than George does. She refrains from saying anything further.

George understands her avoidance of his eyes, so does not press her for the details. He wishes, in fact, there were some way for him to tiptoe out of there. He does not want to be around death.

Lewis tries to bridge this awkwardness when he enters the room to tell his friend Connie will be there soon to take him to the football game.

"If you do not mind, I won't be able to make it," he says, without offering explanation, thereby pushing his friend out of the circle of immediacy, but also preventing him from having to spend the entire day feeling uncomfortable at a time when the family has drawn close. "Dinner will be at four."

"Is there anything I can do to help?" George offers.

"No, just enjoy yourself," Lewis tells him. "I apologize again for not being able to join you." He leaves George to finish dressing, and returns twenty minutes later to inform him Connie is waiting downstairs.

When he goes down and is given over to Connie's charge for the afternoon, George sees some unspoken understanding passed between Lewis and Connie that makes him shudder. It is merely a holding of one another's eyes for a second longer than normal, with a barely perceptible nod, but it communicates some secret intent, in language he does not know, reinforcing his feeling of being an outsider there. He sees how much deeper the bond is between the two of them. They are telling each other something or agreeing to something in conspiracy, he thinks to himself, wondering in briefest panic whether it involves him.

"I will see you tonight," Lewis says to both of them as they get into the car, and he heads back into the house.

Connie pulls the vehicle into motion, behaving toward George with the same cordiality and distance Lewis did, before remembering his manners and asking, "Did you have a good night's sleep?"

"It was fine," George answers, sensing his presence is an intrusion.

Connie focuses on the road, leaving George to try and fathom the mystery he feels around him and his own floating place within it.

"Did Lewis tell you?" Connie asks finally.

"Not really. What happened?"

"His brother, Nathan, was killed last night."

"I did not know," George says, thinking that this is nothing to keep secret, and trying to imagine how he would have behaved if his own brother were murdered. "That's a shame."

"No," Connie says, "it is more than a shame. It was a nigger."

"Did they catch him?" George asks.

"They most certainly did," Connie informs him, slitting his eyes in concentration. "He is sitting over in the jailhouse right now."

"How?" George presses for more information. "What exactly happened?"

"It does not matter how," Connie says, rolling down the window, and taking a pouch of tobacco from the breast pocket of his well-starched shirt.

"I know what you mean," George sympathizes, thinking of his own brother and the men he knew in the army. There is no design to loss.

"No, I don't think you do," Connie goes on, looking out the window. "You see all of this?" He waves his arm toward the depressed landscape along the highway and the fallow, withered fields of autumn. "Unless you grew up here, you cannot know."

"Know?" George asks, confused and worried still to be kept in the dark.

"How much more than a shame it is."

"Well, what exactly happened?" George presses again for the details.

"This was once a great country." Connie speaks in distraction, extending to George the tobacco pouch. George is hesitant, but takes a plug of the shredded leaves and puts it in his mouth. "Don't swallow," Connie instructs as George rolls down his window.

"It is still a great country," George muses. "It will be even greater."

"No," Connie argues. "Maybe the North or the West will be even greater, but the South has been dealt a blow it will take a hundred years to recover from. It is nothing more than a spittoon now, and was made that and dealt that blow by an aggressor who came between the rights of the South, laid out in the Constitution, and the rights that the men who settled the South were able to wrest from nothing but wildness."

"What does that have to do with Lewis's brother?" George demands. "You said he was killed by a single man."

"No," Connie says. "It was not a single man, but part of that conspiracy to subjugate the South. It was a nigger."

George nods, thinking he understands.

"He wears an army uniform," Connie adds, explaining further the insult.

"Well, what happened?" George agitates, impatient to know.

"Okay. Nathan Hampton was at work," Connie tells him. "At work—do you hear me?—doing nothing more than any other man does to have bread and electricity and life, when a nigger come along and knifes him."

"It cannot be that simple," George argues, because he is still on the outside. "Not even a colored would kill a man for nothing."

"There is no reason on earth a nigger could ever have to put his hand to a white man," Connie says, looking over at George. "Now, I know you live up north, but you seem like a decent fellow, and if Lewis says you are decent I take him at his word, and treat you as I would any other of my friends. Do you know why?"

"Because of your friendship with Lewis," George says.

"Yes, but it goes deeper than that," says Connie, "much deeper. It is because of the link one man has to another, and that is the link that allows us to be more than the beasts of the field. Imagine if you had to fight the entire German Army by yourself. Could you do it?"

"No," George says thoughtfully, remembering being bogged down in the hell of the French forests.

"Well, neither could you build a city or, more likely than not, stay alive any longer than a simple beast of the field."

George nods, because he understands something about the link between people, and what it is to be severed. "It would be a nightmare. It would not be society," he says.

"Now, say a colored come to tear that down. A simple godforsaken nigger."

"But didn't they help to build this?" George asks. "Isn't the South as much Negro as it is white?"

"A nigger would no more build a thing of his own free will than would a snake. Do you think we could have won the war with an army of niggers?" Connie asks rhetorically, neither expecting nor needing an answer. "This country has worked because it was governed by men who saw further, and knew how to use all God had given them, white men all, to the best advantage. Imagine if someone came into your office, your place of business, that you were minding, you hear me, with gun or blade to claim and take away your life."

"I do not see how it is the same," George says. "If a wild man does something evil, then isn't he alone at fault?"

"He is indeed at fault," Connie tells George with perfect reason, "and he will pay for what he has done, just as the killers of Christ paid for their wickedness, and this will not take two thousand years to achieve either."

"What do you mean?" George asks, trying to sort sophistry from bedrock in Connie's words, as the conversation takes on surreal edges to him, under the buzz of the tobacco.

"What I mean," says Connie bluntly, "is that God gave to man rules to live by, and laid out an order, a single order, for the world. When that ordering is upset, and it is, then it must be restored, or else all will perish with that single wrong deed multiplied."

George does not agree, but he is a guest here, so nods in curiosity as well as politeness. He gives the people who have invited him into their homes the benefit of the doubt, even if they do not possess the full discipline of intellect. "You mean you're going to . . ."

Connie does not answer, but lets the question die as he spits his tobacco juice out the window, and wipes briskly at a stain on his beautifully laundered shirt. He wonders whether this nervous man next to him is trustworthy, but he extends to him the fact of being Lewis's close friend and fellow survivor.

"Isn't there a law against that?" George asks.

"Yes," Connie answers him, furthering his hospitality by giving to George secular words he may better understand, since he does not seem to know the rigors of mother-wit or Bible. "There is a law, my friend, and it is preterlegal."

This is it, George thinks, as they pull into the parking lot outside Hemingway Stadium, and he experiences a great rush of adrenaline, as before a great mission.

When they take their seats in the stands, George feels this same excitement oozing from the crowd, but also an additional tingling inside himself when Connie greets the other men he met in the bar the night before. They exchange the same knowing look he saw pass between Lewis and Connie, but George feels he is part of their union now, as he rises and falls with that crowd every time one of the players on the field accomplishes something or fails to.

By the time State has finished thrashing Ole Miss, he cannot escape the energy pulsing within himself, any more than he might have turned off the war machine once it was set into motion.

"I will go along as observer," he tells himself, trying to separate George from what is to happen, "to see what it is like." Even then, though, as he thinks about Connie's words, he suspects he has learned some anger in himself the peacetime world otherwise denied itself utterance of, and even words for. He knows now it is allowed a space he has not seen or been able to find before. He will do it because he is Lewis's friend. He will do it because he knows it is a way back into the fellowship of man.

When the last wave has crescendoed through the Mississippi State fans, as the team leaves the field with its twenty-to-nothing victory and the Golden Egg trophy, George thinks again to himself, "So this is it."

They make their way out of the stadium and the pandemonium of fans. They pile into Connie's car and venture back to Meridian for dinner, in a mood of almost euphoric silence, tasting in their mouths, each according to his own proclivity, a breach in the fabric of the world that need not be named again.

Lewis paces the length of the driveway after George and Connie have left for the game, thinking about what he has set into being. I will do this for my brother, he tells himself, then tries to calm down as he remembers his phone conversation with Connie earlier that morning.

He does not recall how the words first came to his mouth, but he knows he said they should kill the bastard who did what he saw done to Nathan.

"Why don't you?" Connie asks. "There is nothing to stop you."

Lewis said the words in anger, but with Connie's question realizes, in fact, he could.

"Just get a few friends and go over to the jailhouse to get him out," Connie goes on. "It is what I would do. It is what any man would."

Lewis knows this is more than sympathy. He feels in it a ferocious challenge. He imagines what it would feel like to do such a thing, circling the phone cord around his fingers, tight as a ball of mercury, imagining the killer's neck clenched beneath his hand.

"So I can count on you," he says to Connie.

"You can."

He paces the length of the driveway, knowing now it will happen. He tries to will a calm.

As he turns to go back into the house, Deputy Richman pulls up, removes his hat from his excited head, and gives to Lewis a consoling look. Perhaps it aims at empathy as well, he cannot say for sure.

"Do you know how it happened?" Lewis asks him, eager for news, as if knowing the details might make simple his complex emotions.

"Well, the only one who saw anything was the nigger boy who worked with him," Richman says. "He claims Nathan and the other nigger had words." Richman stops to measure Lewis's face as he speaks, seeing his coil loosen and tighten according to the words that come from his mouth.

Although he bore Nathan no special love, he knows the Hamptons to be good, hardworking people. Nothing, he says, can excuse what has happened. He tries to be gentler with Lewis than is his usual way. "Well, Nathan and the nigger is arguing over something," he continues in softer voice, "and, according to the nigger child, Nathan pulls out his buck knife."

Lewis does not respond, but takes these words in stride.

"Nathan, so the boy says, goes for the nigger at the throat, like to put him down, and the army nigger, somehow he gets hold of the knife, and, well, that is what the nigger child says."

"And you take his word?" Lewis asks. "You just take him at his word?" His brother, he knows, was many things, but not a senseless murderer.

"I take his word as proof he is a liar," Richman answers. "Besides the color of his skin, he has got the sinner's face."

"So that is it?" Lewis rubs his temple, looking at Richman. Not even a woman, or money, or principle and honor of manhood, but killed over simple running of the mouth.

"Well, a nigger can't testify in court," Richman says to Lewis, "at least not testify and be believed. But you should see the army nigger that did it. He is sitting over in that jail right now, smug as a god-damned Gila monster. And the little liar, right back there behind his mamma's house, talking to me like he happy to have seen it.

"If it was my brother," the deputy trails off, "I would get both of them."

"What do you mean?" Lewis demands, because he did not tell Richman about his plan and is nervous that it has gotten out already. He is not certain how the town would feel if they knew about it. He prefers that they, even his parents, make up their minds whose life was more valuable after they see the murderer swinging. If they do not approve it before, he knows, they will afterward, once the thing has been done and decided.

"Well," Richman replies, "you see all these nigger soldiers coming back from the war, spreading whatever evil they got over in Europe. You put a uniform on them, and a few words in their mouths, and they start to think they just as good as white men, and start spreading that evil all over the place. You should just see the one they got over in the jail. I'm telling you, he is one satisfied sonofabitch. Chest is probably more full of medals than yours was." Richman pauses, measuring Lewis's response. "Medals that the army done gave him, along with God knows what kind of ideas.

"Will look you in the eye, just like he ain't got good sense, and talk just as proper. Now, you imagine a platoon full of them, and you tell me they ain't brought something wicked to us that the little nigger ain't caught.

"Wouldn't no Mississippi colored dare talk to a white man the way that little sonofabitch talked to me a while ago if he hadn't had some outside evil poured out over him."

Lewis looks at Richman and rocks back and forth on his heels in thought. He had not felt the need for permission any more than he already had, but here it is being offered to him by the Mississippi State Highway Patrol.

"Is Cox in?" he asks, looking at the deputy to see that he understands the invitation being proffered.

"No. He's had federal pressures on him lately. It's just me and whatever posse you feel the need for."

Lewis nods.

"Will your daddy be there?" Richman asks.

Lewis shakes his head. He has not thought to ask his father. It seems like too much to have a man face his son's killer, and his own father has a weak heart. That, and he also knows the generational torch has been passed. This is a thing for young hands to carry out, in the old style; a thing for him to put down as it ought be done.

He looks again at Richman, measuring his trustworthiness, as well as his right to be there. "Seven-thirty on Frontage Road."

"Do you have everything you need?"

Need? Lewis had not thought about it before, but of course they will require tools. Ropes, and torches to see by. He wonders whether it is incumbent upon him to provide them, or whether each man must bring his own. "I think there should be some stuff in the garage we can use," he answers.

"Do you have enough men?"

"How many does it take?" he asks, wondering if there are rules and regulations to this as well.

"Whatever number you wish for," Richman says, "but I would guess about a dozen, minimum. He's trained in killing, for one thing, and for another, it belongs not just to the family, but also to whoever was close to Nathan. Hell, bring everybody you can get ahold of."

Lewis realizes this could become as complicated as planning his wedding must have been. He wonders whether there must be one set of ropes for friends and another for family. "Damnit, Richman," he curses, because, as he thinks about it, he realizes he does not know who his brother's close friends were. He thinks how he never will. He has been deprived of this. "How complicated does it all have to be?"

"It ain't no more complicated than going down to the jailhouse and taking him out. But there are procedures to go by, just as with anything else. You have to decide how many men you want, what hour, and what method you will use. A man don't just leave jail and lynch hisself."

"Okay," Lewis says impatiently, "I will take care of it. Frontage Road, seven-thirty. Don't tell anyone else."

"Lewis," Richman asks, "is this your first time?"

"I have never had cause before," Lewis tells him, staring vacantly past the deputy's face, his mind elsewhere.

"Do not be nervous," Richman counsels. "There will be men there, besides myself, to make sure it doesn't go wrong. So just know you will have people there to midwife you through if anything gets out of hand."

Richman leaves, giving Lewis to understand that this is not only death but also matrimony, birth, and initiation all at once; an *uber-*ritual he has not known to exist as such, and never before thought might come to his life. But just as with any other rite of passage, as he moves toward its gates, he finds them opening to receive him. He wonders with brief abstraction how he will be changed, who he must be, once he has passed through their marker, as he had in other moments before.

He returns inside and asks Adele whether she has seen his parents. "Mrs. Hampton is upstairs resting," the maid says, "and your father went out back for some quiet." Adele passes her eyes rapidly over Lewis and sees an agitation she has not seen surface since he was a child, when he had gotten into trouble, or his dog had been run over by a car. She knew then how to speak to him, but is now less certain. That look is tinged now by a whirring edge that tells her, Do not come near.

"Is that how they look when they do it?" she thinks, before reprimanding herself. "Not Mr. Lewis, no, he would not." She realizes she no longer knows, and is afraid of this man whom she has known since he was a child.

She knows him as decent, but does not know what he will do, so goes no nearer, in either word or gesture, than you would the moving engine under the uplifted hood of a car. Lord, she wants to be anywhere today but here, where death sits in vigil, wrapping its wings around the house.

"Thank you, Adele," he says, heading out back to his father, then stops in polite afterthought to ask, "Are you making your cobbler?"

"Don't I every year?" she asks, as he smiles. No, see there, she tells herself, Mr. Lewis is not a part of all that other mess.

Lewis goes out the rear screen door to find his father sitting in deepest thought and lament on a bench in the backyard, his hands folded in front of him like a stone statue. Lewis touches his namesake on the shoulder. The elder man looks around to his son.

"How are you?" he asks.

"As well as might be."

"Did George go with Connie?"

"Yes, about twenty minutes ago."

"And your mother?"

"Upstairs, lying down."

"Good." He drags his hand across his face, wiping away invisible tears that have not yet fallen.

"Daddy," says Lewis, "was Nathan still best friends with Julian?"

"No, Julian moved to Mobile," his father says. "He was running around lately with a fellow named Terrence Briggs, who lives out by Eastville. Why do you ask?" he finishes defensively, as if one son is somehow implicating the other's habits as being responsible for his death.

"Just curious, no special reason," Lewis says, looking at his father and seeing his age come to show almost overnight. "Why don't you go get some rest."

"I am fine here," his father tells him. "I'm waiting for Louise. She's supposed to be coming down from Arkansas."

"Well, if you are all right, I think I'll go for a drive to clear my head," Lewis says, making his way back into the house to retrieve his car keys.

The elder man looks at his firstborn as he makes his way across the lawn. "Where are you going, Lewis?" he asks.

"Just out for a drive. I'll be back before dinner. Get yourself some rest."

"He knows what he does," Lewis's father thinks, watching his son's car pull out of the garage. "He is a grown man."

He doesn't think it right that he be away from the family, but, he tells himself, going back and forth between knowing and being oblivious of his son's intent, "he just needs some time to let it sink in. He knows what he does."

Lewis drives south to Eastville, stopping at a tumbledown grocery store to ask where he might find Terrence Briggs.

"You might find him anywhere," the grocer says, "but he lives a few blocks from here." Lewis is not in a joking mood. The grocer shuts up and gives him an address about a quarter-mile away.

He gets back in the car and continues down the potholed road until he sees a creaky wooden frame house with children's toys scattered about the patchy lawn. He parks and climbs a set of stairs to the second floor.

When he knocks at the door, Terrence opens it and stares rudely, before finally inviting him inside.

Lewis enters a rusty room that was probably salmon-colored

when first painted, and accepts a seat on a milk crate at the low table. Terrence turns off the hot plate, where he had been fixing himself dinner, and sits down across from his visitor.

Lewis knows Nathan ran with a rough crowd, but he did not know his younger brother spent so much time in the company of men like this, who seemed only a couple of steps removed from criminal.

Terrence offers Lewis a cigarette, which is declined. "What can I help you with?" he asks then, not liking to have anybody in his bachelor home who thinks they might judge him, or who he feels might do so.

"My father tells me you and Nathan were pretty close," Lewis says to the younger man.

"I suppose we were," Terrence responds guardedly. "What do you need to know?"

"I thought you might like to come along tonight," he says simply.
"Where?"
"The jailhouse."
Terrence looks at Lewis, and nods. "What time?"
Lewis gives the details, telling him to bring whoever else he thinks should be there. He wants to keep this quiet if he can. He gets up from the milk crate and goes out the door. He descends the stairs of the sagging building. He gets back into his car.

When he arrives home, he is exhausted. He gets in bed, not certain he has prepared carefully enough, but thinks six men ought to be plenty enough to handle one nigger. He wonders whether or not he should tell George, whether or not an outsider can understand. He sleeps fitfully, possessed.

When he wakes up, it is three in the afternoon, and he hears the voices of relatives downstairs. He washes his face and goes down to greet them. The night before and the morning seem so far away, he wonders whether he has dreamed them, but from the way his aunt Louise greets him, so gently, he knows they are real. He wonders what he has done.

They all sit around the living room discussing Nathan, as his mother goes to and fro in the gathering crowd, making certain everyone is comfortable. She stops at her son's chair and kisses him on the forehead, worried about the look on his face. "You're going to be okay," she tells him.

"Lewis, there's a phone call for you," his father says, coming in from an adjoining room. His father is dressed to receive visitors and looks far better than he did the night before. Not so Lewis, who looks to have slept every bit as poorly as he actually did.

On the phone line, Dolores greets her husband and wishes him a happy Thanksgiving, telling him how much she misses him. "I wish we were together." Her voice catches in her throat.

"We will be together every holiday after this," Lewis tells her again, placid at the sound of her voice. "We have had tragedy here."

"My brother was killed."

"I'm so sorry, Lewis," Dolores says, then asks what exactly happened. "I wish I could be there with you."

"It is okay," he comforts her, who gets so worked up with emotion. "I will be home Sunday evening. You can come back up with me for the funeral."

She tells him again how sorry she is, and how she wishes she were there, and they behave toward each other with every tenderness of newlyweds. When he hangs up the phone, he goes back upstairs to dress for dinner.

"What have I done?" Lewis asks himself, knowing it is uncaged and set in motion. "It will go ahead now even without me."

He has killed men before, but never with his own premeditation. Is this what it is like to make all those abstract lines on a map into movements of real men, and to try and control them? he asks himself, misguided or no, as he pulls on a pair of lovely brogues he will not have the chance to change out of before meeting the others out on Frontage Road to avenge his brother. He never once has said to himself the word "lynch," but he knows, even in this fog, it is what he is doing.

When he goes back downstairs, George is just returning from the football game, with his look of excitement, as though he has been a fan of the team all his life, instead of just taking up an interest.

"I'm glad you had a good time," Lewis says to him, while George goes through the solemn rooms to change. He is tired after the two-and-a-half-hour trip back, but when he and Connie reapproached Meridian, he began to feel a crescive anticipation that is still there, lighting his face like the hidden side of the moon.

"So here is where it will happen, and how," he said to himself, looking out on the quiet downtown streets. "I will see how it really is." He has developed by now an almost intellectual detachment from where he is, and his own body, to be observer. He has butterflies in his stomach. He feels anticipation grow, as before a great battle.

When he comes back from changing, George looks at Lewis with a sly smile to let him know he is in as well for the evening.

Lewis acknowledges him with the same slight nodding he gave to Connie. He takes courage from the fact that George is going along with him, and does not question or prod as he did before. That he shall not be judged, or have to find some way to hide it, but also that his own misgivings may not be so well founded. He simply did not know before how it was done, because he had never before held the reins of another's destiny so close, even when he commanded them to war and battle: Then there was a superior who might override his hand. He finds he is now that superior. He must do this right.

They sit down to dinner, and George feels less like a stranger in the house than he did this morning, because the table has expanded to include family and friends alike, shifting from him the burden of being the lone outsider. Within this expanded circle he belongs, and gives thanks for that when his turn comes and he rises to give witness before the assembly. "I thank the Hampton family for opening their hearts and home to a stranger, even under the cloud of calamity."

When Lewis rises, he gives thanks for family and for friends, but also for a God Whom he knows to be just, and Who he knows will see to it that justice will be done in the death of his brother, as in all things. He asks the Lord to give them strength. Amen.

It is the sign that restores to all of them some ease, to see Lewis so well in control of himself and holding up. His mother knows better her son. She looks at him with suspicious eyes, fidgets without ease in her seat.

EIGHT

Lewis sits tensely after dinner, amid a conversation that strains for buoyancy, nursing a glass of brandy from the bottle George has given them. It does not relax him, and he drinks the liquor too quickly, less to calm his nerves than simply to pass the time. When he has finished his second glass, he nods to his friend without adornment. It is time to leave.

"We're just going to go out for a while," he says, hugging and kissing those friends and relatives who will not be there when he returns.

"Where?" His mother turns her head nervously.

"Just over by Connie's for a visit," he says, just as, when he was younger, holiday dinners ended with him and his friends meeting up to see a movie, leaving the well-being of family for the merriment and abundance of friends. It is a feast day.

In the garage, he searches about until he finds an old rope that once held a backyard swing for him and Nathan when they were children. He throws it onto the floorboard of the car, along with a flashlight.

"You know, George," he says, offering his friend a way to avoid the pressure of feeling he has to do something he might not agree with, "you are not bound to go."

"I've never let you go into danger alone yet," George says. It is true. But Lewis knows there is no danger involved for himself tonight. Still, to have George there with him gives comfort, even if George was never so adept a soldier as he.

He is up to this, he tells himself again, getting into the car with hesitation. He will do this for his brother, he goes on, speaking in his mind until it begins to seem normal.

As he approaches Frontage Road, though, the symmetry of his brain tears again—between settling matters in this way, and some other fashion.

What wrong is there in waiting for court justice? he asks. Maybe we are moving with too much haste. He asks whether they have all the necessary information. He asks himself whether what he does is a sin. Whether what they do is murder. He asks briefly whether or not he offends in some way rules and laws men have agreed upon as sanctified to live and abide by.

He probes into those dark alleyways of his mind he had sworn off, and he answers all questions with the simple answer that it is his duty. The colored has transgressed the order of the world, he answers himself. Besides, it has already been set in motion, and not merely by his words that morning, or on this clear night in Southern November, but long ago, when the order that is upset was formed. It is his duty. He does this for his brother, whose blood has been spilt and severed with unforgivable cruelty.

He goes back and forth, within himself, between these various points, until the last becomes most convincing. He will think no more about it.

They drive through that beautiful old town, and out to the empty stretch of country road, where they meet up with the rest of the group as arranged.

When he pulls up and looks around, Lewis is surprised by the number of men who have gathered here. He marvels that his own word, and the depth of sentiment felt for his brother, have brought the number from the six he himself told, to the thirty who wait for him.

He scans the assembly, buzzing with the pressure of his new command, but finds, just as Richman had said, there are others there to pull up the slack. He is comforted by their presence as well as variety, and feels a lightness in his breast. Not all are men who knew his brother and ran with that rough lot. There are also older men he has known and respected his entire life, and would not have expected to find here. He feels better. "So it really is an initiation," he tells himself. They are here to see that it is done properly.

The thirty of them go over the details with him, and they decide to get the boy from his house first, then over to the jail and on out to the reservoir. They check to see that there is enough rope, as well as guns and bullets, to equip any expedition. They are ready.

Their eyes lock, briefly, then look no more at each other, as each concentrates on strengthening his heart for its task. Lewis leaves his car on Frontage when Richman tells him out-of-state plates are easier to remember. No one will be around, but just in case. He does this, and they redistribute themselves through the seven cars. They begin toward Darktown.

"Have you ever done this before?" Lewis asks of no one in particular. Who else is being initiated this night?

"It is nothing to be nervous about," Connie answers, following Richman's directions to the little boy's house.

"When?" Lewis wants to know.

"Earlier this year," Connie says, looking at Richman.

"It was as deserved as this," Richman adds, lending support.

"Don't worry, Lewis, it is all going to be fine. You will see."

Lewis's thoughts in the back seat of the car, though, have begun to double back on him. He thinks how easy it would be for the mob behind them to turn their attention to one of their own. He thinks how thin is the structure that keeps any one of them inside of it, rather than on the receiving end of the fury that motors down the highway, pulling him along.

"How are you back there, George?" Connie asks cordially, looking in his rearview to see George fidget in his seat.

"Me? I'm fine," George answers, feeling as he did before he saw his first stag film, before his first drink of liquor, before losing his virginity, before his first battle. He knows he will soon be inside the experience, and back inside his own self—instead of surrounding it as he does now, waiting. To be connected to something again.

"This is it." Richman points to a cinder-block building with its tin roof painted a vibrant blue. The car comes to a halt. The ones behind it stop as well. The low hum of engines purrs through the darkness.

Four men emerge from the appointed vehicle. Their footfalls crunch over the unraked front yard, through the remains of a summer vegetable garden, to the front door. George looks out the window. Connie and Richman open their doors, then stand on the sideboards for a better view. Lewis stares ahead into the purple early darkness, not admitting to himself it has begun.

When they reach the door of the house, one of the men knocks. The other three ready their guns, in case there is trouble from the inside.

A colored woman's face appears at the door, bearing a spontaneous smile to greet her unexpected guests, but blanks just as quickly with fear when she sees what is outside her door.

"We don't want any trouble," the one who has knocked at the door says to her. "We just want the boy. Hand him over and we will be gone as simple as we come."

"No," Frankie's mother says, shaking her head slowly, with two full left-to-right turnings that repeat as she says that word again and again, "No," until it seems she is about to let loose her mind with all the force of a zeppelin exploding into gaseous debris. "He didn't do nothing."

"We don't want no trouble," the man says again.

"No," she screams at that line of cars in the front yard, until a gun butt crashes into the side of her face, silencing her. The four of them move her slack body out of the way, and enter the small cinderblock rooms to begin searching.

"Come on out," one of voices coaxes the boy from wherever he is hiding. "Come out and take what's coming to you, unless you want your mamma to take it for you."

Behind the potbellied stove, Franklin squeezes himself into a smaller and shrinking ball, holding shut his eyes.

"You're only making it worse," he hears himself called to again.

His eyes open involuntarily, and he sees a pair of boots standing nearby, then looks up as far as he can without moving his head, at the thick legs growing out of them. He tries to think of ways to escape. He hears his mother sob again, then another crashing blow.

"Nigger, you better get out here. Your mamma seem kinda frail."

Frankie does not move, but holds his breath until he hears his mother call out his name. "Frankie," she says. Lord. Lord. Lord. He hears the furniture that has been fit into those tiny rooms being overturned, as the heat from the stove burns against his shins, singeing his leg hair, enveloping him. He thinks about Nathan, about the stranger, about all he has seen, and the screams they pull from his mother.

"Here I am." He presents himself in a show of bravery. "Let my mamma go."

A voice laughs, and a hand pinches the back of his neck. The man guarding his mother pushes her aside. She is a thin, beautiful woman with finely etched features, but she is not who they came here for.

"Where y'all taking him?" she pleads.

The four men do not answer, but walk out of the house with the little copper-colored boy. At the lead car, they shove him into the front seat, where he is pulled in between Connie and Richman.

"I didn't do nothing," he says, pleading, as they drive off down the potted, jolting road.

Richman strikes the child's face with an indignant hand. "Don't speak unless you spoken to," he yells at Frankie. "See, what I tell you?" he says to his companions, calming down.

Connie nods his head. Lewis and George are silent in back. Lewis tells himself this is only a child, George to himself that this is how it happens, as he stares at the back of Connie's neck, then looks over the seat in front of him at the back of the boy's nappy, shaking head.

"This is what you call a bad nigger," Richman says, taking Frankie by the scruff of the neck and turning him around so that George may see.

George looks into the child's face with clinical detachment and recoils. He has never been this close to a Negro before. "And ugly besides," he curses the boy in revulsion. "Don't look at me."

"Goddamnit, didn't I tell you he didn't have no manners?" Richman says, pulling Frankie back around by the handle of his neck and slamming him into the dashboard like a rag doll. "Now, apologize to the man."

"I-I-I'm sorry," Franklin stammers through his fattened lip.

Richman slams him into the dash again. "You sorry what?"

"I-I-I'm sorry, sir," Franklin says, casting his eyes down, as tears flow through them that belong no longer to him but to his captors.

"I-I-I'm sorry," Connie mimics the boy's babbled words while Richman laughs and George and Lewis try to, "s-s-s-s-sir."

"I bet you is," Richman goes on taunting him.

Fuck you, Franklin thinks to himself in a moment of trembling atheism in which he remembers the bargain he tried to make earlier that day with God. The whole day he had thought he would be kept safe, especially as he sat down to Thanksgiving dinner and cleared his plate, thinking danger had passed him by.

"See what you have brought to Meridian," Connie cuts in, looking over at the boy's fallen head. But he is less interested in the child. He wants the man who has brought murder among them.

"Meridian children are generally better raised than this one," Richman continues to George, who is feeling in his mouth the satisfaction of having cursed the little nigger, but in his brain wonders how this has all happened, and that a child can be treated so.

"Niggers can't be well raised," Connie corrects him, looking out the window. George nods and agrees, not knowing how such words find his tongue, but unable to stop them, any more than he can get out of the car and end his own presence here.

He feels a tenseness gathering within himself that he recognizes. It wants to spring forth from the car, or else bash the hateful boy on the head. For no better reason than he feels like it. It is a feast day, and he knows if his hand could only strike bone he must feel a great wave of ataraxia, or if he could reach out a hand to clasp the door handle he might be truly released. He sits there and says nothing more. He is as frightened as the child.

Lewis watches silently. He thinks they have maybe beaten the kid enough, but says nothing, because the boy is not innocent. He is their rightful spoil.

"So you saw him get killed?" Lewis asks patiently, settling into his seat. "And you said nothing?"

Franklin is quiet in the front seat of the car, pressed between the two men.

"Answer him, boy," Connie prods. "It was his brother you killed."

"I saw him stabbed," Franklin says. "I didn't know he was gonna die."

"But you didn't tell anyone either, did you?" Lewis asks. "Are you too stupid to know stabbing leads to dying?"

"I was scared," Franklin answers, composed in the space of being questioned, as if an adequate answer might make them release him.

George closes his eyes, knowing that it must be so, but that it will not matter; the thing must soon reveal itself completely.

"Not as scared as you're about to be," Richman says, the river wall of hatred and violent instinct coursing unchecked within him.

Lewis is quiet again between those points of symmetry within himself, thinking that they ought not beat the boy so, since it was not his hand that did the killing, and that the boy belongs rightfully among the spoils. But he knows what began as word from his mouth has grown larger than any one person's ability to control.

"You are awful quiet," Connie says to him, resenting Lewis's withdrawal.

"I am just waiting for the one who did it," Lewis replies as the car comes to a stop in front of the jailhouse. He looks into the Virginia creepers that cover its walls. This is his business tonight—the grown man, not the child.

Six cars pull in around them. Thirty faces peer at the building and one stares away. Inside sits the sign of all they hate. They know they must have it.

The four men who went in before to retrieve the boy walk up the stairs of the jailhouse. They trust Richman's information is reliable, but if the warden does not turn him over peacefully, they are prepared to fight for what is theirs.

Warden Halloday, a solemn white-haired man, sits at his desk reading an article in a two-month-old *Saturday Evening Post,* smirking at one of the cartoons.

When the door of the jail opens, he looks up to see four men before him with shotguns and pistols drawn.

His hands go numb, he loses sensation in his fingers that turn the page, and he feels all of his limbs as useless as his lame leg. He knows, before they speak, what they have come here for and do with his prisoner tonight.

"But this is Meridian," he says.

"Give us the keys," one of the men answers him. "If you don't, we have fifty outside who will come in and get them."

"You can't do this," Halloday says.

"Don't make this any harder than it needs to be."

"There are laws. This is Meridian."

Down the corridor, Mather hears voices rising toward the warden, as if someone has come to receive payment on a debt, and Halloday's voice fills with the sound of wringing hands, as if he cannot meet the terms and knows he has borrowed from people he should not have.

"Are you going to hand him over, or do we have to burn this whole goddamned building down?" they ask Halloday.

"Can't you just let the courts handle this?" Halloday says, thinking of those fifty men outside and his wife in the back room washing dishes.

"We have waited a whole day. Time done come."

In his cell, Mather realizes what they are arguing over is him. He cannot believe his life has come to this—that the machines of time and history and chance should turn their wheels against him so violently. That he will perhaps never again be home. That this is his last battle. Like the others, he meets it with resolve.

The men come down the corridor with bookish, limping Halloday in front of them. It is a tiny jailhouse, with only four cells, three of which sit empty, and they could have found the prisoner by themselves, but they command Halloday to open the gate for them, to demonstrate their power. They did not know Nathan, but they know the beast inside has killed a white man. The warden turns the key on Mather's cell. The four men enter. The beast will not go peacefully, but puts up a fight. Four men are too many even for him to subdue.

"So this is a hero nigger," they say, laughing, as they drag him, hog-tied in the metal clasp of handcuffs, out of the cell and into the night, where he is shoved into the back seat of a car.

Mather looks and sees the boy from the filling station in the front with his head bowed down, refusing to look at him. The men in the back seat make room to receive his bound body.

Six cars pull away from the jail in single file, without a headlamp on among them, and no sound to speak of. A ring of brightest fire shines in the sky above Mississippi. It is the moon above the world. It holds them and guides their way with clarity to make any undead thing contemplate the meaning of life.

The six of them sit all in this ancient half-illumination of the larger, auspicious heart, fear and expectation sparking, ignis fatuus, between them.

Mather feels an incantatory power men have felt since time's beginning as the four other men each submit to, or are submersed in, the larger engine of the whole, like pack-hunting animals gathered under a primitive spell whose bonds and tribal affinities can be seen playing out their wanting of blood, but which is not, not ever, understood in plainspoken language or logic of diagram and symbols.

The mob passes over the train tracks, past small country stores, tumbledown tackle shops, and barbecue joints, on out of town, and there is nothing else on the road tonight except their vehicles, their faces, and fear's ancient prayer lantern.

When they are finally beyond any dwelling of man, one of the cars lets loose a burst of sound from its horn. One by one the others answer it, until the sound rises to a chorus that passes gaily back and forth between them, only slowly disappearing among the pine and dogwood trees.

Mather's raw face is calm as he reaches still for an impersonal language of history and deities, because the immediate working of that engine of death is more than he can voice. To think too much of it is to risk cowardice and panic. He instead tries to force his mind to carve some sanctuary within itself, of either fond memory or blankness. He thinks of his family. He prepares to fight. Anything, as long as it is a back road away from the intersection of himself and this present moment. He knows that to look any other way would be to acknowledge an imminence of death. He does not want to kill again, and he does not want to die.

"You done broke something, nigger," Connie says as they continue out toward Lake Okatibbee.

George feels himself tensing to be so close to the dead, and a double revulsion when he sees him in uniform and reads the medals on Mather's chest.

Lewis stiffens, to be so close to his brother's killer, and looks at Mather's bruised face with hatred. He feels the cage door within his muscles finally spring.

He looks out on the roads of his homeland as they pass through the world, and tries to grow calm and patient. Connie produces a flask that Lewis gave him as a groomsman at his wedding, and it passes from one hand to another silently. Lewis drinks from the flask in turn, and is about to pass it on when his hand pauses under Mather's nose.

"Do you want a drink?" Lewis asks, extending the flask to him.

Connie brakes the car involuntarily and looks at Richman. They fear for a moment Lewis is losing his will, but know the engine of the thirty will work with him.

"We are about to hang this thing, and you want to offer it a drink?"

"I just thought, as long as we are doing it, we might as well have some sense of propriety," Lewis answers, either not yet given over to the machine, or else in another place, deeper within its workings.

"Well, how about it, nigger?" Connie smiles. "You want to die sober or drunk?"

George watches as Richman pinches Mather's nose and takes the flask from Lewis's hand to fill the black man's mouth.

When the flask is emptied, Richman throws it aside and reaches into his pocket. He pulls out a blue-tipped match, which he brings to life on the door of the car. Before anyone can speak, he thrusts it to the center of Mather's face, where its orange flame catches hold of the ninety-proof and fills his mouth with fire.

George turns his head to see Mather thrashing in the seat, trying without hands or room to move to put the fire out. Richman and Connie laugh as Mather shakes with a violent, beastlike instinct of contracting muscles. From inside the fire, Mather wants only to escape it, to keep from giving himself over to the flame. He is an unconquered hero. He will not capitulate. Not ever. He suffers the burning on his skin but knows, even if it should envelop him entirely, that unless he falters it will not have what it wants of him. It will not have him.

When the flame has finally abated, Richman rolls down his window and sails the bottle into the night. "Goddamnit," he hoots, laughing joyously, "that was almost worth a good flask."

"How about it, nigger? You think your drink was worth it?" Connie asks.

In the front seat, Frankie's only movement has been to watch from the corner of his eye as the bottle glinted into the trees. He is hoping somehow they will forget he is there.

What must a man do when the world has turned against him?

I must resist, Mather thinks, and he lists for himself the reasons for doing so even though he knows tonight what it is to be completely alone in this world.

Lewis draws courage from the bond working between them. I do not have to do this alone, he says to himself, looking out over the streets of his homeland.

"If you were Christian," Connie tells the captive when the flame and all conversation have died away, "you would be praying to the Lord just now to forgive you for causing not only Nathan's but this child's death as well."

Mather does pray. He prays for himself, though he knows he is already doomed, and he finds other thoughts, cold, hard as Arctic diamonds, about what he has seen and been through. Yet he also finds a generosity toward that little boy, finds he is praying for him as well, in the middle of these other prayers. He should not be seeing this. He should not be here.

"I'm the one who did it," he tries to say, under the painful pressure on his burnt tongue. "Why don't you let the kid go? He didn't do anything."

The boy from the filling station does not look at him.

When Lewis hears the Negro talking, he finds words in his mouth that have come from some other place. He remembers all the battles he has fought, and he remembers his brother, and he remembers the duty he has to protect his homeland. He balls his fists and blitzes, pummels, them into Mather's burnt face. "Gird thyself," he says. "Gird up thyself like a man." He is caught in rapture, but hard behind that, something splits and tears away. My God, my God, what have I done? But mostly he is in his Pentecost of rapture.

Mather is still beneath the numb pain that pulses against his face and mouth as they begin to blister. I am not supposed to die like this, he thinks to himself. I am supposed to die by bullet, or bayonet, or collective death-whistle of unleashed bomb, but not here; not like this. And even though he has not done so since he was thirteen, he finds himself thinking these thoughts to his father's God, because only the God of his father might decipher prayer from a moment like this.

Lewis will serve his duty and avenge his brother's death, and he will do it in the old style, according to the tradition of taking might and will to grievance and disannulling force of all that his hands have worked to accomplish, and all that his father's hands as well. He will serve them.

"Gird thyself like a man, nigger," he commands again, blitzing his fists in uncontrolled rapture. For if he does not, who else will lift this? "My God, what have I done?" asks something in him that is no longer Lewis, but a shadow from which he might have sprung and might still spring from.

"Just save a little for the rest of us," Connie says, pleased to see Lewis is over what he took to be his earlier jitters, and looking at George. "You see, niggers spoil easy, and once a young one come into contact with one like this, then he ain't got no more business living. But what does the law do when they see something that vile? They take that vileness to jail, like any ordinary criminal. The warden feeds him, and they usher him to the electric chair, some weeks or months later, as courteous as if he was about to have tea and biscuits with the queen. But the code that's been broke don't belong to the state. It belongs to the same thing as Virtute et Armis."

The others continue listening to him in appreciative silence as the cars behind them make their way down to the bank. He is their philosopher and sage tonight, and when he says "Virtute et Armis" they know exactly what he means, more certain than if he had said, "The dog is big," or else "Incipit Vitae." He gives them a sight of their forebears, their sacrifices and co-promises, and this is enough to rile them up and steel their resolve, as it should be for anyone.

To lynch, he goes on, is not taking the law into one's own hands, but to take justice and retribution to a place beyond the law, into the realm of valor; and to make men again the instrument of commandments. "Because I would no more let the government do my killing than I would let it make my babies," Connie goes on, as they pass into the lush woods.

Lewis listens to Connie, and lets himself know and feel that his responsibilities to these men, whom he has grown up with and fought with, are as real as his obligation to his own child, who rests in his wife's life-giving womb down in New Orleans. He will inherit a world, not a wasteland of decay and rotten filth, he tells himself. No man will shame him so, or cause him such fear—nothing will.

"Well?" asks Connie, who seems to be as much in charge of the lynching party as anyone might be said to be in charge of an assembly such as this one. "Are you asking for forgiveness or not?"

Lewis elbows Mather in the side of the head, and Richman asks where up north he is from. They give him the chance again at confession, which Mather spurns. But he knows. He has failed his family. He has come into something larger than himself, and when a man's country turns on him, he questions, what must he do?

Mather Henry Rose will die.

He grows delirious, but asks them again to spare the little boy, whose time to see the ravages of permanent winter has not yet arrived.

Lewis burns red as a firetruck, but controls himself and tries to hold back the machine of wanting. He must do this, but in its proper fashion.

The car comes to a halt at Lake Okatibbee. The moon holds five men and a boy as it did on other nights, here and in other lands, when we were young.

They leave the vehicles, dragging their captives with them, as they would any other enemy who has upset the covenant with God.

"He is yours," Connie says to Lewis.

"Gird thyself," Lewis says again to Mather. "My God, what have you done?"

They will speak to God tonight.

NINE

The town will make up its mind when they visit the next day and see the charred remains under that tree. They will know it was done for them, so that lawlessness and wickedness do not walk upright through Meridian with greater might and surety than their ability to defend themselves and be free of it.

Mather feels a pair of hands, literally cold to the touch, pry him from the fear-stinking car. He feels another presence as well, but his eyes are swollen from all the blows he has taken, and he sees nothing but distant lights that come from their lanterns and torches. His only other stimuli in the canyon of men are their whoops and hollers, and the increase in the little kid's crying as he realizes he won't be able to bojangles himself a way to wake up again tomorrow.

Thirty-one men circle their quarry in the cold air around the lake and hallo, the bonds between them strengthening before being unloosed on the killer. Richman holds on to Frankie and commands him to watch, to see what he has coming to him.

Mather is pushed from hand to hand and flies around the width of the circle, as if in a children's game, as the snare snaps and descends, their blows falling everywhere upon him, until the air at the bottom of that pile is slowly sucked out. When the men finally withdraw, a breeze rushes in to Mather, reviving him. He holds this breath as the next group of men put their hands and boots out in place of the last, in a slow, excruciating death-dance, held at bay as the posse wills.

It wills it for a moment, catching its own breath, then sets upon Mather again, until everyone has gotten a good blow into his dying body. They lift him, then throw him back to the ground with grunts and cheers. There is much cheering.

Frankie watches, Richman's hands holding open his eyes so he can see the hero. "You are next," Richman says to him. "We brought you out here to watch this, in case you were thinking about growing up to be some kind of fighting nigger too. Now, you think you'll do any better?"

Frankie says nothing as a trickle of piss worms its way down his leg into his shoes.

Mather breathes laboriously, listening to the cries for lifeblood and death-gasp lying in wait beneath every other word they say, and he hears.

"He is yours," Connie tells Lewis again, when Lewis has withdrawn from the avenging pile of men upon that beast. "Go in there again."

"He is mine," Lewis repeats to himself, pushing his hand-stitched brogues into the black man's face and uniformed ribs, as the other men give him way and urge him on, and blood drops spatter his shoes, soaking into the stitches and wetting the tops of his toes inside them. "Kill him," they say. "Kill him as he did your brother. Kill him as they would have in olden days."

In this moment, Lewis feels his doubts decrease and himself surge to become something greater. Not only self, but also brother and soldier and husband and father. He becomes every man in Mississippi, and every man in the Old Confederacy, who has ever been humiliated by an outsider telling him who he must be and what he should do. He becomes tonight every man in his platoon who died that this murderer might come home. As he hears the crack of bones beneath his shoe, he is not himself, but Lewis increased a thousand times.

"My God, what have I done?" he asks briefly as he begins to weary, because events must be interpreted and given meaning, either to fit and be accepted, or else to be rejected from the space of men, and this interpretation reinforcing who and what they are, so it is not the event that makes their culture—anything is liable to happen anywhere at all—but the meaning they give to it, which makes them what they are and gives them their self-imagining.

"He is yours," Connie says again, backing him up, until Lewis is tired from kicking, and the pulp beneath his foot no longer has even integrity enough to resist the prodding of his shoe. When it is brought to bear again, there is no satisfaction, but a slow sinking in of the toe, as if in mud.

We will return this beast to the mud, Lewis says to himself, looking about and seeing that George is there and Connie is there and men he has known all his life, whom he has respected and whose place he one day will take, are there. So this is what it is like, he thinks, because he is being initiated tonight and will no longer suffer humiliation from his wife, or uncertainty in the world, but will look his father-in-law in the eye again, as he did before he had the will of another power worked upon him, and Lewis—named for kings and explorers; for ambition, and the spread of greatness to the extinguishing of time; named for his father, for America—became lackey to others instead of maker of design, as was meant to be. He levies another kick, then pauses to catch his strength, looking out through their eyes and feeling an intense pressure against his fingertips in the open air, not knowing what is pressing on them.

"Stand him up," Connie instructs the others, but they no longer hear him, only voices from inside their own cells, because nothing else in the civilized world—not war, not sport—works like the thing that is working through them tonight, except, and only perhaps, the climactic pulse of lovemaking. And, as in any unorchestrated orgy of lovers, they reach to clasp each other in unspoken communion of passion, but longing in louder ritual. No one needs to give instructions anymore, because they move with single purpose.

Rope and wire are produced spontaneously. And it is the right time for them. The fire builds itself. The noose comes around Mather's neck, and the tired lynchers gather around him in more orderly fashion. Tonight they will speak to Him, as one, in His voice, until they are heard.

As they pause, waiting for the creature to be risen back up, someone lets loose a staccato yell that is a thing of such pure evil it makes the blood of the less enthusiastic members of the gathering stand still. Mather hears this scream as well, and all it contains, as nearby voices discuss the proceedings.

"Should we hang him first or burn him first?"

"I think hanging is always supposed to come before burning," another voice answers quietly—reasonably, George thinks, becoming sick in his belly as he listens, because they are performing some sacred rite whose head priests never left exact instructions. They remember them nonetheless, and he finds himself remembering as well. So we do not turn ourselves and each other into this, but never escaped it entirely before, he thinks, as a primordial slime sloshes in his queasy stomach.

Mather Rose thinks of nothing, not wife, not family, not even the sequence of events in his life; he just wants to hold off dying a little while longer.

Richman takes the end of the rope and fashions an expert noose. His fingers are agile and gleeful as he slips it over the beast's bloodied neck, and other hands take its end to loop it around a branch of the tree.

"Lewis," Connie calls, holding on to Franklin in Richman's stead, "would you like to do the honors?"

The crowd cheers him as he walks forth toward Mather and the lynching tree. He pulls at the rope until the dying man is stretched out, his body held by nothing more than the strength of his two big toes.

Lewis pulls, and knows somehow his life will be better after this, if only for a season, as he sees that thing with more medals on its uniform than his own reduced to tears and blubbering, which would fill an ignorant or weaker-hearted man with unspeakable shame.

George watches and knows tonight power is increased by power, and they will have that which they now take, like ancient shamans eating the organs of the defeated. Like timeless warriors eating an enemy's heart. They will eat of this and live as endless as they do.

Connie stands back, drawing pleasure from the sight of his brethren experiencing this for the first time, as it will never be again. He hugs the back of Frankie's neck with his hand and feels in his fingers the vibration of the boy's knocking knees.

Richman, no one's second tonight, looks at the boy from time to time, wondering what blasphemous union of white man and nigger bitch produced this evil spawning, and walks in every manner the ghettos and dark corners of his mind, even in ways that would surprise and shock his fellow lynchers. He is barely able to contain himself at the thought of letting loose the child's life as soon as this monstrous Yankee beast stops its thrashing, pleading, and generally unmannish behavior, as he sees it, before the knotted noose. "Die like you got some dignity, you black sonofabitch," he hisses, because he wants Mather to put forth some display of pride that he might strike down again. "You know what that is?"

Mather cradles his head from the barrage, and blubbers something, if there was only one less of them, six less of them, he might have a chance, but there are too many in the clearing, and so nothing he can do. He, American, is a hero, and will die as heroes do. "Ain't nobody here you know by name," Richman says, and punches him in the face with the belted knuckles of his hand, just in case they let coloreds into the afterlife and this one might have some thoughts about showing up there. "Ain't nobody here you know, you black sonofabitch. Die." He hates him in this life as well. And this time smashes the base of his hand into Mather's mouth. As if God would listen to a nigger, but just in case they have tainted heaven as well, or slip and let a nigger in, and this one has some notion left over of standing and testifying after he has snuck into heaven, or picked someone's pocket and stolen the key. "Die like the man you think you is," he says, working every muscle of his mouth. It is beautiful murder, this.

"It is time," Connie calls out, because he wants every pleasure that can be received from this ritual, but not to be out here all night, killing a thing that will not die.

As Lewis raises Mather's body higher up from the ground, a small goblinish thing repeats that evil staccato cry. "I got a right," Sydney Harris yells, breaking free of the two men holding him back. "I got a right," he says again, as he opens a bottle across Mather's already unrecognizable face, because his hands alone are not strong enough to deliver the blow he would like to give. He has never been part of anything before, but he is a part of this. "Same as any other white man in Mississippi."

He lets loose that scream again with goblinish glee, as if it has been sent forth by some wild and evil being who is not Sydney at all.

The men applaud as he draws back from the killer and rejoins their circle. Terrence looks at Lewis and nods.

Lewis pulls the rope taut over the tree, and Mather's feet rise from the ground.

"Do you want to confess?" Lewis pauses to ask harshly, with fervor he thought he had lost with the end of the war. "Do you want to ask for redemption and mercy before you fall to hell?"

"Okay," Mather's mouth works, knowing that pride and truth are as useless as anything else, as useless as crying, as useless as fighting.

"Quiet, gentlemen," Connie instructs the restless crowd, and Lewis gives the rope slack. "A moment of silence for the dead."

Mather speaks so softly they can barely hear him. "Let the boy go first, then I'll tell you whatever you want to hear."

Lewis looks at the other men for a second, deciding what to do. "I told you the nigger wasn't any good," Connie says at last, after this final refusal. "He had one more time to do right, and goddamnit if he didn't waste it."

A shout goes out, and Lewis feels the rope moving in his hand. Mather's body rises farther and farther from the ground, and the free end of the rope races to be fastened to the tree.

"Gird thyself," Lewis calls up, because nothing except the Biblical, and even there none but Job, can express what torturous anger he feels, or the violence unleashed here tonight. Gird up they loins now like a man; and declare thou unto me.

They are God's rough words to Job, which he read earlier that day from his mother's Bible when he wondered, after waking from his long night, whether he had the right. He saw in them that he did, but with that right a responsibility. He stops the pulling and asks again for confession.

Mather is not well versed in the Bible, and to his mind all around is doggerel and lunacy, until he hears he is being asked again for confession and final speech. The men doing the asking can tell just by looking that this is a heathen, with no love of God in his breast, so "Gird up thyself," Lewis screams again when Mather does not answer them immediately. "You have broken something." He has broken their hold of the world over their homeland, and brought murder among them, leaving Lewis Hampton a man and his parents' only living son. He will do this for them as he does for his brother, he tells himself, even as he asks just what it is he does.

Mather will not be defeated by these men, or any other, not ever, but gives himself over to what he has faith in, his history and the future of what it has wrought—himself only a passing flicker in the light that flies forth from that axis of time and humanity's heart. He does not beg, would rather die than give them peace in the tragedy they create, lacking imagination and courage to believe even in their own creed, let alone one that belongs not to their own immediate desires and fears or even those of their God, but a faith larger than the personal and divine, a "we" writ larger than God, and dwarfing all kings, but his lips begin to move in painful, near-silent confession as he thinks of that boy. The spirit among the men in the clearing as they listen is religious in its ecstasy. They have broken him, and are vindicated.

"Just let him go," Mather says again, deliriously. He does not know whose child is being brought to harm by unwashed and unlettered crackers in this anacivilized wilderness, never to face his own walk, never to go home again. He has given up hope for himself, but that, that is not right, and even they must know so in their communion of man and man, and whatever else is held under this night, in the room created in that space on the shore of the lake by the emotion and history between them. The child sits outside of that, or inside it more fully than they, and should be released.

Lewis looks at Mather in his war uniform and sees less the symbol of all depravity and the mark of Cain or Ham than simple enemy. He looks outside that assemblage, not knowing all the rules for hosting a lynching party, but wonders, through insanity of present temper, whether the nigger is entitled to any of the honor system of ordinary fighting. Does this nigger's plea belong within the boundary of regular combat, or would he treat me just as he is being treated? Lewis asks himself, coming close but stopping just short of the disaster of empathy, having no one else to ask. Not even George, who knows so much about the war of North and South and how they behaved in war generally, can answer him, because George is lost somewhere in the tangle of faces and limbs surrounding the lynching tree.

Mather does not want to die. His life does not belong to these thirty-one but to another circle, thousands of miles away, as far away as a man could walk to be free of such knowing and such sight. But he knows he will die nonetheless. The sight Mather sees now is of a death valley not meant for the eyes of the living, but seen again and again all the same, and watched by the men around it.

"Look at your hero," Richman says to Franklin. "Look at him good, because this it what it will be like for you, and you won't be able to see it so well from the inside." He laughs. He has not had such a good time in months.

Sydney cracks loose the wild staccato cry that comes from some-where deep inside and will be respected after this evening. George shivers from a brain chill and the numbness at the ends of his fin-gers. Terrence drinks a beer. Allister sinks exhausted into the wet, overgrown grass and laughs, as Lem does a little nigger dance in commemoration of their friend as he was when he had cheated time or defied death on evenings prior to the last. Lewis's chest puffs as he tries to catch his breath. He wipes freezing sweat from his brow and looks around the crowd. Connie holds the back of the boy's neck with pincer fingers. The child watches as Mather's head lolls down his burnt-up chest, and against the ragged uniform, a man without a friend in the world.

Mather does not want to die. He wants to go home again. Home is the City of Light, and the Queen of Angels he is not ready to meet. Mather's toes stretch out to find the ground that was only moments ago beneath them. The men are silent in that circle surrounding him, their faces all lit by the brilliance of this night. Of the moon reflecting off the surface of the lake, and giving back to her her own image, placid as the dry bed of Tranquility, and the reflection of a sun somewhere on the other side of the world, in an unflagging light and ancient beacon prayed to by lunatics and shamans since first word was heard from first man.

It echoes now in their ears and in the chest of Mather as he is strung and returned to that from which he rose. He stretches out to find the ground disappeared.

It is silent.

You hear the tightening gasps of Mather. You watch as he dies. He does not want to die, but the life flows up from him nonetheless— what other sense could it make—as some primitive sacrifice to America.

Two insects call out to each other, and the torches from the lynching party hover around his face. He is no longer Mather Henry Rose. He is the sign of all they hate and all that oppresses them. You watch as he dies. He was the sign of freedom restored.

You watch as Lewis kills.

See Mather. See Lewis. All the world between them. He is not Lewis, but a boy sent out to fight, and come home told to be a man. No idea in heaven what that is. They figure it out as best they can. This is what he does. According to the divination of the signs sent down to him, and sent down to his father. He belongs now to the machine that would interpret those signs, according to the wants of their burden. According to the tradition. According to devotion to that history.

Mather's legs kick out, and a trickle of blood streams down the face of the man who once sailed the wrong way around the world, and has come home now. He is the sign of their love for each other, and the charge they have been given to go out in the world and force it upright and away from entropy. Emptiness.

This they do now like lawgivers, who have seen into the breach of lawlessness.

He is the sign of a love for entropy and death that extends back to Rome, and beyond. He is a sign to be freed from that circle.

He is not Lewis who reaches so, no, not Mr. Lewis. He is Lewis extended according to the demands of devotion. He makes this sacrifice so that he may become a great Southerner, colossal and divine as America; so that all the shadows circling around his life may be vanished. His brother's murder properly appeased. Because if such a thing might be done to his brother then it can also befall him. His homeland. He will sleep better after this, or not, but will perform his duty. He looks around at what it has asked of him and feels in that shadow heart of his a young boy crying, but he is a man, and in his own breast feels a swelling of what he must contain. It is too small an imagining of the world.

The machinery of the crowd whirs and hums and sings the name of whatever on high might listen, as each of them is extended beyond "I" to become "we" and stretches further to lift that "we" up to the divine.

They will speak to God tonight.

They will speak to Him in a voice He understands. Until He answers them back with some new sign. If it is given, they will read this new sign according to another system of divination, or else by the way of interpreting he gave to their fathers. Filial piety is real as this rope. They are not evil. This is not murder. It is too long since He has spoken to them, a very long time, and they seek from Him this communion in their own voice. God listens to white men. Doesn't

He? They keep from damnation. From the abyss and what they know it to contain.

Mather sputters. His eyes bulge from his face as one of his friends' used to, a man who brought a bottle of whiskey to a cold New Year's Day at the Battle of the Bulge. Blood trickles from his lips. The breast he once pressed against his wife's falls uncommon still. There is no ground beneath him. He does not want to die, but if he must, let it be in battle.

All that sustains him now is force of will in the tense muscles of his neck. They keep the rope from cutting in. He tells Gans he does not want to ride today, but move over just in case. Maybe save him a seat on that train. He prays to his fathers' Gods.

They pray to one much like Him. They pray from a different verse.

"Burn him," one of the voices says, as the wiggling from that hanging man slows down, and he falls in perfect line from the rope to the patch of ground below.

"Not yet," Connie counters over their cheers, relinquishing Frankie to the man standing next to him. "When I was a little boy, my grand-daddy had himself a coonskin purse. He was so proud of it they buried him with it. But it was the prettiest thing I ever saw, and tonight I aim to have one exactly the same."

He will have it. He squints and walks over to Mather, then takes the knife he has brought for this purpose alone and traces the out-line of the soldier's back, from the nape of the neck to the line above his buttocks. Slips his fingers up between the skin and muscle and pries loose a clean sheet in a single motion that leaves the muscle and tendon of the back exposed, dripping not-yet-congealed blood, as you would with any animal that has lost the chase. He throws it over his shoulder, and does not care what they do with the rest of it.

"Burn him now," Connie commands, standing back to admire his trophy. He flushes with a pride that puts an unspeakable burden on your heart. "I have always wanted this," he says again, his eyes nearly brimming over. "Burn him."

One of the men without souvenir throws a sparked match onto that pile of beast and coal oil that sends the skinned soldier thing up in flames, and fills the air with the odor of singeing hair and burning skin as it climbs the length of the hanging corpse. From the inside, Mather can no longer see them. He relaxes the tensed muscles of his neck. He feels something cold and stinging on that exposed interior space. He feels it grow hotter. He tells his God and his dead he wants not to die, but maybe hold the train at the station just in case. In case he needs a ride to the City of Light or back to the City of Angels, or to his own country in the middle of the ocean, where he is not perfect, because he has failed his wife and children, and he has learned a hatred here in Raceriotland that would not bring that unwashed and untutored cracker back to life even if it could, but he is nonetheless a man. Greater. He is why you live in near freedom.

A ring of brightest fire shines in the sky, and another down below.

A cheer goes up from the crowd. They have done good. They smile and watch as the charred maze of their spoil falls back to earth in a pile of burn tissue like droughted fields.

Someone prods the head with a stick, and another man comes forth with pliers, saying only, "Nigger teeth is lucky," as he performs death's dentistry.

They are pleased as they each receive a tooth from the body, but hold it a little against Connie that he thought to have a purse before they did. But there are teeth enough to go around, and the pliers continue their feast on the corpse, bringing forth ivory from the black jungle of death.

The crowd stares in awe of what they do, and the millions of feelings those thirty-one men produce are still ignescent over the lake as they divide the body, and receive their tokens and heirlooms, and are satisfied, but are not yet done with killing.

"Your ass is mine now, boy," Richman says, looking at Frankie and the piss that glistens down his legs, as the deputy goes to retrieve him. He approaches Connie to take that filth that belongs now to him.

"No," Lewis says, from beneath the whir of the machine, wondering whether he can pull back what his words have unleashed. "He is not ours to have."

"Of course he is," Richman says, because he is who he has come here for.

"C'mon, Lewis," Connie says. "He is ruined. He has seen our faces. What do you want? To let him just leave?"

"That's right, it's already done," someone calls from within the crowd.

"It's not done until I say so," Lewis says. "If I let you go, you're not going to run back home to your mamma and make a lot of trouble for her, are you?" he asks the boy.

"It don't matter. He has seen it, and after a nigger has seen something like this, there ain't no good in his living."

Lewis ignores Richman, and gives the kid a shove. "Run, boy," he says. "Go on. Get as far away from here as you can."

"Come here, boy," Richman says. "Goddamnit, Hampton, that is my nigger. Just because his brother died on account of yours don't mean this is all even."

Lewis had not known this one was related to the boy who went into the army in lieu of Nathan. It is arbitrary grace, this. Because he can. It is not done until he says so.

"Go on, now," he says again coldly, looking at Frankie. "Get yourself out of here."

"Give me that nigger," Richman screams. "Come here, boy, before I come over there and get you."

"Get out of here," Lewis commands, straining to hold back that mob.

"Come here, nigger," Richman says, leveling his shotgun on Frankie.

Lewis takes the barrel.

"Stay out of this," Richman calls. "That nigger is spoiled."

"Then ain't no sense in you having him," Lewis says, as the others in that multitude take sides, according to who and which faction they have loyalty to, or see power in, and their level of satiation.

"Get out of here," Lewis yells to the black boy, who is less child after this.

Frankie does not speak, but looks between the men, and beyond them to the smoldering ash and blackened corpse on the ground, as does Lewis, and as does George, and he does not need to be told again. He is barefoot but begins to fly over the cold, prickly ground with greater and greater speed. His loose limbs set into motion through the grasses around the reservoir. Shot scatters in the air around him, over his head, propelling him forward, until he knows he can run forever.

He feels a white-hot burning screeching around his skin, and a hand grasping and seizing at his heart. The hive of shotgun pellets buzz in his ear, and he is frightened as hell, but he will not stop running, not ever. He feels the burning pierce his skin, and a stinging in his side, but even it does not slow him down. He feels that hand releasing him and his lungs fill with crisp, true air. He runs with more meaning and more speed than even he thought he was capable of, as laughter flies up from the crowd at the ungainly sight he makes, and dies down the farther and farther away from them, into the dark woods carpeted with fallen branches and pine needles, he goes.

He feels he can run forever, but knows he will not run too long.

Behind him, the light from the fire grows dim.

A ring of brightest fire shines in the sky. It is the moon above the world, and it guides him, shining brighter than stars, because it casts its glow for America, and for the heroes of Mississippi.

But also for us, as it did on other nights when we were young. And if, fifty years from here, when the boy would be sixty-five or so, and the men would be all in their seventies, one of the ones who were there approached his deathbed and needed it, not so he could get right for any kind of afterlife, but needed the record, not all the way straight, no man or child has that power in him, or any other who was there that night, but needed it, so it would all be less crooked, less dark and cowardly cast over his homeland, and so told the thing, as unslantwise as he could—especially given that man can be such a slantwise creation—who would—could even his own children forgive and absolve him? Who would do that? Maybe even a thousand years from that night. And what if he did, but it brought neither truth nor reconciliation to it, but simple pain and self-deceit back to a shattering surface, explaining nothing?

Richman and his friends lower their guns, and Connie strokes the trophy thrown over his shoulder. Richman makes to move toward Lewis, who shakes his head. Do not try that. George and Allister and Terrence look after the boy, and someone prods the body with a stick to see if there is anything more to be gotten from it. There is not.

"You owe me something," Richman says, not ready to let go of a thing once he has gotten it within his power. "You owe me a nigger."

"He don't owe nothing but your poor aim."

"C'mon let's go home," someone says. They ball their fists around the tooth each hand holds. Lewis looks back at that outstretched pile of blackened killer, into the orbs where his eyes were; what is done is done. The torches and flashlights pass over them all a final time, as they are, as they once were.

"C'mon, let's go home."

They will.